SHANNA GERMAIN

The Poison Eater

A Numenera Novel

ANGRY
ROBOT

ANGRY ROBOT
An imprint of Watkins Media Ltd

20 Fletcher Gate,
Nottingham
NG1 2FZ
UK

angryrobotbooks.com
twitter.com/angryrobotbooks
Every heart a death

An Angry Robot paperback original 2017

A catalogue record for this book is available from the British Library.

ISBN 978 0 85766 634 5
EBook ISBN 978 0 85766 636 9

Set in Meridien by Epub Services.
Printed in the UK by 4edge Ltd.

For Monte, who gave us the world

Eternity is a long time to go hungry, and the newone has known nothing but this gaping ache.

A shadowed moon circles in its chest. It can feel the pull of something lost. Broken fingers furrow the soil of the body, seed fist to flesh.

The sutured outside-in beast pants beside it, voidmouth, its tongue a gaping star.

The scent of fear buried in bone. The voice of someone long ago calling its name. A shivered shard of black, sharpened skypiece.

The newone remembers its mission. Go. Seek. Devour.

It has eaten everything it has ever loved. What is left?

I. ebeli

MEMORIES

Poison never lies.

But Talia does. Every time she takes the poison, she lies. False words are the only weapons she has left, and she wields them with precision, but not with pride. Every time, she tells the guards that she sees danger in the woods, creatures in the clouds, something coming, something dark. Not too specific. Just enough menace. For those who are looking, those who believe, there is always a danger to be found outside Enthait's walls. And Talia is the one who finds it for them.

She would lie this time too. She had to.

In the small room that she'd come, over time, to think of as *hers*, Talia picked a small spraypen off the small table and marked a circle, no bigger than the pad of her thumb, on the wall. That one made seven. Seven moons. Seven poisonings. Seven lies.

Talia still wasn't used to writing with her left hand, and all of the circles were misshapen in a different way. She touched each one with the pad of her left thumb, the most recent smearing as it took on the texture of her fingerprint. Seven down, three to go. *If* she lived through this one, that was.

Lying about the poisoning was a given for her. Living through one was not. Most poison eaters lived through one, many through four or five, less through seven, and no one – as everyone was so fond of reminding her – had lived through all ten. No one but the orness. They called it the killer, the tenth poison. As if the others weren't.

Even to Talia, whose sense of right and wrong was no compass to guide one's life by, the system seemed… broken at the very best. And something else entirely at its worst. But it was a system that served her needs, at least for now, and she would play its game until she won – or until it killed her.

There was very little in the room other than herself. A bed. The small table that held, in addition to the spraypen, a hexed armband and a broken blue-black blade. A cobalt cloak upon a hook. Two doors, one to the street and one to the tunnels. And Khee, the former warbeast, curled about himself and snoring lightly on a blanket in the corner, his weirdly angled legs and long neck forming an impossible circle. The striped implants that laced his fur were unlit, settling into a shade of brown only slightly paler than his natural color.

Talia picked up the hexed metal band and pulled it over the empty space where her right hand used to be. It glowed pale blue as it settled around the skin of her upper arm. Ganeth's handiwork. The Aeon Priest had wanted to recreate her a living hand, but she'd refused. She had reasons for wanting to remember her loss. That negative space was as important to the entirety of her self as the etchings along her spine or the streaks of red hair that grew from the scars on her scalp. She wielded these with neither precision nor pride, but with some combination of shame and memory that formed no word.

She had not been able to turn Ganeth away from building this, though: as she reached for the cobalt cloak hanging on the wall, the hexes covering her forearm spread apart and reworked themselves into a mechanical semblance of her former hand. The transition was silent and took a mere second – barely long enough for her to marvel, as she often did, at Ganeth's skills – and then she was using both hands to pull the cloak over her head.

The cloak was not hers. It belonged to the station of the poison eater – those who had worn it before and those who would wear it after – but the metallic fabric settled and shaped itself around her as though it had been made for her. It had taken her weeks to figure out how to flow the fabric with a thought, but now it was second nature, a passing trifle in the ritual of getting ready.

Ganeth had showed her the mechanism once, a weave of thin metals inside the fabric that pressed to her skin, and while she could make the material bend to her will, she still didn't *understand* it.

At the soft rustle of shifting material, Khee raised his head, blinking, his long upward-curving tusks glinting with sleep drool.

Khee was no longer the warbeast he'd been when they'd found each other. Since the night they'd walked side by side through the city's gates nearly a year ago, his stripes (she thought of them as his *moods*) rarely glowed anymore. Sometimes when he was sleeping – dreaming, she thought – they'd pop bright yellow or blue, light up the room in tiny flickers, wake her from her own fitful sleep. But mostly they stayed quiet.

He'd grown full and sated, a little soft, maybe even a little sweet. But then again, so had she. Sometimes that gnawed at her – *the vordcha will come for you* – but most of the time she was able to push the thought away.

She was working on it. Small steps. Small thoughts. First the poison eater, then the orness, then the aria. When the vordcha came, she would be ready.

Khee stretched and yawned, showing off a row of natural teeth and, behind that, two rows of crafted ones. One set was enough to kill. Two were enough to kill slowly, painfully. Only the vordcha would think it necessary to add more. Or perhaps they did it for fun. Because they could. She thought she had some answers about the vordcha, but how they thought, *why* they did things – for that, she had only questions.

Khee blinked her way, four bright blue eyes asking.
now?

"Soon," she said.

Talia flexed her hexlight fingers and the pieces slid back into the shape of a band around her arm.

Then she bent her head until her chin touched her chest. She hadn't come here with any gods of her own. Only the gods given to her by others, gods that had betrayed and sacrificed her, and so she said no prayer now other than her own name. Not the name she owned now. Not the name she'd been given by her former captors. The name she'd been born into, a secret name of a people she no longer remembered. She whispered it toward her heart, so quiet that not even Khee could hear.

And then the only thing she knew that even resembled

a prayer. "And only the orness, the keeper of the aria, shall remain."

A knock against the door, soft and low enough that she knew instantly whose hand it belonged to.

"Come, Seild."

The girl scarcely waited for the sound of her name to leave Talia's lips before she rushed into the room. Barely tall enough to carry the long flickerstick against her back without it dragging on the ground. Her cloak did drag, but it carried no sign of the tunnel she'd just passed through. Seild stopped in front of Talia, as was custom and proper, but her gaze couldn't help sliding toward the creature in the corner.

For the poisoning, Seild's usually wild hair was pinned and wrapped into the shape of two curling horns on the sides of her head. Talia almost laughed to think of Isera getting her daughter to sit still long enough for that piece of costuming.

Talia was generally bad with ages, but the first time she'd met Seild the girl had said, "Finwa. I'm Seild, I am six, and I am the youngest member of the zaffre."

Talia hadn't known half the words the girl had said. Like most people she'd met, Talia spoke the Truth. She also spoke the code language that she and the other martyrs had made up to keep plans out of the minds of the vordcha. But Enthait also seemed to have its own turns of phrase, cultural threads woven through the language. She'd pulled at those threads a lot since then, unweaving them, trying to reweave them. The patterns were more complicated than she'd expected. *Finwa* was usually *hello*. But sometimes *please*. And other times another, more nuanced, sentiment that she still didn't quite grasp.

Zaffre was an easier word, at least. Concrete. Simple. Enthait's defense force. Patrols. Protectors. Guards. They served the wishes of the elusive orness, who served the wishes of the city. And Talia, as the poison eater, served the wishes of them all. Or, at least, she was supposed to.

Most in Enthait revered the zaffre, hoped their children would grow up to be a member some day. Talia knew Isera felt differently. And yet here was her only daughter, already wearing the mark. To be the poison eater's escort was high honor, decreed by the orness herself. Not even Isera's desire to keep her daughter safe was strong enough to turn the orness' decision. Talia wondered, not for the first time, why the orness had chosen someone so young. That, in turn, begged the question of why the orness had chosen her, Talia, an outsider to the city, to be the poison eater. Or, really, why the orness did any of the things she did. Mystery upon mystery. Only a few of which she'd been able to solve.

"Moon meld you, Seild," Talia said. The formal greeting of her position still felt strange in Talia's mouth after all this time. The vordcha had formalities and rituals, but they were wordless and bloody, metal and mech. But then, the vordcha were not human and cared not for human things.

Remembering herself and her duties at the sound of Talia's voice, Seild pressed her thumbs to the spaces above her eyes and raised her half-brown, half-gray gaze to Talia. Her mismatched eyes were identical to her mother's, a startling contrast in their otherwise symmetrical faces. At first, Talia had thought the mismatched eyes to be a blessing, passed mother to daughter. Now she knew the truth. Or something closer to the truth.

"Moon meld ebeli, memories cleave the marrow. Moon

meld iisrad, shades ward your eyes–" Seild began. Talia waved the formal gesture of address aside. The girl was well-trained and would do her duties – she knew the list of the ten poisons backward and forward – but the recitation took forever, and it was obvious Seild only had eyes for the creature in the corner. And he her.

"Tell it to Khee, yes? I need to finish preparing."

There was nothing left for her to do. But, of course, the girl didn't know that. There was so much mystery, so much hidden ritual, surrounding the role of poison eater that even she felt like she didn't know the whole, or even the half of it. How could anyone else be expected to?

"Go," she urged, when she realized the girl was still standing there.

Seild's delighted grin lasted only a second before she was running to the corner, toward the languishing beast.

"Slow, slow," Talia cautioned.

The girl caught herself up short. After the two's first fateful encounter – not surprising that a bouncing, screeching girl and a former warbeast weren't the best mix – Talia had taught her to greet Khee quietly and let him make the first move.

Seild went down on her knees – oh, the dirt she would hear about later – in front of Khee, and with as much propriety as a girl with a too-big weapon and a too-big bundle of energy could muster, said, "Hello, Your Softness."

Khee caught Talia's gaze.

like.

You and me both, beast.

She didn't know if Khee talked to the girl, if Khee talked to anyone but her, and she never asked. But some signal must have passed between the two, for a moment later they were a giggling, growling ball of fur and formal clothing.

Someone from the zaffre – most likely Isera – would have the girl's head for her disheveled state. As the youngest member of the corps, Seild was expected to be a role model for every child who someday dreamt of wearing the blue and bronze uniform of the zaffre. Seild's cloak, at least, was still clean. Too bad Ganeth hadn't also given her dirt-proof everything else.

Talia might need to interfere and take the blame. It would be worth it, just to have seen the two of them at play. She watched Khee lower his triangular head, ever careful of his sharp, upwardly curving tusks, to the girl's stomach until she giggled and hugged his whole head to her. The beast's barbed tail thumped the floor softly. Seild scratched around one of the hard metal stumps at the top of Khee's head until he huffed a rare breath of contentment.

"What are these?" Seild asked.

"He had horns once," Talia said.

"What happened to them?"

"A story for a later time," she said.

The girl kept her gaze lowered on Khee as she parted his fur and ran her hand over one of his now-brown stripes. Talia knew from experience how those odd striations of his body felt. Smooth as synth, but softer. Warmer. More alive. What she didn't know was whether those parts of his body felt different to him, or whether he'd had them so long they seemed natural. The parts the vordcha had put in her felt both foreign and somehow part of her. Even now, after she'd pulled them from her body, she felt their dissonance.

Seild was quiet, paying far too much attention to her

own hand running through Khee's fur. Talia knew little of children – hadn't spent time with them until she'd come here, not since she was a child herself – but it was clear the girl had something on her mind.

Talia waited as long as she could before she cleared her throat and spoke.

"Seild, it's time for us to go."

The girl's words were muffled in Khee's fur. "I don't want you to go. All the poison eaters die."

Seild's bottom lip was trembling, and she drew in a wet breath, the rest of her words tumbling out in a rush. "Today is seven. Today is seven. Lots of the others died this time, and I don't want you to die. I don't."

Talia was surprised that the girl knew about such things. Where had she heard it? Certainly not from Isera. On the street, likely. The whole city was abuzz with today's poisoning. It was true – it had been a long time since a poison eater made it through seven. Maybe as long as the child had been alive.

"Come, Seild," she said.

The girl didn't, her head down and fingers still in Khee's fur. Talia could tell that she was doing her very best to honor the zaffre and her mother and herself, and not to break into tears. It must be hard for her, Talia thought, to be so young and carry such burdens. She went to her and knelt at her shoulder, catching Khee's unreadable gaze over Seild's head.

"Yes," Talia said. "All the poison eaters die. But not this one. Not today. Not with you as my escort."

Reminding Seild of her duty brought her back to herself, as Talia had hoped it would. The girl softly wrapped her hands around Khee's snout, then leaned in and kissed him on the side of his head. Khee's lips curled back in surprise, but he didn't bare his teeth as he would have for most other creatures entering his space. Likely unaware of the gift she'd just been given – a beast designed for destruction letting another creature bring their mouth so close to his – Seild stood, brushing the dust and dirt from her knees and palms.

"I will protect you," Seild said, serious. She steepled her fingers together. It was a promise gesture Talia had seen others use. In the gesture, Seild was her mother's daughter, right down to the uplift of her shoulders and the strength in her mismatched gaze.

"I'm sure of it," Talia said. She was tempted to brush the remaining dirt from Seild's pants, to right the carefully molded hair that had run askew, but it would only serve to make the girl nervous. Instead, she picked up the broken blue-black blade from the table – it was only as long as her pinky, but the jagged edge was as honed as it had ever been – and tucked it inside her armband. Its cool sharpness calmed the too-fast beat of her pulse.

They went out by the tunnel door, Seild leading, her flickerstick giving enough light to see the ornate patterns beaded along the side and top of the stone walls. Talia had touched one of the beads once as she went by – an orange one the size of a tooth – and she'd had the distinct sensation that it had somehow opened up and *snapped* at her fingers. Now she kept to the center of the tunnel, careful not to step on the drag of Seild's cloak.

Enthait's tunnel system was a maze Talia hadn't yet mastered. It seemed you could get almost anywhere in the city without venturing aboveground, a bit of privacy and secrecy that she would have appreciated and taken advantage of if she wasn't always getting lost and popping out some door into some random city street on her way to somewhere else.

Thankfully, this tunnel only allowed her one path: from the poison eater's door to the clave, the circular building in the center of town where the poisonings were held. Seild's guidance was a formality required by the ritual, but not by Talia's poor sense of direction.

Each beaded section represented one of the ten poisons, but Talia could never remember which, so she'd dubbed them all with a name that had meaning for her. Here was Khee's section, beaded in the brown and once-blue stripes of his fur. Here was Seild's, red for some reason that she didn't know, but the beads were scattered, windblown, in a way that spoke of the girl's movement. Isera's was orange. Ganeth's blue. The orness was a pale green, the color of deep wood moss. She named each one in her head as she passed it.

Last, they crossed what she thought of as Maeryl's section, rolling swirls of blue and silver, like the sea. Talia had never seen the sea, but Maeryl had described it to her so many times she felt like she knew it, what waves were and how they smelled of salt, and why blue and silver were Maeryl's favored colors.

At the tunnel's end, it widened so they could stand abreast in front of a large metal door flecked with ten symbols in a circle. Talia licked her thumb and touched it to the symbols in turn, saying the name of each poison as she did so. Two holes, each slightly larger than a human fist, irised open on either side of the door.

"Ready?" Talia asked.

Seild nodded, then raised her tiny fist and put it inside

one of the circles. Talia did the same with the left hand. Something licked the base of her wrist, pressing wet and warm against her pulse, and she shuddered. Beside her, Seild wrinkled her nose and made an involuntary noise of disgust.

This was just one reason that some believed Talia shouldn't be in this position. Whatever lived inside this door only opened for two living hands, and she had only one.

There were other reasons. She was an outsider. She walked around with a mechbeast at her side. *A mechbeast that you mentally talk to; don't forget that.* And then there was Burrin – the leader of the zaffre and the orness' only son – who clearly wanted, who clearly felt that he deserved, to be the one standing here with his fists buried in the door.

The pressing flesh withdrew and, a moment later, the door clicked open to reveal a sprawling round room. No. *Room* was far too small a word. The clave was easily the largest building Talia had ever been in. A giant sphere, the walls and top arching up with ancient red ribs that ran from the floor which Talia stood on all the way to the faraway top of the clear domed roof. She didn't know what it was originally designed for, but whatever it was, it must have been a spectacle, for the building could hold far more people than those who lived in Enthait's walls. Perhaps three times as many.

Not everyone who lived in Enthait came to watch the poisonings, but many did. They were gathered now along the sloped edges, up and up, sitting or standing as space allowed. It was tradition to attend. And, she thought, a bit of blood lust. You never wished for the poison eater to die – at least not out loud – but you didn't want to miss it if it happened either. She'd heard the stories of the deaths. Or at least she'd heard the beginnings of them; she always tried to step out of earshot before they started recounting the actual demise.

Designs etched in the clave floor echoed those of the door she'd just passed through. The ornate etchings were lit from beneath, creating upward swaths of pale light big enough for a person to stand inside. For the poisoning, all of the positions were held by the greyes, the ten highest-ranked members of the zaffre.

Burrin stood in the shine of the closest beam, his back to them. He was a head and a half taller than Talia, lean and sharp as a blade, though she'd never seen him use one. He seemed to prefer a set of long, round-handled sticks with barbed ends. Likely something Ganeth had made just for him, though Ganeth hated making weapons. She imagined that when the leader of the zaffre – who also happened to be the only surviving son of the orness – asked you for anything, you said yes.

Next to her, Seild saw Burrin and faltered in her stride. The hairs along Khee's arched neck ruffled up, and he stepped forward to press himself into Seild's side. Talia didn't know if he was seeking comfort or giving it. Seild's duty was done here, and there was no need to press her into the light, despite all the time her mother had taken with her hair.

"Stay," she said, more for Seild than for Khee. Khee would do his own thing – he always did – but she knew him well enough to know that he would not seek the center of all these people without absolute need.

Leaving the two in the shadows of the doorway, Talia

stepped forward into the circle. The clave, which had been filled with low murmurings, erupted into a cheer as the crowd caught sight of her in her cobalt cloak. They were cries of luck and hope. For her. For the city. Most of all, for themselves. "Moon meld us!" "Finwa, Poison Eater!" No one called her name. She wasn't sure most of them knew it. That was just as well by her.

Talia stepped forward. The globed glass ceiling let in the late afternoon light, hot and bright. It caught the dust swirling up from her steps across the floor, the shine of people's faces in the crowd, the sharp glare off the zaffre's weapons and armor.

Burrin didn't glance at her as she went by, but the gazes of the other greyes followed her walk to the center of the circle. Their faces were heavy with expectation, a weight that seemed to grow with each poisoning. The crowd too had gone suddenly, completely silent. The only sound was that of their breathing, almost as one.

Talia knew that Isera stood upon one of the lights, but she couldn't bring herself to look for her. They would see each other after, if she made it through this alive.

When she made it through this alive.

She lifted her shoulders and kept her gaze on the orness as she strode toward the center of the wide space. The orness stood on a low dais, facing Talia. It was impossible to see anything of her features. The crimson hood pulled over her head somehow granted her face constant shadow, even in the brightness of the dome. Every time Talia tried to see the details of her face – eyes, nose, mouth, anything – her gaze slipped away, skittered across shadow forms. At first she'd thought it was a mask, but now she thought it was something more… Ganeth-ish. Still, she couldn't help but try, and fail, each time.

Everything about the orness' garb seemed designed to obfuscate the person wearing it – the layer upon layer of wrapped red and gold that gave no indication of the body beneath, the thin gloves that left only her thumbs uncovered, the jeweled tassels that shifted as she did, distracting the eye.

Only her feet were bare. Thick silver bracelets fastened around both ankles, their pale glitter a sharp contrast to her dark skin. Each toe bore a ring of colored cloth – one for each of the poisons she'd survived. The black one around her pinky toe – awos – the final poison. The killer. For everyone except the orness.

As Talia drew near the dais, the orness made a series of gestures – her fingers moving through the air in a way that reminded Talia of birds taking flight – and the Eye appeared in front of her.

It was a moment that never failed to draw a collective gasp from the crowd. And not without reason. First there was nothing in the air between the orness and the poison eater. Then there was this: a floating orb lowering itself from nowhere, so big that it was impossible to wrap your arms around.

It wasn't that easy to wrap your mind around either.

Depending on where you stood, the time of day, and your own state of mind, the Eye of Enthait looked like the moon, the sun, a child's face, an egg, the inside of an eye, the black of the night. Yellow, golden, brown, beige, white, silver. Some said they could see creatures milling about inside its surface. Others that it was filled with machine parts. Or completely empty.

None of those things were what Talia saw. No one had

ever asked her what it looked like. That at least was one thing she'd never had to lie about.

The Eye slowly lowered itself until it rested just above the surface of the dais. The dais was only a single step off the ground, but every time Talia took it, it felt eternally higher. As if she was not walking onto a solid platform, but was climbing toward something distant and unreachable. She feared she would fall, and find herself with nothing below her but emptiness.

But then her foot landed solidly on the dais and the orness was coming toward her, murmuring, "Moon meld you, Poison Eater."

"And you, Orness."

The orness reached forward and pressed her thumbs over Talia's eyes. When Talia dreamt of the orness – and she did, more often than she wanted to admit – it was this moment that she saw: a tall woman hooded in bloodshadow, the dark whorls of her thumbs coming to take away her sight.

The orness' thumbs gave off a soft heat, as if a fire had just gone out beneath her skin. Her voice in murmured ritual was ancient, tired, but not without strength. She had been the orness a long time.

Not much longer. Not if Talia could help it.

In the blackness behind the orness' thumbs, Talia heard the Eye begin to spin, a low keening whir that made her back teeth ache and her tongue go dry. The noise was always the same, no matter what poison the device created. Talia's reaction was too – a sense of dread in the very depth of her being, the taste of bitter acid in the back of her throat.

"Do you promise to serve the city of Enthait?" the orness asked. "Do you promise to serve its people?"

"I do," Talia said. Bitter-tongued in the blackness.

"You may begin," the orness said. She removed her thumbs and stepped behind Talia in a swift movement that left her blinking, unsteady. Looking at the device didn't help; it moved at a speed that challenged you to take it in, promised you could make sense of it if you just stared long enough, hard enough. But you never could; it was so fast that your eyes couldn't capture any single thing, but hers kept trying, skipping across its surface, grasping nothing but shapes and shadows.

Swallowing down the bile in her throat, aware of the crowds all around her, she knelt in front of the whirring device, closing her eyes against its dizzying promise. Its movement pushed a breeze across her skin as it, too, did its duty.

Each poison was different. The Eye made each one in time with the moon's passage. There was an order, but Talia didn't know it. Only the orness knew such things. How the device chose which poison to make. How it made each one. What shape or form the poison would come in.

All around her, the crowd chanted, soft and low. She knew they bet on the poisonings, although it was forbidden. Which poison. Whether she would live or die. What coming danger she would see in her visions. If she was smart, she would have bet on herself, but she never did.

Of course, she hadn't told them, any of them, the truth.

She wasn't the true poison eater.

The true poison eater was supposed to do more than just survive the poison. You were also supposed to let it connect you to the all-knowing entity that the orness called the datasphere. You were supposed to let it show you all the dangers that were coming for the city of Enthait. You were supposed to protect the city.

None of that happened for Talia. She didn't connect to the datasphere. She never saw Enthait's endangered future. She only saw her own past, spread out before her, choice by failed choice, step by broken step. A beast of her own black mind, coming for her through the toxin.

So she lied, made up bedtime stories of spooks in the night, and sent the zaffre out hunting shadows of nothing. She wasn't proud of it. Most things borne of necessity were not things she was proud of. Her missing arm. The fine scars along the sides of her head. The shard of blue-black blade. But she bore them, if only because she refused to fall beneath their weight.

The Eye stopped with a low whine and a metallic clunk. Waiting for her. Talia reached into – *through* – the hull of the device with her true hand and felt around until she grasped something small and soft. She pulled out a tiny pill filled with roiling black liquid. It smelled of wet ashes and wounds on the edge of going bad. Her stomach rolled, protested at the thought of taking *that* into her body, at the thought of the memories it would surely bring.

She'd done worse in order to survive. She could do this. Six down, four to go. She *would* live through the poisonings. She *would* become the orness. She *would* be the keeper of the aria and use it to destroy the monsters that haunted her dreams.

"Ebeli," the crowd whispered, a hushed hiss, as she held up the pill. A few at first, and then more and more. Until the whisper had no choice but to become a chant. A hissing, writhing demand. *Ebeli. Ebeli. Ebeli.*

Everyone was waiting for her. Waiting for her to be

their poison eater. Waiting for her to save them and the city. Waiting for her to lie.

Finwa, she thought, as she always did when she placed the poison upon her tongue. *I am sorry for what I am about to do.*

THE POISONING – EBELI

Cathaliaste, the last of the Twelve Martyrs of the Forgotten Compass, was falling. In the storm and the blood and the fading sharpness of her frozen blade, there was nothing to be done for it.

They had known from the beginning that they could not win this fight, that not all of them would make it out. But they had sworn that they would go down together, still swinging, their blue-black blades making one final cut of mech and flesh.

And they all had. All except Cathaliaste.

She had tried. She had swung her blade until her arm could no longer lift it, and then she had lifted it anyway.

The martyrs had discovered how to destroy the swarms, bloated gold hunters of wing and sting, awaiting their numbing poison before slicing their bellies with a single quick stroke. They'd learned of the secret place behind the spine where the horned mechbeasts' minds lived, and plunged their blades deep through skin and sinew to find the beating metal thoughts.

They had maimed more than she could count. Killed

enough that the bodies of swarms and mechbeasts piled around them. Lost enough that the bodies of their sisters littered the snow.

Cathaliaste was the only one still standing when the last wave of the mechbeasts came across the snow. The unhuman vordcha were never ones for subtlety, and the things they twisted were not either. They were altered to bring pain and death, and always in that order. The sound of them coming, more of them, always more, as she stood alone, unsistered, unmoored, made Cathaliaste shiver with dread.

The creatures slavered and snarled as they came from the edge of the blackweave, metal horns forward, their yellow war stripes lighting up the night. She met them with her blade, its blue-black steel driving deep. The mechbeasts returned the favor. Sharpened metal horns tore into the exposed places in her flesh. Sharp tusks and rows of teeth sank around her legs to open her skin to the bone.

And still they came. And behind them, she knew, the vordcha waited for the light of day. In the safety of the dawn the vordcha would leave the oily ooze of the blackweave and come for all of them, the living and the dead.

Earlier, as they had prepared their escape from the blackweave and the creatures who bound them there, Cathaliaste had stood with her sisters, finger to finger, and sworn that they would fall as one. Skelohin. Anthleaon. Maeryl. And they would take as many mechbeasts with them as they could lay blade to. They knew they would not win, but they would fall together, and that was something.

But in the end, it was not to be. Cathaliaste's amputated hand and wrist ached, invisible and broken. Her knife hand had slipped into nothing, numb with the fight and the swinging. Her blood dripped onto the white earth, the dropped path a vivid reminder of her progress and her fall back. The friends, lovers, sisters she'd fought beside were dead, already cooling in the snow around her. There was no one left to see her fall.

Two more beasts came for her, leading with teeth and tusks. She watched her knife tumble from her hand as if in a dream, unable to stop its decline.

As the mechbeasts bore down upon her, the last martyr stepped backward over the bright drops, added more, retracing the map of her coming demise. And then she turned and ran.

She scrabbled through the snow, falling and flailing, catching herself and then pushing on. At last she fell face-down, panting, and could not get up. The snow was deep enough that she thought she could drown in it, just bury herself inside the white and be gone.

But she thought of her sisters, dead in the deep white banks, and how the vordcha would come for them with the unfolding of the light. She should be there with them, for whatever horrors came next, she should be there. And she did not want to die alone.

She forced herself to rise, fingers cracking from the cold, the flayed skin on her cheeks and wrist iced along the edges. She had no weapon save her boots and teeth, no plan other than a need to lie among her sisters until the white covered her.

She crossed the blood-spotted field. It had not stopped snowing, and martyr and insects and mechbeast alike were covered. She could only see vague shapes beneath the white and red, couldn't tell who was friend and who was foe. She would find Maeryl, Maeryl whom she had loved and who loved her, and she would lie beside her until the end.

She began to dig, forgetting for a moment the loss of her hand. The impact of the solid snow against the open stump of her arm froze her breath and shadowed her vision's edge.

She chopped the freezing snow with the sides of her remaining hand. Her skin was broken and bleeding, her nails splitting down the center, and still she dug.

Here was Staviane, her red braids and black garb locked at her throat. Here, another sister that she could not make out, still crushed beneath the body of a fallen mechbeast. She crawled through the snow, pushing ice away from faces. Kanistl, who fought with cries of jubilation and who had gone down singing in her home tongue, a beautiful haunting sound that had made Cathaliaste cry as she brought down her own blade. She found Anthleaon's makeshift knife buried in the snow, but not Anthleaon herself.

Finally, she found Maeryl. Her long double-braids were black with blood and gore, and she'd lost much of her face to the grinding teeth of the mechbeasts, but Cathaliaste would have recognized her anywhere. Maeryl who had loved blue and silver, who had loved anything that smelled of salt, Maeryl who had loved Cathaliaste.

Her tears froze so quickly it was impossible to tell them from the ice shards that stung her cheeks and eyes. She scooped snow as best she could from Maeryl's side, making a hollow.

When the hollow was almost big enough to hold her, she lowered her body into it and closed her eyes. She would lie at her friend's side and then she would let the snow cover her and then she would die. It's what she should have done before. It's what would have happened if she had not been a coward, if she had not run.

A flare of yellow light and the low snort of a mechbeast stopped her from falling into stillness. She wasn't afraid, although she should have been. She was shamed and heartsick and aching, but she was not afraid.

The mechbeast in front of her was barely able to stand, one foreleg bent at a bad angle. As she watched from her hollow in the snow, its stripes went dead of light, becoming a brown wash against its hide. One of its mechanical horns had been ripped away, leaving only blood and wires along the stump. The other horn hung crookedly, connected only by frazzled wires that sparked and sputtered.

The beast tried to scramble to a stand and gave a quiet exhale of pain, its labored breath scattering the bloodied snow around its muzzle like pink petals.

She was sorry she'd let her knife fall so long ago. It was the only true succor she could have given. Even monsters deserved that kindness at the end.

"I can't help you," she said. And her voice was cracked with frost. "I can't even help myself. Kill me if you're going to."

The creature's stripes flared, a new wash of yellow across the snow.

wait.

The plea felt like a horn being blown in the space of her chest, and it took her a long moment to figure out that it had come from the creature. Some light still shone blue behind the casings of its eyes as it turned its gaze upon her. There was something... under there... beneath what the vordcha had made it.

help.

It was both an offer and a request.

"No. They will come," she said. "And you will become theirs again."

They were already coming. The sky was growing light. The snow was brightening beneath her.

The creature raised its bad back leg, and aimed it at the dangling horn. She could hear the crack of the already damaged leg bone as it struck the mech, and then the creature's pained breath. The wires in the horn sparked again, hissing as snow fell upon them.

The vordcha built their beasts up for war, just as they built their martyrs up for memory. Tusks. Horns. Heads. Hands. The arm she'd cut away throbbed with the echo of what it had been.

"Wait," she said. Her voice no more than a puff of air and yet the creature stilled.

She raised herself to her knees and dug in the snow with different purpose now, fingers cracked and freezing, the wounds that had begun to scab over breaking open to trail blood across her skin. She cut her fingers on Maeryl's blade when she found it, a slice so quick and fast that she wouldn't have noticed if not for the new gush of blood. Its warmth was welcome, if temporary.

The blood and snow made the work slippery. One-handed, Cathaliaste worked to open the frozen fingers of her friend, but Maeryl had courage. Maeryl had swung until her end, clutching the base of her blade tight in her fisted fingers.

Cathaliaste whispered an apology and broke the fingers of her friend, her sister, her love, one after the other, until she could pull the blade from Maeryl's shattered fist. The curved metal was coated in a sheen of frost and blood, but it was unbroken.

She felt like she should say something, but she didn't know any prayers or words of succor other than those forced upon her by the vordcha, and she would not despoil her friend's death with that. So she leaned down, hobbled and stilted by cold and loss, and kissed the frosted, torn face of the one she had loved. She whispered one single word, a promise greater than any other she had made.

She raised her gaze to the creature before her. It hadn't moved, other than to shift the weight off its bad leg.

"I will help you," she said. She didn't know why she said it, but she felt the weight of its truth in her chest.

The two eyed each other across the snow. We are two wild beasts, Cathaliaste thought. Made in the likeness of our creators.

yes.

She crawled forward, slowly, on her knees. The creature gave up all pretense of standing, sending a spray of bloodied snow up into Cathaliaste's eyes and mouth as it let itself fall. The creature closed its eyes. She hadn't realized how much light the stripes gave off until they were extinguished and she found herself in the dark.

"I can't see," she said.

Stripes of blue flared along the creature's sides. She'd seen them turn orange for fighting, and yellow just before. But never this turquoise. It blinded her and she blinked away the spots in her vision.

"I will give you mercy if you ask it of me," she said.

The hollow in her chest waited for an answer that came only as silence.

She had never touched a mechbeast other than in fight and fear. Her fist wanted to grip the blade, to beat and batter, to destroy. She tightened her hand around her friend's blade, unable to move.

The creature made the decision for her, pushing its head into her makeshift lap. She gasped at the heat of it. Even covered in a layer of snow and gore, the short fur was soft, plush. The remaining horn was half scored, a jagged cut that left it hanging by wires and mech. There was no blood or living tissue inside, but she knew it pained the creature. And her next act would do more so.

She had no idea how to do it. With both hands, she could have taken hold of the horn's end and cut with the other hand. With one hand, she needed something to shore the horn against. She shifted, until the broken horn lay flat against her lap, its curve along the top of her thigh.

"Ready?" she asked.

She had been a survivor long enough to know not to wait for an answer. She drew the blade down through the air, the effort punctuated by her own low grunt.

The blade broke through the horn and wires and sliced through the top of her thigh. She'd known that was a risk and still the pain surprised her into forgetting. It wasn't the worst pain she'd faced in the long night, but it was the pain that made her realize that she had decided to live. There was an anguish in that far beyond the way her skin and muscle split beneath the blade's press, and it was that which pushed the howl from her lips. The creature howled, too, a mournful cry that swept like wind through her chest.

The blade in her hand was broken. She dropped it into the snow. There was steel inside her, a jagged piece of cold embedded in the flesh, but she couldn't grasp it with her frozen fingers.

The horn, at least, had broken clean through. She watched the creature nudge at it, and realized that the snow was lightening.

Cathaliaste lifted her eyes to the horizon. It was dawn. The vordcha would come. She would not die at their hands again.

"Can you move?" she asked the creature.

It stood and took a single step by way of answer. She matched it, impossibly, her muscles driven by something deep and new. Not fear. Not the desire to live. Not even grief. It was something she had no name for. Not yet.

As dawn broke, Cathaliaste, the last of the Twelve Martyrs of the Forgotten Compass, rose and began to walk north with a mechbeast at her side.

Talia woke from the poisonings nearly alone. Bed. Body. The ache of ice against her skin. A sense of thirst. A sense of sick. The lie she was about to tell clogging the back of her throat like the pit of a fruit.

Every time, she wondered if she could do it all again.

Every time, she decided no.

Then yes.

It was hard after to tell what was real, what was now. Shaking the blackhang of memory. Her everything was filled with then – the bloodied hollow in the snow, the fevered ache of her missing arm, Maeryl's fingers snapping inside her own.

Maeryl. There was something in the poison dream that she'd seen about her friend. A detail. A missing piece. But what? She couldn't grasp it. It was like the dream was more detailed than it had been in real life. More detailed, but at the same time, full of things she had missed. She tried to see it again, to visualize herself down on her knees in the snow, Maeryl's cold fingers beneath her own but... there was nothing. It was sliding away. And she had more pressing things. Like preparing herself for Burrin. *Focus.*

Her whole body was dirt and dust. Even her eyes were full of desert, gritted shut, starred with pressure. After a moment, she could feel the rough blanket beneath her, sense her hand clenching, the knuckles aching. She knew this bed, this sideways light that flickered through her eyelids, the scent of her own body's toil and, softer, the acrid taste of the Painter's colors at the back of her throat.

She'd survived. Seven down, three to go.

She opened her eyes. Standing at the side of her bed, the Painter was staring at her. When he realized she was alive, he exhaled, a soft, low sound filled with disappointment.

"I'm sorry," she said. Or tried to say. The words died on the dead muscle of her tongue and sank to the back of her breath. It was what she tried to say every time.

And the Painter, every time, merely nodded and said very solemnly, "Perhaps next time."

"Perhaps," she said, her voice coming back midway through the word, although she knew what she was saying wasn't true. There was something wrong with her. Or, perhaps in this case, right. Whatever horrors the vordcha had put inside her, they had remade her into something that was more than or less than human. She'd pulled out their mech piece by piece, but she couldn't undo the changes it had wrought inside her. It was the only reason she could find for why she kept surviving the poisonings without being the true poison eater.

The Painter wasn't entirely human either. Too long a face, and when you looked at him for more than a few seconds, his angles seemed off, as if he was put together by someone who didn't understand humans. He had only three thin fingers on each hand, the ends of which were frilled like brushes and covered in the colors he'd been mixing, sitting here waiting for her to die.

"Nice brown," she said.

"Your eyes," he said.

He was right.

She watched him pack up his paints and his disappointment, placing them side by side in a tiny box that rested on top of a wheeled device full of tubes and wires. The device was for her – for dead her. The first time she'd woken here, the Painter had told her that if she had died, he would have been able to use the device to drain the fat and marrow from her, and give her immortality in his paint. He'd been so kind, and so very sad, that for a moment she almost felt bad that she'd survived. By now, disappointing the Painter was just part of the ritual, another step in this dance to be carefully followed.

"Next time, perhaps you'll die and I shall be blessed to shine you eternal on the mekalan," the Painter said as he swung the door open.

"Perhaps you shall," she agreed. Although she had no intention of becoming part of his painted wall of the dead.

After he left and she was alone, Talia pushed herself to sitting. It was *thoda* – bad luck – for the zaffre to see her dead, but the Painter would tell Burrin and the others that she was alive and they would come soon. She needed to be ready.

As always, she had no idea what she would tell Burrin

when he asked her what she'd seen. Telling lies, she believed, came best without rehearsal. But every time, she worried that she would trip herself up, get it wrong, and Burrin – smart, suspicious Burrin – would find her out.

The large room – she had come to think of it as the *lying room*, although its true name was Mekalan Hall – was a rectangle of white synth walls, empty but for a bed, two chairs, and a table upon which rested a folded drape of fabric the same blue as her cloak. Her winding sheet.

The far wall was the only anomaly, a single piece of translucent metal, three times as tall as Talia. Three times again as wide as it was tall. The mekalan.

Written across the very top in a fine hand: THE MOON DID MELD US AND WE DID SHINE.

Beneath, the painted ones. The dead ones. The would-be poison eaters, men and women, who had come before her and died before her. So many that they piled up like strata, filling the wall space until they were cheek to cheek, shoulder to shoulder, their painted blue cloaks flowing together so they became one great blue sky dotted with dark stars of faces. The sun flowed through the paint, stopping only at the thickness of the eyes, which were detailed with so many layers they almost seemed to suck the very light into them.

The Painter had mixed their fat and marrow and blood into his colors and given each of them eternity on this wall.

Eternity. The vordcha had talked about eternity, too. To them, eternity looked like carving memory into the body: their memories into her body. Here, eternity looked like painting the body into memory: her body into their memories.

Talia was pretty sure she didn't care for eternity, either

way. She would take her own now over someone else's imparted forever.

The sun shifted, shining cantways through the clear wall, sending colored shadows across the floor and over her feet. Through the thinnest layers of paint, Talia could see the diviners on the other side of the wall, in the street. On their knees, they prostrated before the art, running their palms over the images in complex patterns that meant something unknown to her. They sing-songed, low and melodious, in time to their movements, only the lowest notes coming through the plating.

They were praying for her. Until she left Mekalan Hall and walked among them again, they would believe she was caught in Attor, the space between life and death. Unlike the Painter (and probably a few others), the diviners very much wanted her to continue to live.

Talia touched one of the paintings on the wall, running her fingers over the textures of the woman's face. The wall was hot where the colors were light – the white of her hair, her pale teeth – and nearly freezing in the shadows: the dark folds of her cloak, the black orbs of her eyes.

The woman's name was Uprys, a would-be poison eater who had died shortly after Talia had arrived. Talia had gone to watch the poisoning, not because she was interested in it or even understood it, but because it was something that people did here, and she'd been trying to blend in. If she was honest with herself, she'd mostly gone because when the blue-haired woman on the Green Road had asked if she was going, her mismatched eyes had lingered in a way that Talia had not been ready to protect against.

Talia had been surprised to see that same woman standing in the middle of the clave – a word she'd just come to know – dressed in blue and bronze, draped in light. But she'd been even more surprised to watch another woman enter from what Talia now knew was the door to the tunnel outside her own room, and to hear the crowd begin to chant.

Uprys, a tall, almost gaunt woman, had worn the same cloak that Talia wore now. She was older than Talia, the white shine of her hair piled in little circles around her head. When she reached into the device, she'd pulled out what looked like a shelled creature of some kind. It was hard to see from as far away as Talia was – way up near the top of the curving walls – but when it wiggled in the woman's hand, even Talia could tell that it was alive.

It wasn't until the woman lifted the creature between her thin fingers and brought it to her open mouth that Talia had understood that she was expected to swallow the thing. She'd been unable to suppress the shudder that rose in her, and couldn't understand how it was that no one else around her seemed to feel the same.

Somehow, impossibly, the woman had lowered the creature into her mouth. Talia could have sworn she saw it catch and bob in the woman's long throat, but she had since convinced herself that wasn't possible. She'd been too far away to have seen such a thing, surely.

The woman had swallowed, coughed, and then just... disappeared. Not completely. It was still possible to see her outline, a long draw of lines where she'd been just moments ago. The lines shuddered, contracted, and then broke apart, seeming to whirl into a thing that was utterly inhuman, each line a leg and a mouth at the same time, the outline of a hundred heads. The vision lasted only a second and then the woman was there again, falling to the floor in a spasm of gnashing teeth and clenched fists.

Uprys' legacy was that she'd had four successful poisonings – the last one warning the city of a roving band of abhumans – before the fifth took her. Talia imagined the Painter had been very pleased indeed. Uprys was beautiful on the wall, her face depicting an expression of sweetness and longing.

Beside her was a man named Darad. Talia had met him a few times before the poisoning, and he seemed steady, confident even, that he would become the next orness without issue. Talia hadn't been able to convince herself to attend another poisoning – not even for the woman with the mismatched eyes – but she had heard about it both times Darad succeeded, once even delivering the rare good news that nothing dangerous lurked on the horizon. The next thing she'd heard, Darad was gone and his image had gone up on the mekalan.

And the orness was beginning her search for a new poison eater.

And Talia was starting to come up with her plan for filling that hole.

She touched an unpainted space on the wall. A hole too. One reserved for her face.

"Not this time," she said aloud, just as the door opened behind her.

Even without turning, she could tell Burrin had entered the room first. She'd noticed he always did, when he could. Plus, his footsteps were... unique. He wore boots soled with some type of metal that made every step an announcement of his presence. It was still a surprise to her, how someone whose job it was to protect and hunt might never consider the virtues of not being noticed right away.

But certainly she was happy to use it to her advantage when she could.

"They're beautiful, yes?" Burrin said.

If he was ever disappointed to walk through that door and see her alive, he never showed it.

"Affah," she agreed.

She heard him step closer – one footfall, the next – and then his voice was low in her ear, designed only for her to hear. "And *they* are fools," he said. "Down in the dirt for the not-yet-dead." A thing no one else in Enthait would dare say, most surely not to her.

She said nothing. For a moment, side by side, they watched the diviners on their knees, praying into the unknown for a thing they didn't know had already happened.

"Well, what dangers have you brought us this time?" Burrin asked. As if it was not the dangers she saw, but her very presence that brought destruction upon the city.

She turned. Unlike his mother, Burrin kept no part of his face hidden. In fact, he accentuated the sharp angles of his cheeks and jaw with a soft crimson wrap that coiled about his neck and ran under his zaffre bronzes and blues. His dark eyes – so black they sometimes seemed to run toward purple – were set deep in his head. Everything about him was sharp and striking, like a well-wielded blade.

Two of the other greyes stood behind him.

Talia had taught herself the names of all ten greyes as soon as she'd decided to become the poison eater. Names were important. They had power. Not a power that you could hold in your hand, but something intangible. Powerful the way that air was powerful. She knew many of the zaffre's names too, although nowhere near all. She'd thought at first there might be dozens of them, but over time, she'd started to notice that there were far more than she'd imagined.

These greyes were Imran and Rynz. Imran bore a shaved head, and an ever-present scowl beneath a thick black mustache. Rynz had two dimples on the right side when he smiled, and a gap between his teeth that whistled softly when he exhaled.

She liked both of them – she would have said she liked them better than she liked Burrin, but that could be said about any of the greyes, and probably most of the zaffre as well, even the ones she didn't know. She liked them quite a bit more than that – but that wasn't why she was glad to see them standing behind Burrin. She was glad because neither of them was Isera.

For someone who was brutally bad at *telling* lies, Isera could spot one on your lips before you even spoke it. Those mismatched eyes had purpose. Lying to Burrin in front of her would have put Isera in a place where she'd be torn between her duty to the zaffre and her... whatever it was she felt for Talia.

It seemed that so far, luck of the draw had kept Isera out of the lying room. But if Talia kept surviving, Isera would be in here with Burrin eventually. She just hoped it wouldn't be soon.

By way of greeting, Imran and Rynz put their thumbs to the spaces above their eyes. Talia responded in kind, although she kept her attention entirely on Burrin. He was all that mattered here.

"Moon meld you, Greyes Burrin," she said.

"And you," he replied. He never used her title. Nor her name. Burrin never went by the formalities when he could get away with not.

Talia let her thumbs linger above her eyes a heartbeat beyond what was expected. She never brushed aside the rituals with Burrin; if anything, she went the other way, overly formal, overly perfect. He didn't scare her, as he seemed to others. But he was smart and he was driven – and she was sure she was standing in his way.

At first, she'd thought Burrin dumb and peevish, the spoiled son of the orness who'd gotten his job by nothing more than the luck of his bloodline. But it hadn't taken her long to see that wasn't true. He wasn't like Seild, an impatient child who had to be reminded of her duties in order to return to them. When he skipped the rituals, he did so to make it clear he was above them, that they were unnecessary. As were you. He was as sharp as those sticks he carried. She had to be sharper.

"Greyes Burrin, I hope you weren't kept waiting too long by my lack of death," she said.

A cool game they played. Her pretending deference, loyalty, truth. Him pretending to believe that she felt any of those things. She knew why she played it; she had yet to figure out why he did. She could only imagine he was biding his time. Waiting for her to slip up. Or die.

The words, scathing and burnt – *your mother didn't choose you, she chose me* – rose to her tongue, but she held them there, silent seeds for the future.

"We shall see, once we hear your story," he said.

The first time she'd stood before Burrin, she had been scared. Terrified. She'd taken the poison, expecting either to die or to see a true threat to the city. Neither of those things had happened.

Instead, she'd seen the moment she and Maeryl had

begun to plan their escape from the vordcha. In the poison dream, they'd been in bed together – if you could call the oily substrate they'd piled up a bed – as Maeryl drew fingers along Talia's arm. Beneath the skin, the vordcha's metal and mech made a living tattoo of branches that marked her blood and bone.

Maeryl's mech was elsewhere, hidden in the depths of her head. When the vordcha implanted a new memory in her, she would slide away for days on end, forgetting everything else. Forgetting Talia. Forgetting herself. But in that moment, she was fully present, fully Maeryl.

"We won't win," Maeryl had said.

"We can't lose anything else," Talia had responded.

That was the moment they'd begun to plan.

That first poison dream, Talia hadn't known what it meant. Why had she seen her own past in the poisoning instead of the city's future, as they had told her she would? Afraid, uncertain, she'd planned to tell Burrin the truth. That she wasn't the poison eater, that she didn't see any dangers to the city. She'd opened her mouth to say, "I didn't see anything. I just had a memory. Or maybe a dream."

Instead, she started telling a story about a long-legged hunter stalking its way toward the city. Hungry and seeking. Moving in from the west.

Why? Instinct. Self-preservation. A way out. Yes. But also, there was something she saw in Burrin even then. An edge. She thought it was an expectation that all things belonged to him, or should belong to him. And that if he just waited her out, he would have this thing too. In that, he had reminded her of the vordcha, and she could not bring herself to tell the truth. Could not bring herself to give up so easily.

All of those things had crashed into her and she had spit out their seeds and started this untrue thing growing inside her.

Burrin's foot tapped impatiently, a metallic click. "The Painter said you were not dying," he said. "So...?"

Talia waited a moment, a breath, let Burrin's question settle into the space before she lifted her gaze to his eyes. Those dark pools were impossible to read. She imagined that were she younger, she would have looked there and found herself drowning in that blackness. But she'd known the kind of blackness that stole the breath, that stole the very beating of one's heart, and this was so far short of that the space between gave her a kind of strength.

She lowered her voice slightly and began to tell her story. She never knew what she was going to say until she began, but she could always taste the story on her tongue as it arrived, the taste of cool, clear water running through her.

"Ebeli showed me true," she said. "The coming of a flock of winged beasts, from the southwest." She closed her eyes and began to bring the creatures to life upon her tongue.

She'd sometimes told stories for her sisters in the blackweave. Stories they would first tell to her, disjointed, personal, full of back and forths and confusion, and she would take the threads and spin them into something grand. Something that made them forget, for a moment, the metal bits beneath their skin, the horror beneath their dreams.

She pulled the details of the poisonings from those stories and her own mind, details gleaned and honed, weaving them together as she went, more by instinct than anything else. She pulled in details from books she'd read here, from the tapestries in the market, from the children's tales on the street. Had the other poison eaters told such stories? She didn't know.

Burrin gave her no indication either way. He stood listening but unmoved. No response to anything she said, other than a small tightening of his eyes as she described the creatures' wings, metallic triangles that reflected the orange desert below and the blue sky above.

At that pull of his eyes, she worried she'd gone too far; what if the poisoning wasn't as detailed for the others? What if all they had were vague impressions? It was too late to take the detail back, and so she pushed on. She thought of Khee and added yawning mouths, filled with multiple rows of teeth. She thought of a tapestry she'd seen in the market and talked of talon-tipped claws on long legs. She thought of the poison dream, and when she told him of the rows of stingers along the beasts' stomachs, the numbing poisons, her shudders were not a lie.

Imran and Rynz exchanged a glance. Imran mouthed something to Rynz that Talia couldn't make out, and Rynz nodded. Whatever Burrin might think, they, at least, believed her tale.

When she was done, Burrin nodded, and made a gesture toward the two greyes behind him. Something else Talia couldn't read, but they both bowed their heads and stepped quickly from the room.

Burrin watched them go, then pulled a tiny orb from his pocket. It was dark blue, etched with silver lines. When he shook it in his fist, a piece of thick fabric bloomed from its center. He spread the fabric on the bottom of the bed, running his hands over it to smooth it. Beneath his fingers, it became a map.

She refused to admit, even to herself, how much she coveted this device of his. Not the device so much, but what it promised – the whole world in your hand, available to you with little more than a flick of your wrist. Her desire was a secret she kept buried in the layers of her skin, lest he discover it and use it against her. She didn't even know why she craved it, exactly.

Talia looked at the map on the bed, letting the places on it sink into her mind once again. The city of Enthait from above, looking as she'd never seen it in life, spread out across the middle of the fabric. The clave, the Endless Market, the Green Road, the skars – tall, scythe-shaped buildings that dotted the city – even Isera's house, although Talia didn't look directly at it. Not with Burrin watching her so closely.

Around Enthait, the rusty orange desert – the Tawn – that flowed out for miles before it eventually became grassland and then forest and then the unknown where the fabric folded back on itself. The blackweave was out there, somewhere, in that blank space, and it pleased her to know that on this map at least, it did not appear. It almost made it possible for her to believe, just for a moment, that it did not exist at all.

"Now, tell me exactly where you saw these creatures," Burrin said.

Talia didn't hesitate. She picked a point on the map, off to the southwest, a tiny pinpoint of dust or ink that specked the fabric. That place was as good as any for her lie.

"There," she said. "I saw them there."

• • •

As soon as Burrin left and she could breathe again, she realized she was ravenous, dizzy with hunger. Every part of her body had become a sudden, gaping void that demanded to be filled. A creature of mouth and fist, a beast of hunger and need, she was suddenly, irrevocably sure that she would die if she didn't become fulfilled. She didn't let herself think of how that hunger, that need, was not just for food, but also for something else.

Isera.

Hurrying at the very thought of her, Talia removed her cloak, then felt around for the tiny pocket in its hem. Inside, a small round knob was attached to the coat by a piece of thin wire. She tugged the knob – "Softly, please!" she could almost hear Ganeth say, as he had the first time, when she'd nearly torn it loose from its moorings. She didn't pretend to understand most of the devices he made, and he often had to guide her in their use, lest she destroy something with her carelessness. He treated his creations the way most people might treat their children, and it clearly pained him to watch her interacting with them. She was about as good with devices as she was with children, so that was something he should be grateful for at least.

Her first tug was too gentle, and nothing happened. She pulled a little harder and was rewarded as the cloak tightened in upon itself, vibrating so hard she could feel it in the bottom of her stomach. And then it turned itself... inside out. Except it didn't. It wasn't like when you turned a shirt inside out. This was as though each part of the fabric, the very weave and stitch of it, reversed themselves. In a moment, she was holding a long grey wrap that looked and felt nothing like the cloak she'd just been wearing.

"Most people will know your trappings," Ganeth had said. "Not your face. At least, not while you're alive."

He'd meant to be helpful, saying that. But she hadn't been able to quell the flinch that pulled her spine tight, and as soon as the words were out, he bared his teeth in apology. He wasn't, she had come to understand, very good at those types of things.

Now she pulled the wrap over her shoulders, tugging the heavy hood up so that her hair was hidden and her face was deep in the fabric's shadow. Then she shifted the fabric around her, draping it until it covered her hexed hand. She would have taken the band off, but she had no pockets. And as much as she might have protested when Ganeth had given her the thing, she did find it useful. Plus, she suspected that having no hand might be just as much of a giveaway as having a mechanical one.

When she stepped outside, darkness hadn't arrived yet, but it was on its way. The light from the sun-powered glowglobes shone softly all along the street. Here and there, mirrored orbs, smaller than her fist, bobbed around the shine. She'd never figured out what they were – device? creature? debris? – and no one else seemed to take notice of them, but she'd seen them fluttering, often near lights, at all times of day.

Even though the mekalan opened onto the Green Road – one of the busiest areas of the city – it was mostly quiet. It often was after the poisonings. Few walked the streets. She imagined people went home to mourn their losses, or to one of the bars in the rundown section of the Break to crow about their winnings. And, she thought, something about the poisoning, about the poison eater, about *her*, scared them as much as it drew them.

She didn't know how news traveled so quickly in the city, but it did, and by the time she stepped onto the street, she bet nearly everyone who cared to know did know – whether she'd survived, what she saw in the poisoning, and how the zaffre were planning to respond. Sometimes, it seemed that she, out of everyone inside Enthait's walls, was the last to know. Perhaps second only to the diviners.

Who even now were still touching the wall, singing their prayers. Talia began to make her way past them. None noticed her passing. After she walked by them, she stopped and turned back. She tugged her hood down around her neck, waiting for one to recognize her – whether they truly were fools or not, as Burrin believed, she couldn't bear to think of them down on their knees for any longer, praying for something they didn't know had already come to pass.

Just as she was starting to regret her decision – she was hungry and tired, and attention was the last thing she desired – one of them noticed her. A tiny older man with white paste across his dark brow and yellowing hair placed his fists over his eyes in what Talia understood to be the old gesture of reverence, long replaced by the pressing of thumbs above the eyes. His language was gnarled and twisted, words that slipped through Talia's understanding like water through her fingers. It wasn't the Truth, but it carried the lilt of it, just enough that she felt like she *should* know it, even though she didn't. The other diviners heard it and joined in, putting their fists over their eyes and then, seemingly as one, pressing their foreheads to the ground.

She never quite got used to this moment. Standing, while others knelt before her, their fists against their eyes. Blind. Below. Vulnerable. The first time it had happened, she'd tried to get them all to rise, to go back to their homes and their lives. But they had shrunk from her touch, refusing to stand or stop singing as long as she remained standing there. Now, she muttered a soft thank you, for what she wasn't sure, and shrank back into the shadows of her wrap.

She stepped briskly toward the soft pink lights of the Scarlet Sisk.

Since Talia's very first poisoning – *tursin*, a yellow goo in the shape of a moth that had burst open as soon as she'd put it in her mouth, sending a dry, coughing powder down her throat – since that first time, she and Isera had met after at the Scarlet Sisk, a little nothing bar not far from Mekalan Hall.

The place was dark, private, and rarely busy. There was just enough of a hum in the air to make her feel as though they could talk without being heard, and it gave them reason to sit close, mouths to each other's ears.

It was risky to meet in public, but the effects of the poisoning stayed with her, in her head if not in her bones. She needed time to shake that off, but she also didn't want to be alone. The lasting effect of spending her whole life in a small space with others, she guessed. Always vying for room, but being so used to the press of bodies that you forgot how to make the edges of your own skin. Spending time with Isera at the Sisk gave her time to fill herself up again, become whole, find where her skin began.

That first time she and Isera had met at the Sisk, it was accidental. Talia had stepped out of Mekalan Hall into the street, starving, confused, having just lied to the leader of the zaffre. No one had taught her what to expect or do after that first poisoning. Because no one, she realized now, had expected her to survive it.

Just outside the door she'd been waylaid by the diviners, who'd wanted to surround her that first time, to keep her there, as if to ensure that she truly was alive. Someone else had run up the street, shaking his fists at her, yelling about the shins she'd cost him by daring to stay alive.

Shaken, she'd ducked around the nearest dark corner, walking until she'd found an old stone building with light flickering inside. It wasn't until she'd peered through the windows that she'd even realized it was a bar. A secret business with no sign out front was definitely her kind of place. And when she'd seen a flash of blue curls in a corner booth, she'd pushed open the door and gone inside.

The second time, she'd asked Isera if she would meet her there after, and Isera had not hesitated to say yes. The Sisk had become their dark and quiet haven, a place where they could both feel unwatched, unnoticed, safe. A place where no one would care when their fingers brushed together across the table.

As far as Talia could tell, it wasn't forbidden, precisely, for the poison eater and a member of the zaffre to spend time together outside of the necessary rituals. But it wasn't exactly condoned, either. And Isera was one of the greyes, directly under Burrin's command. Which changed everything.

As soon as her hand touched the carved horn doorknob of the Sisk, she let out a deep breath. It was almost done. Soon, she would be sitting in a quiet, dark corner next to Isera, laughing over something. And that would be the moment in the ritual where Talia felt truly and deeply sure that she had survived another poisoning. That she had pulled it off. That things were going to be all right.

Seven down, three to go.

She pushed the door open, grateful for the dim light and the oddly angled interior space, where booths were tucked into corners and half hidden by heavy fabrics and ornate layers of lights and strings.

Ziralyt was behind the bar, serving drinks and smiling coyly, as he often was. Every visible part of his skin – which was a lot, as he favored low-slung pants and little more than a few long necklaces on top – was covered in pale silver triangles that seemed to shape and reshape themselves upon his skin as he moved. His eyes, too, were silvered, and they shone in the half-dark.

Ziralyt saw her first – he recognized her, even as she was hidden beneath her hood. Which shouldn't have surprised her, as often as she and Isera met here, and as often as he served them both. It wasn't the first time she felt like she was well hidden, only to have someone spot her inside her disguise.

It wasn't so much that she wanted to be sneaky or that she had a hidden agenda – outside of her role as the poison eater, at least. It was more that being the poison eater brought with it a level of attention that made her uncomfortable. Unlike Burrin, she didn't want to announce herself. She wanted the choice to enter a space without disrupting it, to walk unnoticed, to do whatever the opposite was of creating a stir. Not invisibility so much as blending in. She suspected it was, like so many things, a leftover of her life before; any time the vordcha took notice of you was likely to be a bad moment. She had learned to do her best to skirt the edges of their vision, to walk the corners and shadows.

Before she'd become the poison eater, she hadn't considered the ramifications. Some, she assumed, wanted the position for the fame it brought. She'd wanted it for entirely different reasons; the attention was an unfortunate side effect.

Just another reason that she was always grateful for Ziralyt's discretion. Grateful now that he didn't give formal greeting or even stop in his work – which was currently to give light to some kind of drink in a large metal glass. He did call a hail, the same as he might anyone who stepped into his tavern, certainly nothing interesting enough to turn anyone's gaze.

She doubted anyone else noticed the second gesture, a shake of his head that seemed to cause his tattoos to momentarily turn and point toward the back of the tavern.

She didn't think the gesture was just meant to tell her where Isera was. She couldn't remember the last time she'd walked in the door without Ziralyt stepping out from behind the bar to clasp her shoulders and drop his forehead to hers in greeting. The place was busy tonight – perhaps not as busy as she'd ever seen it, but busier than she'd expected it to be, certainly. She didn't think that was what kept him behind the bar, pointedly not shifting his body language toward her. Her hunger dissipated into an unease; it didn't change the empty feeling in her stomach, but it did change her next set of steps from a ravenous rush into something more careful.

Talia gave Ziralyt a small nod, partly in thanks and partly to acknowledge that she'd received his signal, even if she didn't yet understand it. Sometimes living in Enthait was like living inside another person's head, or being inside someone else's story. Even after nearly a year here, after all this time and all her study, there were so many things that she didn't know, so many dangerous places to step that she didn't even know to look for. But Enthait wasn't the blackweave, and that made it better than almost anywhere else she'd ever known.

She ducked her head and began to make her way through the patrons, choosing the walkspaces where there were fewer people and less light. Often after the poisoning, her senses seemed to heighten into a dizzying intensity. Colors and scents grew overwhelmingly bold, sounds clamoring against each other, as if dueling for her attention. She found that to be true now as she stepped through the wide archway into the bar's main room.

A goldglam was performing on the open stage in the middle of the main room, twirling giant golden wings in time to a music that Talia wasn't sure existed outside the dancer's own head. It didn't matter; the show was captivating even without it, perhaps even more so, a languid, sultry flow of muscle and movement that beckoned you to lean in, take a step closer, until you found yourself practically at the glam's decorated feet. Which was, the dance promised, right where you were supposed to be.

Talia had seen the glam here before; the dancer was popular, always surrounded by potential suitors, many of whom were already writing their offerings on the slips of paper to tuck into the glam's large, ornate box. One of them, maybe two, would be lucky enough to be chosen by the dancer, who would take them home in exchange for their patronage.

Tonight, the glam's hair was painted gold, to match the wings, and wound high into the shape of a tree. Tiny rainbowed jewels shimmered from the ends of the branches like leaves just before the fall. As the invisible music raised in tempo, so did the glam's dance. A hard shimmy, a slow head toss, and a few leaves did fall, twirling down, catching the light on their way. One of the would-be patrons reached out a hand and tried to catch one; it flittered away from his fingers, teasing.

That hand was reaching out from inside the sleeves of a blue and bronze uniform. That's what Ziralyt had been trying to tell her – now that she was looking, she saw zaffre everywhere.

Before now, she'd never seen a single zaffre here, other than Isera. Tonight, as she looked around, she realized the place was full of guards. Many seemed half in their cups, their uniforms disheveled, weapons leaned against walls or resting upon tables. The zaffre were not known for frivolity, and certainly not for public displays like this. And not just zaffre, but greyes as well. What were they doing here?

She saw Imran and Rynz, both, standing with their backs to her in a far corner, conversing with someone she couldn't see. *I bet my hexed hand that's Burrin*, she thought, and then nearly laughed at her own absurdity. Burrin, here? No, that was impossible. He would never.

Just in case, she tugged her hood up and ducked around a big, broad-shouldered man – one of the few in here who wasn't a zaffre, it seemed – toward the back of the building.

Isera was sitting at their usual booth, a barely lit space tucked into a curved alcove. The round light on the table touched her features, flickering across them like a kind hand. Her short blue hair was decorated with silver jewels that shone in the dark. The tiny piercings along the angle of her jaw, up the curve of her ear, and along the sides of her brow gave off a similar glow, making her light brown skin turn honeyed in the shadows.

She was no longer in her zaffre uniform, but had changed into a dark purple outfit that Talia had once remarked on for the softness of the fabric. Talia had no doubt she'd put it on just for her.

Talia took a step forward, and then realized that Isera wasn't alone. Two other greyes sat at her table. From their exuberant gestures, Talia was pretty sure they'd either been here for a while or they'd been drinking quickly. She watched one of them, Woris, handtalk wildly mid-story and nearly spill his flaming concoction on the table. She wondered, not for the first time, who originally thought that adding fire to alcohol seemed like a good idea. Isera caught Woris' gesture mid-swing, putting a steady hand against the base of the cup, staying its impending fiery slosh.

Talia had interacted with Woris only a few times, but her impression hadn't been good. He wasn't the shiniest cypher in the bag, but seemed the one most likely to malfunction when you needed him most. She doubted he improved with alcohol.

Isera hadn't seen her yet. With the drink disaster averted, Isera picked up the folding knife she'd let fall to the table. She fiddled with it, opening and closing it, her eyes everywhere but on the blade. It was the kind of thing she did when she was uncomfortable, which wasn't very often. Isera had a hundred tells, ways you could know what she was feeling and thinking without her ever having to say anything. But then she often said something anyway. It was one of the things that drew Talia to her. The quiet resolve, the steadiness of her conviction. She was as honest and forward as Talia was delusive.

That might be what drew her to Isera, but Talia still had no true idea what drew Isera to her.

She stopped in the shadow, unsure what to do. It was risky to try to talk to Isera here, to take the chance of being spotted. But she couldn't bear to leave without at least making eye contact, letting her know she'd tried.

She'd wait until Isera saw her, then she'd go. The thought made her feel nervous, as if she wouldn't be able to mark this poisoning in her mind as completed, as if leaving might come back to haunt her in some way she couldn't yet imagine. She knew it was false belief, that it was only the ritual of it – the way she'd grown accustomed to finishing the evening with Isera at her side – but she couldn't shake it.

There was nothing to be done for it. It was the right choice. Talia took another moment to watch Isera at the table, flipping her knife, pretending to be interested in whatever story Woris was telling now. But mostly she looked at Isera's eyes, the way the firelight danced across those dark surfaces.

At that moment, Isera looked up, caught sight of Talia standing there. Her face opened – eyes first, then smile – then her hands went still on the now-closed knife. It was the most amazing thing Talia had seen all night, but even as she watched, she knew Isera couldn't close it back down. She was radiating joy and relief, and in about half a second, someone would notice.

Time to go. Talia ducked her head lower and turned to step back into the night.

"Moon meld you, Poison Eater." It was Ardit, another of the greyes – were they *all* here tonight? – at her elbow, his hand lightly on her wrist. At first, she had no idea how he'd noticed her, but then she realized which wrist his hand rested upon. Blue light shone up through the gaps between his fingers. In moving through the crowd, her wrap had shifted, revealing her made hand. *Skist. And double skist.*

It took her a moment to figure out how to respond. Every greyes was chosen for something – a skill, a talent, a unique knowledge. She often saw Ardit at Burrin's side, but didn't know him well enough to even guess at his specialty. He was just taller than her, his braided white hair slicked back, dark eyes hooded. He smelled lightly of fermented calafruit and alcohol. He seemed clearer headed than the others. She'd have to gamble on him being with it enough not to ignore a gentle nudge toward proper decorum.

"Greyes Ardit," she said. "I'd greet you properly, but..." She let her gaze pointedly linger on his hand over hers. It was forward of him to touch her, even as one of the greyes. She let the touch go without further comment, hoping that they might get through the formalities quickly, and he would allow her to escape.

She expected him to remove his hand and murmur an apology. Instead, he said, "You'll come and join us."

"I should be going," she said. But her voice was lost in the din of the crowd and he did not let go of her made arm. If she stood still when he pulled, would the hexes break apart? Would the band slide from her arm and leave her standing there? She didn't know, and so she let him lead her.

So much for proper decorum. Next time, her nudge would not be so gentle.

He wove through the crowd with a speed and ease that

was startling – so that was something of his skills – and it seemed they were standing at Isera's table before she'd barely finished speaking. She suddenly found herself in the midst of half a dozen zaffre, all of them raising their glasses silently in her direction.

"I believe you know everyone, or know of them at least. But in case not…" Ardit talked above the din, saying each of their names as if they were new to her, and she did not give him an indication to think otherwise. He introduced Isera last, adding, "But you probably know her well enough already."

Talia was not about to take that dangling bait and ask what he meant.

Isera, who had shifted her attention toward one of the others as soon as she'd realized Ardit and Talia were heading their way, brought her mismatched gaze to meet Talia's.

"Moon meld you, Poison Eater," Isera said. Her thumbs trembled slightly as she brought them to rest above her eyes. Formal. More distant than even the first time they'd met on the Green Road. It was odd to hear that from Isera here, in a place where they'd never been poison eater and greyes, but something else entirely.

Talia would have responded in kind, but the noise of a chant was welling up, making it nearly impossible to hear herself, much less anyone else. It was the zaffre all around her, their cups lifting high in the air, their feet stamping on the ground.

Moon meld us and mold us and keep us from harm
for tomorrow we enter the wilds of Tawn
and face fierce dangers from far beyond

There was more, but after "beyond", it grew rambling and off-beat, the words stumbling over themselves, and Talia couldn't make it out. And then, with a sudden last-gasp effort, the words sobered up long enough to find their way home.

When the eater of poison eats of the ten
she'll see us in her dreams of the dead

When the chant had faltered away, she saw that Isera had slid over in the booth to make room for her. A quick glance at the tight crowd made it clear that leaving was not a likely option. Isera gave her a nod that meant *this is the best way*. Talia trusted that nod, so she slid along the booth until they were sitting together, as they often sat together at this very table, and yet this was wholly and completely different. The length of their thighs touched beneath the table and despite everything happening around them, all of Talia's body sank down to be in those places of heat between them. Isera's hands were back on the table. Knife open and closed, open and closed. Talia had to resist the urge to touch her dancing fingers, her wrist, the blade.

Instead, she nodded at Isera as if they'd just met, had nothing more than a passing knowledge of each other's life. Not as they were at all.

"Finwa," Talia said to the table, and the word was simple enough, but it was also so much more. To the greyes, a proper greeting. Beneath that, a sadness, a reaching out, that was hidden, she hoped, to all but Isera and her.

"Surely you're not all here for Ziralyt's barely potable concoctions," Talia said, tinkling the edge of her fingernail against one of the half-empty metal cups. She felt a little bad saying it; Ziralyt made beautiful drinks and took great pride. If he'd heard her, she had no doubt he would be hurt. It was the only thing she could think of to say. It wasn't as if she could ask Isera what was going on, not without giving things away that she didn't want to give away, and nothing in her experience was helping her figure out what the zaffre were doing here.

Woris leaned in, spilling some of his no-longer-flaming drink on the scarred wooden table. He smelled sweetly decayed, like flowers gone to rot.

"As if you don't know why we are here," he said.

Beside her, Isera stiffened. Talia waited. If someone like Woris wanted to tell you something, she'd learned the fastest way to get them to do so was not to ask, but to sit silent and wait.

It didn't take long. He leaned in, all flopping black hair and sad-flower breath. "We're going to die because of you. Because of you and your *satho* vision."

It's not my crazy vision, she started to say, but of course it was. The creatures she'd described to Burrin didn't exist, they were a figment of her imagination, and tomorrow the zaffre would ride out and try to protect the city by fighting something that could not be found.

"Why couldn't you have just lied?" Woris said. "Made something up? No, instead you had to–"

Whatever came next was cut off by Ardit, who pulled Woris away, draping an arm around his shoulders. Still, the irony of Woris' words wasn't lost on her. She felt it run down her spine like a creature with a thousand spiky legs. Talia couldn't tell if she was the one shaking or if it was Isera. She swallowed so hard it felt like there was a living thing in her throat. Even if there were words she knew to say in response – which there weren't – she didn't know if she could have said them.

Ardit said something to Woris that she couldn't hear. Then loudly, in a voice that carried farther than it should have been able to, he said, "Don't let Woris fool you. There will be no dying tomorrow. Woris is as excited to fight the charn as the rest of us. Aren't you, Woris?"

In answer, Woris pulled back and punched Ardit in the jaw, a sloppy half-closed fist that probably hit harder than he meant it to, the crack of his fingers sounding loud even in the din.

For a moment, she thought they'd fight. Both had their fists up. Ardit's lip was curled. Half snarl, half grin. His voice was low, but it carried across to Talia as if it was meant for her. "Stop, you fool. Save your fear for tomorrow. We'll fight together, as we always do."

A moment later, Woris nodded, allowing himself to be drawn back into Ardit's embrace for half a moment before he reached for his cup again. His face was set, impassive but for a tiny tic at the corner of his jaw. He was scared. Terrified. Putting on a brave face – both of them, Ardit better at it than Woris – but what was it that had them so afraid?

Talia opened her mouth to ask one of the many questions swirling around in her breath but didn't know who to ask it to. Beneath the table, Isera's leg pushed to hers, a quick touch that could have meant anything. She thought it was a warning, and so she closed her mouth without making a sound.

Woris drained his cup, slammed it hard against the table. "Someone get the poison eater a drink!" he said. "If we drink, so shall she!"

Ardit made a circular gesture with his hand above the crowd. She had no idea where it came from, but a moment later, she had a half-filled, slopped-over mug in her true hand. When she brought it to her nose, the liquid smelled of something oily and rancid. Her stomach rolled, thinking of the poison she'd swallowed earlier, leaving her unable to do more than touch her lips to the rim.

As soon as she did so, a roar went up from the other side of the tavern, and then wild applause. The goldglam had begun a new dance, no doubt a zenith to end the evening. Talia couldn't see from where she was sitting, but whatever it was, it caught the eyes of those standing. She felt their attention slide away from her, prey released from the steely gaze of the hunter.

Talia reached and touched Isera's hand beneath the table. Risky, but worth it when she felt Isera's fingers tighten over her own in a quick pulse before she let go.

"What is happening?" she asked Isera, beneath the din.

Isera leaned in, almost imperceptibly, but in a way that brought her voice closer to Talia's ear.

"They're sending all of us out."

"All of the greyes?"

Isera lifted a brow, nodded. Usually it was Burrin, Ardit, and one or two other greyes. After her second poisoning, she'd described a cragworm, a giant burrowing beast she'd read about, and half a dozen of them had gone out. But that was the most she'd ever heard of. Never all of them.

"Even you?" she asked. Isera could fight – all the zaffre could – but it wasn't her specialty. Hers was more… people-focused. She rarely went into the Tawn.

"*All* of us."

Isera answered her next question before Talia asked it.

"It's the charm," Isera said quietly, as if that were an answer that made sense, when it truly made none.

That word. She'd heard Ardit say it, but it had slid by her. She repeated it, made it a question.

Talia watched Isera fiddle with her knife, sliding it between her fingers before she answered.

"The creatures you saw," Isera said.

For the first time, Talia noticed Isera's hands were trembling. Oh. It wasn't boredom that had her playing with her knife; it was fear. Talia hadn't recognized it because she'd never seen Isera afraid before.

A shiv of her own fear slipped into her, cold and hollow. *Wait. You made them up. These things that are so dangerous. They're nothing.* Sometimes she told her lies so well that even she forgot.

"How…" She was trying to figure out what she wanted to ask, how to do so without giving herself away. "How do they know what it is?"

By way of an answer, Isera drew a triangle shape on the table with her finger. The shape of wings. Wings Talia had made up, out of stories and memories. On a whim. *Oh, Talia.*

"We leave at dawn," Isera said. She let the knife fall to the table, lifted her mismatched gaze in a quick catch of Talia's eyes. "You could come before."

It was an invitation that Talia wanted very badly to accept.

Talia opened her mouth, tempted to tell the truth, to put it out there, everything she knew, everything she was not. She would tell Isera, and Isera would… what? Tell Burrin? And everyone would know she was a liar, that she was not the poison eater after all.

What punishment, that? She didn't know. Surely there had never been another like her. Liar. False seer. It was unthinkable to betray the city so. They would have to devise a whole new punishment just for her.

Whatever punishment they came up with, it would be nothing compared to this: she would not become the orness. She would not gain access to the aria, she would not be able to kill the vordcha once and for all. And elsewhere, a dozen new children would replace her and her sisters in the oily murk of the blackweave. A dozen new children would be opened and filled with mech and memories.

For as long as the vordcha lived, they needed martyrs. As long as there were martyrs, she needed to become the orness.

She couldn't tell the truth. She couldn't risk it.

So much finwa, so much sorry for what she was about to do.

So she held her tongue, unwilling or unable to put the truth out there. Beneath the table, Isera's leg touched hers and Talia realized that her whole body was shaking, trembling, a leaf on the verge of falling.

And still Talia said nothing. Ardit gave a signal, telling all the zaffre it was time to go, to sleep it off and be ready to rise before the dawn and ride. Not even when Burrin stepped forward from the corner – Talia's breath stopped, fell from her mouth like a living thing, he *was* here, why? – not even when he stopped and caught her gaze, hard eyes holding her own for two beats too long. Not even when Isera stood from the table and looked at her, a gaze that said how very much she knew, and how very little, and radiated all her fear and dread.

All things that Talia could have saved her from. And still, and still, Talia sat there, her face hooded in her reversible cloak, and she said nothing and did nothing. And it wasn't long before the tavern was empty but for a false poison eater and a golden-winged dancer and a man painted in arrows pointing nowhere.

CLEAVE

After leaving the Scarlet Sisk, Talia found herself in front of Isera's house, her fist raised to knock on the black synth door. She'd waited until everyone was gone from the bar and the streets were empty before threading her way through the city northward.

Isera's door was inscribed with a shining silver spiral, designed to be seen from anywhere on the street. Everyone knew what the symbol meant.

For criminals or would-be criminals, it said, *The person who lives here is a greyes. Take your business elsewhere.*

For law-abiding citizens, it said, *A greyes lives here. Knock if you are in need.*

Caught somewhere between those two things, Talia lifted her knuckles and knocked.

Isera answered so quickly it was as though she were waiting on the other side of the door. Talia thought – hoped – that were true. She was still wearing the purple dress from the Sisk. The way it wrapped her shoulders drew attention to the long hollow of her neck, the strength of her chin.

"Finwa, Poison Eater," she said. The formal, and required, greeting was one that Talia heard many times a day. And yet, when Isera let it roll from her tongue, accompanied by her wry smile, it was utterly different. Somehow more personal and private than even her own name. It almost washed away the forced formality of their greeting in the Sisk.

"Moon meld you, Greyes Isera." They went through the rituals – thumbs over eyes, words passed between them – but here there was an impatient undercurrent beneath the exchange. The gestures felt like a necessary, but overly long, step to ease the transition from what they had been to the world to what they would be to each other. There was always this moment between the two of them, when they shook off their roles, their formalities, and found their way back to themselves. In a way, Talia supposed that was its own kind of ritual.

"Come in already," Isera said, her laughter hushed, pulling the door wider, gesturing Talia inside.

The front room was lit by large metal moths mounted on the walls. Each time they flapped their wings, the room filled with dancing yellow light. They were so beautiful that Talia had thought they were real, living creatures the first time she'd seen them. It still took all her will not to hold out her hand, hoping for such beauty to land upon it, if only for a moment.

That was before she could hold out her hand, as she did now, toward a completely different beauty. Isera took her hand, curling their fingers together. She was still trembling. Her row of rings scratched tiny cuts across Talia's palm.

"Where's Seild?" Talia asked.

Isera gestured toward the back of the house, behind the

dark green curtains that hung across the hall. Asleep, then. Probably for hours.

"The poisonings have a cost for everyone," Isera said. In the flicker, her grey eye reflected shimmering streaks of light. "For Seild, it's only sleep. What's their cost for you, Poison Eater?"

There was a word Maeryl had taught her long ago. *Onas.* It meant *one who hides nothing and sees all.* It wasn't an Enthait word, or even one in the Truth. But it was the perfect word for Isera.

Rather than answer, Talia asked a question of her own. It wasn't what she wanted to ask, not yet, but it was a step toward it. "You're scared about tomorrow?"

"Yes." Isera lifted one shoulder, the beginning of an attempt at nonchalance, but it fell away. "But I'm good at what I do. As are the others."

How to tell her not to be afraid? How to explain that the beasts were nothing more than figments of Talia's mind? She didn't know.

"It's just a few creatures," Talia said. "Perhaps it will turn out to be nothing. Or… I could be wrong about what I saw. I'm never quite sure what the poisoning is telling me." It was the closest she'd come to telling Isera the truth. The words had weight, but she couldn't tell if they were growing heavier or lighter as she said them.

"The charn are not just a few creatures. Don't you read those books that you're always borrowing from Omuf-Rhi?" Isera's voice tried for soft teasing, but it fell flat, gave way to the same fear it had carried earlier.

Talia *had* read the books she borrowed from Books & Blades, Omuf-Rhi's shop. She'd offered to help him out around the shop in exchange for reading privileges, and she took full advantage of it, reading as many as she could, as often as she could. She'd scoured them for clues about the poison eater, the orness, the aria, but she couldn't remember seeing the word *charn* in there.

"You've fought them before?" Talia asked.

"Moon meld me, no," Isera said. "I only know the stories."

Talia had more questions, but Isera stayed them with her words. "The truth is that, yes, I'm scared. But talking about it won't make me less so." She gave Talia a dimpled smile that was, at its first moment, forced, and then opened up into the real thing. "There are other things I'd much rather talk about. Well, not *talk* so much as…"

Isera stepped closer. The soft swish of the fabric against her skin was, for a moment, the only sound in the room. As she shifted in the fluttering light, it was hard to tell that her eyes were not the same color. They both looked the grey of the moonlight in shadow.

Sometimes just looking at her was enough to knock the breath from Talia's lungs. She didn't know how she felt about that. It was dangerous – but there was something about *this* danger that drew her in. That made her want more and more.

Talia took a long stride, closing the space between them. Isera often smelled of clean sweat and steel-oil, but that was only a top layer, superficial. Easily washed off. Not that Talia minded – she liked the scent on her. But it was her public scent, one that everyone got. Tonight, she smelled only of herself, a soft mixture of cyrria spices and green boughs that always seemed to beckon Talia closer.

Isera lowered her head. Talia did the same until she was

touching her forehead to Isera's. They stood that way a long time, breathing.

"I see what you're doing," Isera said.

"No, you don't," Talia said, hoping, praying to the moon or the mech or the datasphere or whatever one might pray to that actually worked, that it was not true. The moment Isera saw through her, all of this would end. It was as good a reason as any to stop, to step away and walk out right now, to never be so close to this woman again.

Step away.

But her feet would not go. And when Isera moved forward and lifted her mouth to Talia's, the only thing her body would let her do was respond in kind. Isera's hands pushed up Talia's spine to the back of her head, pulling her in.

Isera was not Talia's first. She'd slept with some of her sisters in the blackweave – it was one of the few small comforts the vordcha had not taken from them. She found pleasure there, and escape certainly, but being with Isera was different. Not even with Maeryl had she felt both this powerful and this afraid.

She was never sure if she worried that Isera would split her open or put her back together. Or perhaps both, one after the other.

That hesitation stayed her hand for a heartbeat, but after another kiss, after the rough tumble to the stone floor that had them laughing as the floor poked into Talia's hip and then grasping for clothes, corners and clasps and anything else they could get their hands on; after that, it didn't matter. Afraid or not, they were here, Talia was here, and there was nowhere else she would choose to be instead.

They didn't undress. Merely opened the places of their clothing that could be opened and met their bodies together there, heat and desire tangling together. They were fast and as furtive as their passion allowed, aware that any moment, someone might knock on Isera's door, seeking the help of a greyes who was currently half-clothed and digging her nails into the bare back of the city's poison eater.

Isera was a lithe and restless lover, all moving muscles beneath Talia's hands and mouth. It was easy to tell the things that pleased her. She talked constantly, a steady soft stream of praise and pleasure. Talia was more pleased when she brought Isera pleasure than when she found her own, partly because her own came so easy here – a thing she had not yet figured out how to reconcile – and partly because Isera was such a pleasure to watch, the arch of her body, the half-closed eyes, the way her neck lengthened so you could see the thrumming beat of her pulse.

When Isera peaked, she was loud enough that she clamped her own hand over her mouth, laughing a moment later as she came down.

They both stilled momentarily to listen for the patter of sleepy feet coming down the hall. There was no sound other than their own hastened breath.

"You're beautiful," Talia said after, because she didn't know what else to say to quell the pace of her heart against her skin, to soften the pounding of her blood.

Isera lay on her elbow in front of her, one hand trailing over Talia's shoulders and down her back. Her fingers found the intricate ridges over Talia's skin, traced one of them down toward the wide swath at her spine. Shame and fear tried to flare up, but somehow Isera's touch kept them at bay.

"Someday, you'll tell me this story."

"Someday," Talia said. Unlike with the Painter, she didn't know that this was untrue. Would she tell Isera of the vordcha, of the martyrs, of the complex pattern scarred upon the spines of them all? Her answer – maybe – gave her some kind of hidden feeling that she didn't dare look at too closely.

"What does it look like?" Talia asked. She'd seen her sisters' spine scars, all of them different, none of them given meaning that made sense, but she'd never seen her own, could only trace the edges of it with one hand.

"A tree," Isera said. "It looks like a tree."

Isera ran her fingers along the outline of it, slow and steady enough that it began to take shape. The thick base at her lower back. The long trunk that rose up her spine. The delicate branches that threaded toward her shoulders. Such a thing couldn't be beautiful, and yet, beneath the stroke of Isera's fingers, it was. Almost.

"I should prepare for tomorrow," Isera said finally. The reluctance in her voice made Talia smile.

"I wish you wouldn't," Talia said.

"And I wish you wouldn't eat poison every time the moon changes." Isera's voice was teasing, but there was a sharp truth hidden inside the words, like a stinging bee wrapped inside a flower. Isera shifted, and began to pull sections of her outfit closed around her, buttoning buttons, closing clasps. The soft slow movements were gone, replaced with the efficient strength of a fighter. "But I understand why you do it."

She didn't, of course. She thought Talia did it for the

good of the city, for the good of Seild and Ganeth and the others. For the same reason that Isera was zaffre and let her daughter be zaffre.

They finished dressing in silence, their furtive movements interrupted only by the sudden sound of Khee snoring from the back room. Talia couldn't help but laugh, and Isera soon followed. "I didn't even know he was here," Talia said.

"He comes in the evenings sometimes. I think he helps Seild go to sleep. But usually he leaves before dawn."

Talia had wondered where he'd been going lately. She'd have guessed hunting for sport along Enthait's outer walls, where little green lizards sometimes ran to and fro between the stones. This seemed better somehow, more complete.

Isera leaned in, laughing quietly. "Sometimes she reads to him. But really it's more like her telling him a nonsensical story and him sleeping through it. She doesn't seem to mind."

They listened to Khee snarl in his sleep from the other room for a moment.

"I wish I had faith that would be me shortly, sound asleep and dreaming," Isera said.

"I could stay," Talia said, and then regretted it because she knew the answer. Oh, the heart gone to rot and softness. So soon.

Isera shook her head, her only response. The jewels in her hair had come loose and one tumbled down to her shoulder. She plucked it and put it back with the smooth efficiency that defined most of her movements. Fucking. Fighting. Even fidgeting.

The way of her made Talia want to guide her all the way

back down to the floor, breath to breath. She clasped her hex hand to her true hand to keep herself still.

"Who will watch her?" Talia said. They both knew who she meant.

"Ganeth offered."

"Of course." She was oddly both saddened and relieved to hear Ganeth's name. She would have watched Seild, of course, although in all honesty she had no idea what it meant to watch a girl that age and likely would have botched it badly. Not to mention that Seild's face would remind her every moment of her mother, the woman that Talia's lies were about to send into harm's way.

Not harm. Lies.

As if they were not the same thing.

Standing there, she wanted more than anything to tell Isera the truth. All the truths. That she wasn't the poison eater. That she wasn't just some traveler, exploring the world, as she'd told her. That she had sliced off her own arm and cut out pieces of her own skull, in the midst of fire and snow and pain, to free herself from a danger she barely had a name for. That she was a fugitive, a killer, an unspeakable beast that had done unspeakable things.

The words sprouted on her tongue, and then withered before she could give them life. Rather than putting words into the air, she took Isera's skin into her mouth. The soft curve of her lip, the coil of her earlobe. She took in as much of Isera as she could, until she could tell herself she was full. Isera met her, sighing.

Talia was the first to pull away.

"Moon meld you tomorrow, Greyes Isera." Talia was aiming for humor, but it fell short, landed on serious and scared instead. She felt a stab of panic, a thin slice to the edge of her breath. What was she sending her to?

But of course, there was nothing. She'd made the dangers up, just as she'd made up every threat before this. They would find nothing, as they always did, and assume the threat had moved on or met some other untimely end. Isera would be safe. All of the zaffre would.

But you won't. Because eventually, someone will see through you. Through your lies. Burrin, she thought. *Because he was looking. Or Isera, because she was not.*

"I'll look in on Seild if you'd like," Talia said.

"She would like that." Not the same thing, but enough for now.

The two of them touched fingers, one of the few things that Talia had brought with her from her sisters. They stood that way for a long moment before Talia slipped out into the night, pulling the marked door closed tight behind her.

Sometimes the city sang. No. Sang wasn't the right word. The city's sound wasn't one of mouth or lungs, throat or tongue. It was stormvoice – thunder crack and cloud breath and the patter of red rain across a bloodied blade. A beautiful and terrible chorus that made Talia's bones ache in response.

Most days, Enthait sounded like any other city – the call of animals and people, the passage of wind across the walls, the snap of banners and the turn of wheels. But when it despaired, when it hungered, when the winds swirled around it in fear and dismay, the city sang.

People had told her she'd get so that she'd hardly hear it – and it was clear that most of them had long ago reached that stage – but for her that day had not yet come. She wasn't sure it ever would; perhaps it was a result of coming here so late in life, while most others had grown up inside these walls, surrounded by this song of sorrow and steel.

The greyes – Burrin, Isera, the others – had been gone five days and the city was singing fiercely. The sound threaded through Talia as soon as she stepped out of the tunnels onto the Green Road. She staggered into the crowd, more startled by the singing than by the sight, barking her shoulder against a nearby pillar. It took her a moment to right herself again, to figure out where she was in the hustle and bustle of noise and light. The city's chorus had blurred her vision into tears, and she blinked them away in time to its steel-slick pulsebeat.

She hadn't meant to emerge from the tunnels here, into the push of song and sound, but she also wasn't that surprised. Every time she took a correct turn through the tunnels, she took an equally incorrect one. If it wasn't for the sense of secrecy they offered her, she'd be tempted to leave the tangle of their angled passages behind for good.

She'd been aiming for the Eternal Market – it was the best place to hear news of the city and she'd been hoping to learn more of the zaffre, the charn. She was on the exact opposite side of the Green Road.

The weather was surprisingly cool and windy, a rare break from the desertlike weather, and Talia was half-hidden in tan pants and a worn-down coat. A dark blue scarf around her neck, her long braids wrapped up inside a second, darker scarf. It wasn't likely that she'd be recognized, so it couldn't hurt to walk along the Green Road to get to the market. It had to be better than trying her luck again in the tunnels.

Even though it went nowhere but back to itself, the Green Road was always busy. Like so many things here, *road* wasn't the right word, as she'd eventually discovered. It looked like a wide strip of translucent green material. As far as Talia could tell, it ran a perfect circle around the clave, making it a common meeting place.

Talia had spent a lot of time here when she and Khee first arrived in the city. Then, she hadn't known what the poison eater was. She barely knew the name of the city. She and Khee weren't planning to stay any longer than the time it took them to heal, lie low, and find or steal enough food and supplies to keep running.

Running where? She didn't know. Somewhere very far. She didn't have a grasp of how big the world was, but in the stories she'd retold for her sisters, they'd come from lands of red ash, ice walls, forests so vast and thick you might never find your way out. Maeryl's blue-silver sea-city called Qi. Even Talia's own small village buried deep in the mountains of the Black Riage. It seemed the vordcha could go anywhere, *would* go anywhere, to find what they were looking for.

Talia had wanted badly to believe that she and Khee were not what the vordcha were looking for. That the vordcha had forgotten about them. But she knew that wasn't true. The vordcha were surely hunting them. Not for revenge. That was far too... human. But for property. They had owned her. Thought they owned her still.

She'd cut off her arm, sliced out bits of her scalp, released Khee from his horns – every way she could think of that the vordcha might use to track them – and still she wasn't sure that they wouldn't come. Weren't already coming. They were relentless and smart. They would find a way. So the goal was: heal, gather supplies, run until they could no longer run.

And then she'd met a woman with mismatched eyes on the Green Road and everything had gone upside down.

She'd come to find food. *Steal* food, to be true. She'd found the market less than ideal – too crowded and full of things for the taking, so people were on their guard. Even the best of thieves had a hard time there, and with only her left hand, she wasn't sure picking pockets would ever become a bragging skill. She missed her right hand, even as much as she'd hated all the mech inside it. Her hair had started to grow back, at least, although the bright streaks of red along her scars were taking some getting used to. She had them covered with an elaborately stitched grey hood she'd borrowed from a passerby.

The Green Road was better, easier. She mostly didn't steal for herself – but Khee, Khee was starving. So hollowed she could see the curves of his teeth inside his closed jaws. He was better – sleeping less fitfully in the tiny place she'd found for them in the wall near the run-down part of town. But he was still too weak to hunt – not that she'd seen much in the way of prey in the city. So she was hunting for him. It was the least she could do. She didn't remember much about their passage from the blackweave to the city, but she was pretty sure Khee was the only reason she'd made it here. Although how he might have done that in his state was something she didn't know. Perhaps when he was healed, he would tell her. She didn't think it likely, though.

She'd stood still, upon the road, letting the throngs pass her, brush her, jostle against her. A predator hidden in plain sight. Man, child, family, two men in blue and bronze uniforms looking stern and official. She rejected them all. She wasn't swift or clean, a clumsy one-handed fumbling with packages or wrappings. Her best prey were those not paying attention.

Two young women walked by, talking excitedly with their hands, giggling together, several bags over their shoulders. One was pulling a mechanical floating box on a long string. It was piled high with packages and folded bits of fabric. Clothing, mostly. Not that she couldn't use something to wear that wasn't stained and broken. But that wasn't what she needed.

One of the packages caught her eye; it was wrapped in yellow paper inside a clear synth bag. The paper was dotted with reddish pools. Meat. It was even near the top of the pile. And on her left side. Clearly, whatever gods lived in Enthait – was this a god-filled place? She didn't know – were guiding her hand today.

Swiftly, she slid past the women, plucking the package from the box in a single, nonchalant sweep of her arm. Without looking back, she continued on her way. If they noticed, they would come after her whether she stopped or not. It took her half a second to tuck the package into her empty sleeve, where she'd rigged a holder of sorts. She nearly smiled at the weight of it. It had been two days since she'd brought something back for Khee. This one, this one was good. Fresh. Heavy. *I'm coming, Khee.*

The woman in front of her appeared so swiftly that Talia barely had time to react. She put both hands out, realized her mistake too late, and dropped her right arm to her side. The package inside her sleeve shifted and bulged. She barely breathed, expecting it to fall to the ground between them, but the straps she'd rigged up held and caught.

"Sehwa," the woman said. A word Talia didn't know,

but she guessed from the woman's tone that it was an apology of sorts. Mostly, the language here was one she was familiar with, even if the accent was slanted to her ears. But it was sprinkled throughout with words and phrases that sounded like gibberish, soft-voweled things that fell off her tongue at odd angles when she tried them and gave her away as an outsider. "I thought you were someone... else."

The woman was wearing a blue and bronze uniform – the same as the men who'd passed her earlier. Her short hair was the same blue as her clothing, standing up in small, crafted points all over her head. In the middle of her forehead, a silver spiral was painted upon her skin. Talia would have found herself mesmerized by it, but for the eyes beneath it. Mismatched. Grey and brown. Staring at her intently.

Or rather at her stolen hood.

Talia could have ducked her head, bowed, did whatever people did here to show reverence or apology. But some instinct told her this woman would not be swayed by her attempt at being demure.

Talia lifted her face fully. She knew everything this gave away; she'd seen her reflection in a glass-faced building just this morning. The bruises and cuts still half-healed across her cheeks. The broken lip that occasionally opened and bled for no reason. The single puncture at the front of her neck, festering still, pulling tight in protest at her movement.

Despite that, despite it all, she met the woman's gaze with as much strength as she could bring to bear. "Perhaps I *am* someone else."

A moment of stillness and then. Reward. One tiny

corner of the woman's lips lifted. She might never again wield the swiftest blade or have the fastest of fingers, but words were weapons that never failed.

"That may be," the woman said. "But you are not the someone else I thought you were."

"No?" People crowded by them, but not as close as before. They opened up and made room for the woman in the blue and bronze. And, by the same motion, for Talia, too.

The woman continued to regard her, long enough that Talia's heart beat three, four times in her chest. Slow, thick thumps against her breastbone in time to her breath.

"No," the woman said. "I'm quite sure that person does not have a stolen bit of meat for an arm."

Talia blinked in surprise. If she'd seen malice, even aggression, in the woman's face, she would have run. Bolted back toward Khee. A race that she surely would have lost, not yet knowing the city, not yet having her body back.

If she'd seen authority there, she would have lied her way out of the conversation. She'd done it with a shopkeeper in the market just a few days ago. He'd thought she'd taken a bit of fruit. She had, by way of distraction, convinced him she hadn't. In truth, she actually hadn't – but a substantial bit of jerky did seem to find its way into her pocket while they were talking about fruit. Certainly something she could do again.

But in those mismatched eyes, what she saw was a curiosity. That, more than anything, made her fold her forthcoming lie up and slip it back into her pocket for safekeeping. There'd be another time to use it, she was sure.

"It's for another," Talia said simply, hoping that would be enough.

The woman blinked, hard, twice. There was a sound like wings between them. The pupil in her grey eye tightened into nothing, a pinpoint of black, and then disappeared, leaving a solid steel-colored orb.

"Does that person look as unwell as you?"

The woman ran her odd gaze across Talia's face as she answered, "Not a person, but yes." Talia considered. "No, worse."

The woman blinked again, and a second later, both pupils were back to being the same size. She tilted her head to the side, touching two fingers lightly to the side of her eye as if it pained her.

"Why are you telling me the truth?" she asked.

The package in Talia's sleeve seemed like it was growing heavier, tugging her down. "Why are you believing me?"

"It's part of my job," the woman said. "To see true."

Talia didn't know what that meant, but she didn't want to show her ignorance by asking. There was something about this woman that made her want to know everything, to have all the answers and spread them out before her, like a hand of perfect cards.

"I thought you were a..." Talia looked for the word. "Guard, of sorts."

The other woman had lifted her eyebrow at that. She had a crooked smile that brought one side of her mouth higher than the other, and created a deep dimple in one cheek. Talia tried to keep her mind on the conversation.

"I suppose I am," the woman said. "A guard, of sorts."

She put both thumbs to her eyes – it was a gesture Talia had seen others give to each other, but until that moment, none had given it to her.

"Greyes Isera, zaffre, in the service of Enthait, the orness, and the poison eater."

It was clear the woman – Greyes Isera – was waiting for her to respond in kind but Talia's mouth seemed to be something she no longer owned. She knew she was no longer Cathaliaste, no longer martyr to the vordcha. But who was she? She had started thinking of herself as Talia somewhere between the blackweave and Enthait, but she didn't think she had ever said the name aloud. Maybe to Khee, maybe in the snow and ice and shatter. She had a vague memory of such a thing.

What does it matter? Soon, you will be elsewhere and no one will remember the name you gave to another today.

"Talia," she said, despite everything that told her not to. "I'm Talia."

"Talia." Isera's accent stretched the name longwise, gave it weight that it hadn't before. That corner of her mouth curled up. "You aren't from here, are you?"

"Are you going to do that eye thing again if I answer you?" She looped a hand in the air, made it smaller on the second circle, mimicking as best she could the way the pupil had shrunk in on itself.

Isera laughed at that – loud and true, a sound that rose up into the air on tiny wings and, oh, for the first time since she'd run and fallen, for one tiny moment since she'd buried her friends beneath the bloodied snow, Talia felt something real. It washed over her, hot and white and full of pain. She staggered, her knees buckling forward. She caught herself before she fell, but it was an ungainly move that showed the stiff pain of her body.

Isera had reached to catch Talia's stumble, then clearly thought better of it, for the arm she would have taken hold of was no arm at all.

"That question was for duty," she said. "This one is for pleasure."

"Then no." Talia considered a moment. "Was it my accent?"

"No." The woman waved a hand covered in blue rings, but didn't elucidate further. "But I can tell you've been on the Green Road, based on your... skills."

There was a pause.

Talia chose not to fill it.

"Have you seen the gardens?" The same hand pointed downward, toward the wide green swatch of road. Talia followed it and saw nothing more than what she always saw – stippled green glass, reflecting light in an unusual way. Enthait was full of materials she'd never seen before, many of them far weirder than that. And it was certainly no garden, unless that word had a different meaning than the one she knew.

"Look again," she said, as if she could tell what Talia was thinking. "You'll see it."

Talia didn't – and then she did. She was looking through the glass, down. And down. There was nothing directly beneath her feet except for the glass she stood upon. Far, far below, she was looking at what looked like the tops of trees. A tiny shape that absolutely could not be a person, so far down she could barely see them, moved across what could absolutely not be a long, long ladder.

All this time standing here, walking here, stealing here, and she hadn't noticed the long fall beneath her feet, the steep sides that slipped down and down. It was as if someone had shifted an optical illusion, and now she couldn't unsee it, the vast distance between her and the ground.

She was aware of the pounding of her heart, the loss of breath that made her face feel hot and swollen. She needed to get off this road, and quickly. It was impossible to believe she would not fall. But she was hemmed in by crowds that flowed around her, packages and pets and people. There was nowhere to go.

Only Isera stood, not moving. This time, she did take Talia's arm. Through the fabric, she felt the pressure of her fingers, solid, strong, holding her steady.

Isera whispered a word, soft vowels that slipped through her without staying, without casting understanding, but that seemed to urge her to breathe. Talia did so, deep and full, then looked down, in the space between her boots and Isera's.

Green everywhere. Not the surface of the road – in fact, she thought that was translucent, completely clear. But far, far below, a layer of green. She thought the whole thing went as far down as the skars went up, perhaps farther.

The more she looked, the more she saw – that the green wasn't just green, but the white and yellow and red of flowers and fruit. The entire space was filled with growing things. The figure she'd seen *was* a human, climbing down the side of the wall, along a ladder that extended and extended.

Until that moment, she'd not thought about where the city got its supplies. The market was full of vegetables, fruit, various meats, all things she'd stolen or considered stealing. She'd seen the meat animals on the west side of the city – the tall aneen and the wooly yol – but now that she thought of it, she'd never seen anything growing in the city besides the occasional pot of scraggly herbs by someone's front door. And while she was sure that something grew and lived in the Tawn, she couldn't imagine that much – plant or animal – thrived in that red heat.

The more she watched, the more intrigued she became, until she was nearly bent over, looking through the glass. As she saw people moving through the plants, everything suddenly clicked into place. She had no idea how things were growing under there, but it was clear that they were. There was likely a water source too, perhaps the very spring that fed the city. Now that she thought of it, she'd never heard tell of a drought or even a worry over water, which should have seemed surprising, if she'd thought about it. The vordcha hadn't needed food or drink – at least not that she could tell – and the sisters had become good at scrounging for themselves.

When she looked up, she saw that Isera was watching her, that half-smile, those mismatched eyes.

"I've never been able to show anyone that before," she said. "Most everyone I know is from here, or has been here longer than I've been alive."

Talia was afraid Isera would ask the obvious next question, and she found her breath failing her, as if it couldn't find its way back into her body.

She didn't. She let go of Talia's arm and gave her a small nod, then asked a question that Talia was not expecting. "I'll see you at the poisoning, then?" And for the life of her, Talia could not figure out what a poisoning was or why she was suddenly nodding and saying, "Of course."

That felt like a lifetime ago, and like yesterday. Talia didn't need to steal anymore, and she'd grown accustomed to walking over the swath of growing things beneath her feet. It was part of the city she'd come to know – but would not allow herself to love. There was danger in that, a danger she didn't want to think about. And so she threaded herself through the crowds, leaving behind the Green Road to see what she could learn of the zaffre.

The Eternal Market was called that because it ran constantly – day and night, an endless cacophony of taking and giving, of wanting and wanting to be rid of. But it was also a spiral, a long blackglass street that turned and turned and never seemed to find its center. You walked inward and inward along the ebony surface, and then suddenly you were on the outermost street again. If not exactly where you'd started, then nearly so.

She'd walk the spiral and pick up something for Seild along the way – maybe the saltpetals she loved so much. And something of a meatier variety for Khee too. Khee had gone to Ganeth's shortly after the greyes had ridden out; she was pretty sure to be at Seild's side, although the beast certainly hadn't said as much. And Ganeth, well... There was nothing that Ganeth seemed to covet except for devices, and she wasn't going to find something like that at the market. At least not that she could understand well enough to select something from.

Hundreds of stalls, creatures, carts, and more permanent shops ran along both sides of the road. The space was so crowded and overgrown that half of the stalls and stores floated above her head, marooned by tie-offs to the stalls below. Baskets on extending poles and trained climbers

– both human and not – allowed for easy access to the products above.

Above the market rose four of the tall, curved spires – the skars – that filled Enthait's sky. They towered hundreds of feet high, curving up toward the sky like weapons from giants. Some were thick, some thin, some with holes or carvings, but all looked deadly sharp, tapering to a point. They seemed to draw weather to them, as their tips were often obscured by the presence of fluffed clouds. The skars had no other use that Talia could see, although she sometimes wondered if it wasn't they that caused the city's song, using the wind the way a flute might use a player's breath.

Each skar was named in a complex system that Talia couldn't keep track of. Something that was both alphabetical and numerical, and involving lineage, placement in the city, and some other thing that made no sense to her. But thankfully, each one also had a common-use nickname – the false skar, the crescent skar, morning's skar.

In the shadow of the skars, entwined in the singing of the city, the Eternal Market moved at its own rhythm, an ebb and bustle that she thought of, thanks to Maeryl's stories, as something like a tide. She moved through it as small things learn to move through power, unresisting, letting the curves and patterns of the crowd guide her path where they would.

A young boy with curly brown hair and a green-furred creature with six limbs and two prehensile tails raced each other up the side of an herb stall, competing for the shin or piece of bread they'd get if they returned fastest with the desired goods.

She was glad that Khee was at Ganeth's, probably

being spoiled by Seild. Even more than her, he seemed to find the crowds of the city overwhelming, slinking his body carefully through them so as not to be touched. He said little during the times when they moved through the city – not that he ever said much – but one time shortly after they'd arrived, they'd come here. She'd gotten lost and had fumbled through the market for what seemed like ages before she found their way out. After, he had merely said *no* and somehow in a single word had conveyed how overwhelmed and over-touched he'd been. He'd never joined her at the market again.

She wondered what it had been like for him, before. The vordcha had kept their martyrs penned in like beasts. She had no idea what they did to their actual beasts.

Thinking of him, she stopped at a meat stall, counting out a few shins, all of them courtesy of her job at Books & Blades – being the poison eater was not a paying position – for a few thick strips of jerky that smelled of spices and flame, and a hunk of something so fresh it was still dripping blood. She didn't ask what it was, just double-checked that it was well wrapped before she tucked it into her bag and moved on through the crowd.

The greyes had been away for five days, which was longer than usual, but nothing so far out of the ordinary that people should be remarking on it, and yet they were. It seemed that everyone had heard that the greyes had gone out in full force, and the air was buzzing with talk. No one seemed to be saying the word *charn*, although she kept her ears open for it.

Nothing else came up that provided any clues. Perhaps she'd hear more by the time she got to the spiral's end. If nothing else, it strengthened her resolve to scour Omuf-Rhi's books for some clue. What she wanted to know was what part of her made-up story had resembled the real-life creatures that they were so afraid of. She felt that if she could just figure out what detail she'd pulled out of her brain that had made Burrin think *charn*, she would have a place to begin.

Just before she reached the saltpetal stall, she ran into a group of children gathered in a circle. Two costumed actors stood on a small round stage in the middle of them. One was dressed in the makeshift wraps of the orness, a dark mask over his face. The other, dressed as Talia. Or rather, as the poison eater. It wasn't uncommon to see these types of reenactments, but this one for whatever reason had drawn a large crowd. She tucked herself into a corner to watch for a moment.

"I see…" The poison eater put her hands into the air, mimed as if pulling threads of thought from her head. "What horrible danger do I see coming for our beautiful city?" she asked the children.

They yelled out answers excitedly. *A seskii! A face! A cloud! Candy!*

If only, Talia thought. Some of them clearly hadn't quite mastered an understanding of danger. Which wasn't a bad thing. It showed how protected they were. She didn't feel jealous about that, but more a sense of wonder. What must that kind of childhood be like? She couldn't even imagine. Didn't want to imagine. Such a thing might break her.

The actor ran with the funniest of answers, much to the delight of the children. "I see candy. Piles and piles and piles of candy. Coming out of the sky. We will all be covered in candy. Buried alive in candy. Oh no, what shall we do?"

"Send the greyes!" The kids were nearly in unison. Only one lone child chimed in with "Eat it!", which was met with laughter by the other adults watching. Everyone knew this story. It was the culture, the belief, that the city was built on. Thrived on. Survived on.

"Yes! We'll send the greyes. The greyes ride out into the desert on their faithful mounts..." The clumpity-clumpty of fernowalker feet came from behind the small stage. The kids laughed in delight. "And what do they find?"

So many answers Talia couldn't make them all out. Apparently, it didn't really matter what they found because the actor threw up her hands and yelled "And they fight!" and all of the kids stood up and swung invisible swords at invisible foes.

"But... there are so many." The actor's voice got lower and lower as she talked. The kids, one by one, stopped fighting and stood, still and quiet. Talia was beginning to see the appeal of this particular performance. "There are too many... the zaffre cannot win. Only the orness can save them now. And so they ride back to the city–" This time there were no feet sounds, just the actor's quiet, serious voice. "And what do they say?"

"Orness, save us!" It was the part of the story that everyone seemed to love the best. How once there came a danger so great that neither the poison eater nor the zaffre could save the city. All was lost. Until the orness activated her special device, which wiped out the danger – and the city too. Although Talia noticed the stories often left out that last part.

The actor dressed as the orness stepped up in answer. "I

am the orness, the keeper of the device. And I shall save
Enthait from this destruction!" She lifted a large, ornately
carved star that seemed to be made of folded paper over
her head.

Cries of "The aria! The aria!" went up from the gathered
children.

She threw the object down and it burst into a little pile
of colored smoke and shiny jewels that scattered on the
group.

Near her, a ragtag bunch cheered as the jewels rained
down on them. "We're saved! We're saved!"

Such true believers. Only children would believe so
fervently in a solution that had no repercussions.

You believe. And you're not even of Enthait.

It was true. She did believe. But she also understood
that her actions would have consequences. To her, to the
city, to those within its walls. She would do what she had
to. As she always had.

Talia bent to pick up one of the jewels fallen at her feet.
It reminded her of the jewels in Isera's hair.

"Hey... that's the poison eater." A girl near her. *Astute
little thing.*

"Isn't," said one of the boys. "She's taller. My ma took
me and I saw her, in her robe." The voice slightly lower.
"My ma bet five shins on her to die."

"I bet ten for her to live." The girl again.

"You didn't. You're satho." *Crazy. Liar.*

"Am not."

"Prove it."

Talia turned, looked right at the girl and gave her a nod.
She was scrawny, her clothes too big, and a thin white scar
ran along the side of her throat.

"You bet smartly," she told the girl in a mock whisper, one she was sure would carry to the others. "I don't plan on dying anytime soon." She flipped her the jewel – it caught the rainbow light as it arced. The girl snagged it out of the air, as sure with her hand as she'd been with her words.

As Talia walked away, she heard the girl run with it, not even missing a beat.

"Told you, Osler. You owe me a saltpetal."

And shortly after, the boy's grumbling agreement.

Ah, Talia. You've just helped create another liar. Well done.

To stand near the saltpetal stand meant being surrounded by the caramel-sweet smell of flowers being burnt. Saltpetals weren't a delicacy Talia had come to enjoy, or even stomach – she found the bitterness of the nyryn petals beneath the salt and sugar coating left her mouth stinging and her stomach roiling. It was clearly a learned delight, appreciated most by those who'd grown up inside Enthait's walls. Seild and Isera loved them, ate them by the handfuls, Seild all the way to the point of stomach ache, if no one was around to stop her.

The crowd was heavy. She was pretty sure that while half came for the delicacies, the other half were there for the man serving them up. A group of barely grown women in line before her showed themselves off in brightly-colored clothing, tittering and bunching around the stand like songbirds. At first glance, she'd thought they were from the Upper Crescent, full of money and themselves, but it was just pretend. Their hands were too clean; scrubbed with the sole purpose of taking away working dirt.

Saric served them, said something she couldn't hear,

and they scattered, blushing, banging into each other, jostling their bags of saltpetals.

"Children playing grownups," Saric said to her once they'd gone. "But you, Talia… you are no child. You couldn't stay away. And I am the better for it." Saric's grin was fast and loose. Typically, his compliments too. He'd learned long ago that she would buy his wares without the sweet talk, but he couldn't seem to help himself. Or perhaps he didn't want to.

She didn't mind. It was all in fair play, and he was, mostly, worth the banter. He wore his hair pulled back into a braided tail at the back of his neck, showing off finely muscled shoulders, lithe arms. For all his tone, he moved with a softness that appealed to her. If she didn't find the sugar-salt scent of his work cloying, she might have taken things further than flirting.

"They begged me to come," she said, teasing. It felt good to smile at him. He knew who she meant – Isera and Seild were regular customers, and had dragged Talia with them more than once to convince her of the error of her digestive ways.

"Such is the way of those, sending someone else to get what they already know they can have," he said. His green-hued eyes lingered on hers for a moment, an invitation. Perhaps for her. Perhaps for her and Isera, both. It wasn't uncommon. She found the pulse in her neck thumping beneath the skin as heat prickled her skin, but she could hear the group of children take their places in line behind her, still talking about their bets, and she held her tongue.

When she didn't respond, he lowered his gaze back to the heaters where piles of nyryn petals were swiftly losing their pink, turning a soft brown in the heat. "I'll scoop you some of the fresh ones," he said. "If you don't mind waiting."

She didn't. She watched him move between sun and shade as he carefully turned the petals over the heat with a small, soft spoon. Somewhere behind her, a musician began to play, some kind of wind instrument. Metallic and pitched, the song wove through the city's own song, echoed it softly. If she wasn't careful, she was going to fall in love with this city, with its people – and that was something she could ill afford.

When the petals were the color of caramel through and through, Saric scooped them equally carefully into a clear bag. From a small jar, he added a top layer of long yellow nuts, crisped on the ends. The bag steamed with dappled heat.

"For you," he said. "And yours." He meant he was giving her the petals for free, a gesture that she had no doubt had meaning beyond what it seemed. She tried to wave away the offering, but he placed it into her waving palm, gently but firmly. A man used to pressing delicate things into an uncareful hand.

"Mihil," he said, holding the bag out steady in a rare moment of stillness. "For our safety. It is the least I can give."

The guilt that she felt most acutely behind her eyeballs pinged her, a tight thrumming ache. Safety? No, that was not what she offered. Yet to say no would slight him, and she had no desire to do that.

Sighing, she closed her fingers around the packet, let the scent of him and his offering waft over her.

"I…" she began.

Before she could offer a proper thank you, a loud clang

came from behind her, the kind of sound that was sudden and sharp enough to momentarily still all voices. The children scattered in a whoosh of small feet and whispers. It was nothing – an automaton falling from one of the higher stalls, part of it shattering to the cobblestones below.

But as she turned back, she caught movement out of the corner of her eye.

A streak of white braids pulled back tight to a scalp, the body beneath wrapped in blue and bronze, ducking through the crowd. She knew instantly that it was Ardit. It had to be. What was he doing here, in the city? The greyes didn't really have a hierarchy, beyond Burrin being at the top, but it was clear that Ardit was Burrin's second. So why wasn't he out with Burrin and the rest?

A sick feeling spread through her, landing at the bottom of her stomach. Did Burrin suspect her deception? Had he asked Ardit to stay and keep an eye on her?

She had to get out of sight, at least for a moment. See if Ardit was following her.

Or if you're just being paranoid.

Also possible. There was one way to know.

She dropped her gaze to the packet that she and Saric still held between them. He was still looking at her face, as if the spectacle in the marketplace had turned his attention not at all.

Murmuring a quick thanks, she pulled the packet from Saric's grasp, aware that one or the other, perhaps both, of them was crushing his delicately preserved gift. She stuffed her packet of broken petals beneath her arm, and made long strides forward. She needed a hidden space, a place where she could see Ardit, but he couldn't see her. The crowd was bunched up, making it hard to get through. So she ducked her head and joined them, letting them carry her forward, hidden inside their mass and movement. Ardit was somewhere behind her, moving in this direction, but she didn't dare turn back to see.

As she went, she kept her head down and scanned the long wall of stalls for one she knew. The shadowed space of a covered stall beckoned, one that was hung along the sides with shimmering blankets, each woven with a different image. She slipped between the crowd, then ducked between two blankets and stepped into the darkness.

"Talia," the woman inside said. She didn't look up from the blanket she was spinning. Two rings on each finger flashed as she wound the threads across the points of them. Blue and gold and red, thread on thread, and then she pulled, her fingers interlocking and breaking apart, and added another stripe to the growing blanket across her knees.

Angha was one of the tiniest women Talia had ever known. And one of the fiercest. She'd watched her chase after a thief once – a young man who'd had the misfortune of choosing Angha's stall to try to steal from. Angha had knocked him to the ground in three strides, wrapped the almost-stolen blanket around him, and forced him to *sago*, an odd and complicated ritual of submission that she had only ever seen kids force upon each other.

Now that same boy worked for her. He nodded to Talia. His cheeks still flushed when he saw her – she'd never ribbed him about that day, but it was clear he remembered it as well as she did.

Talia pressed her thumb briefly to the space above one eye in greeting to them both. It was still an odd gesture, after all this time and all these many greetings. She doubted it would ever become habit or instinct, but it was at least becoming comfortable, one of the many ways she knew how to make herself fit in.

In her other hand, Talia still clutched the bag of petals, now powdered to a fine dust. Inedible. She should go back and buy a new bag from Saric when this was over.

Angha was looking behind Talia, through the space between the blankets, toward the crowd and the zaffre. Talia didn't know what she saw, but whatever it was made her say, "Druv, keep a lookout for one moment, please." The boy didn't even ask what he was looking out for. Just ducked between the same two blankets that Talia had come in through – both depicting the baubled building that was the clave – and stepped outside the stall.

Once he was gone, Angha twisted her rings off and set the rug aside before standing. She barely came to Talia's shoulder. Talia was pretty sure the rug she'd been working on was bigger than she was. Probably weighed more as well.

"Are you running?" Angha asked.

"Walking swiftly."

"Trouble?" It was a double-edged question: are you about to be in trouble? Are you about to make trouble for me?

"I'm not sure," Talia said. She didn't know why she felt comfortable telling the truth to Angha, but there it was. Perhaps because Ganeth had introduced them, and she trusted Ganeth, although she wasn't always sure why. Also, she knew that sometimes the fastest path to what she wanted was the truth. Even if it was a road that she rarely chose to walk.

Angha stepped forward, pushing aside the blankets for a better view of whatever was happening behind Talia.

As Talia stood there, she found herself scanning the tapestries. Surely it was here that she'd seen the image that had inspired her description of the creatures. A blanket hanging on the far end of the stall caught her eye. It showed a replica of the mekalan. The former poison eaters were all stitched upon the fabric. Perfect detail. The darkened eyes. The blue cloaks.

Her face. Her own face was there. Almost as good as the Painter would have done it. The red streaks in her dark braids. The triple sets of earrings she wore. The brown of her eyes wasn't quite right, though. Too much gray. Not enough tan.

She wanted to reach out and touch it, her cheeks and lips, the scar at the front of her throat, to make sure she was standing here, really and truly, and not locked inside Angha's horrible death wrap.

Angha watched Ardit over Talia's shoulder while Talia watched herself ripple in the wind over Angha.

After a moment, Angha stepped back. She followed Talia's gaze, clicked her teeth together.

"Sehwa," she said, lifting her tiny shoulders in a shrug. "Just business. You'll be in demand when you die."

"I'm sure I will," Talia said. Her words did not belie her heart, as it wavered and faltered inside her chest.

"Druv will take you through the back," Angha said. "Should you wish it."

The boy was there beside her as suddenly as he'd left.

"No," Talia said. "I'll go myself, through the front."

It was a stupid choice, the unsafe choice, but she couldn't bear to take help from this woman that she'd trusted, even in a small way, this woman who had made her death face to sell for a few shins. She'd rather face Ardit and find out the truth, even if it wasn't what she wanted to hear.

Talia pulled her hood down and squared her shoulders. Then she stepped into the sunlight, blinking.

Ardit was half a crowd away, coming fast. He glanced her way and her breath caught. But she didn't flinch. She didn't back down. If this was the end, she would meet it head on. Her poison dream played in her mind, how she'd run, how she'd failed Maeryl and her sisters. Not this time. Let him come.

She took a tentative step forward, began to bring her thumbs to her eyes. A gesture of reverence, yes, but also a show of no harm. I don't have a weapon or a cypher. I have nothing by these hands and these eyes and they are yours.

That's when she realized Ardit wasn't alone. Another of the greyes was at his side. As they drew closer, she saw that it was Rakdel, the chiurgeon. Normally, Rakdel was hard to miss. Everything about her was thin except her cheekbones, which curved out of her face like the sides of a bowl. Her hair was black, slicked and tucked under, giving the impression that it was short, but something about that carry of her head made it seem otherwise; there was weight back there. A proudness in the lift of her spine as she moved.

At this moment, Rakdel barely looked like herself. Her blue cloak was soaked, as if she'd just come from a storm, hood plastered to her head. Her sword – held up high above the crowd – was slathered with a dark green substance that seemed to shift on its own, dripping down before pulling itself back up to the metal. Looking at it too long gave Talia a sharp twinge behind her eyes.

"Stand away," Ardit was saying to the crowd, as he wove through the gathered people with his usual skill. "Stand away. Don't let us touch you."

A moment later, he caught sight of Talia standing there. His glance was hard and fast, and then he was throwing a small metal disc into the air. It opened mid-fall, releasing a barely visible shield around the two greyes. The shield pulsed, and the crowd imperceptibly opened up around it, giving them room to move through. If he was still speaking, she could no longer hear him.

They stopped as they reached her. Ardit seemed about to say something, his eyes pulled tight and his mouth opening – but then Rakdel said something to him, she couldn't hear what through the shield – and he let it drop. Then they were hurrying past, the invisible bubble of their sphere just barely brushing her shoulder on their way by.

Talia let out a breath she hadn't known she was holding. She still didn't know anything – what had happened to Rakdel, if Burrin suspected, why Ardit was here, what was going on with the rest of the greyes – but she felt like she'd just barely missed stepping on a detonation by some unknown force of luck. The sense of bare escape made her lightheaded.

She let the crowd close in and swell around her as she watched them go for a moment. They were heading north out of the market. Not in the direction of Rakdel's home nor in the direction of the zaffre headquarters, but toward the Winnow. What was there? Working class houses, mostly. The moonmarket. A handful of small shops – weaponsmiths, mechmakers, Aeon Priests. And Ganeth... Ganeth's workshop was there too.

Before they were lost from view, she made her way

quickly out of the market and headed north, following them from what felt like a safe distance. And all around her, the city sang its promise of steel and sorrow.

They did go to Ganeth's, but around the back and through an entrance she hadn't noticed before. Once they were inside, she walked by it. The door bore the mark of the greyes, but much smaller and more subtle than the one at Isera's. This mark wasn't designed for those passing by, but for those looking for it. She was tempted to push her way in, to find out what was happening, but she'd learned the hard way that Ganeth's workshop was rife with dangers to the uninvited.

She'd go through the front. Still likely to give her answers, but hopefully with less chance of accidentally blowing something up.

Ganeth's shop was like none of the other places around it. Where they were brick or stone, his was striated wood and metal. Two stories, with odd-shaped windows. The wood, especially, marked this as a place of importance, for there were almost no trees in this purpled shade within the whole city of Enthait. The Tawn's desert stretched wide around the city, and then the plains of the Emerald Wilds extended another two or three days' walk before there was so much as a semblance of forest to be found. And, Omuf-Rhi had told her once, even that was whitewood – not the thick red wood slabs that interspersed the metal here. He'd said the only trees like these were the ones beneath the Green Road.

It wasn't Ganeth who cared about such materials or shows of status; the sense of importance was a loan from the orness. Although Ganeth had apprentices, and a few other mechmakers like himself worked on the easier devices and defenses for the city, Ganeth was the city's official Aeon Priest. That came with benefits. And, she was sure, costs. Like making weapons when you didn't believe in war.

She waited as long as her patience could bear and then she pushed open the front door of the shop. The door chime released a scent that tasted of metal and berries, and a ragged buzzing sound that was probably supposed to carry far enough for Ganeth to hear it back in his workshop. It never seemed to, though, or perhaps he chose to ignore it. Either way, neither man nor child nor beast greeted her at the door when she entered. The taste of panic, acrid and sour, rose in the back of her throat. What if whatever that stuff was had gotten to Khee and Seild? What if, in waiting, she'd endangered them instead?

"Hello?" she called.

"In the shop!" The slightly distracted sound of Ganeth's voice was enough to bring her pulse back to its normal pace. She stepped through the store, aware of all the devices on shelves and tables, hanging from the ceiling or floating in the air. The numenera, he called them. Cyphers. Artifacts. Things with no names. Others with complex names that said what they did or didn't do. Reality spike. Heat nodule. Some moved or made noise. Others were still and silent.

Most of Ganeth's patrons wanted frivolities – gadgets or toys that did odd things, the occasional special item for a loved one, something that heated or cooled food in their homes. Those weren't Ganeth's love. His love was creating new things, a thing no one had ever created or thought of. Any time he had to repeat a device, recreate it, he felt like he was doing an injustice to the object itself. But of course that's what everyone wanted, even the zaffre. Something they already knew, a thing they'd seen at their neighbor's or friend's. Not that she blamed them. It was part of the reason she was here, sunk into Enthait and sinking faster. Hiding herself beneath the rhythm and repetition.

The first time she and Ganeth had met, he'd told her, "Everything wants to become something."

She'd been brought here by one of the zaffre – one that she was pretty sure she'd never seen since – for a training session with her new cloak, following the man's blue garb through tunnel after tunnel until they'd ended up here, where he'd dropped her off in front of this cluttered and yet perfectly organized shop. And in front of a giant hulk of a man. Who at the time had been wearing a body suit the color of yellow flowers that covered even his face. She hadn't been sure whether to be scared of him or delighted.

Ganeth stripped out of his suit faster than seemed possible – he'd shown her the secret of that later, some kind of instant removal device sewn into a pocket – and placed two objects into her hand before he'd said so much as a hello.

One was a small disk inscribed with words she couldn't read. The other was a glob of grey substance that started warm and grew colder the longer she held it.

She didn't dare move. She'd seen objects similar to this – well, not similar, but in the same category. They'd always been weapons. Was this her first test as the poison eater? Was she supposed to dismantle them before they blew up in her fingers? She had no idea.

He watched her for a long time, her face, her fingers. And then he took the devices back from her.

"Just checking," he said.

"Checking what?"

"If you could hear them." She almost laughed when she realized he meant the devices. But then again, she could hear a living creature that, as far as she knew, didn't actually talk. So who was she to say that these didn't talk either?

"Hear them?"

He fiddled with the devices, pulling bits out with a tiny tool and inserting them into another. Something about it – the precision, the insertion – made Talia shudder. She felt something deep in her body... and realized it was the same gestures, the same process that the vordcha had used. Only in that case, she'd been one of the devices.

It made her instantly and fiercely dislike this man, even though she knew nothing about him. It was a full-bodied, full-boned distaste. She had to close her eyes momentarily. She breathed. She told herself it wasn't the same. She could do this. She would do this. Even if she didn't like him, she could learn to tolerate him, pretend. It's what she did. What she was good at. She swallowed back her fear and revulsion. She couldn't bring herself to smile, but she could bring herself to stand there quietly and lie.

He brought the devices together, and then handed the new, single item back to her. It was a box now, a little bigger than the others, with a sheened coating of thick fluid. The coating was sticky and she expected it to come off on her hands, but it didn't.

"Just touch the orange thing on the side," he said.

She pressed her thumb onto it. It let out a small squawk, like a creature freed from a trap. The top opened and a tiny fluttering mechanical bird, no bigger than her thumb, came out of it. It flew around her twice, fluttering above her head. It landed on her shoulder, sang three clear, clean notes, and zipped out of sight. The box in her hand disintegrated into nothing.

"They all want to become something. They tell you, and then you try to make them that thing. Sometimes the thing is useful, a cypher, an artifact even. Sometimes it's not. Sometimes it's just a surprise." He pointed in the direction that the bird had flown. "I expect it will come back at some point. Down the road. Probably when you need it most.

"Or maybe when you absolutely don't."

His sheepish grin made her laugh, despite herself.

"I'm Ganeth," he said.

"Talia."

"I thought you might have the ability to hear them," he said. He sounded a little disappointed or sad, but not overly surprised. "Most don't. I've never met a poison eater who did. But something about you… I would have guessed you were connected to mech somehow."

She shook her head, oddly sad to have disappointed him. Not sad enough to tell him about the mech that the vordcha had once filled her body with. "I have little experience with that type of thing." It was largely true. But mostly not. Just that most of her experience had been on the other side. Trying to tell someone else what she didn't want to become and having them not listen. Or care.

"Ah well. Come and have your cloak fitted, if you're going to be the next poison eater. Don't take it the wrong way when I say I really liked the last one, though. He was funny."

"I won't," she said. But of course she did.

That was seven poisonings ago now. Ganeth had never

told her she was funny, but she thought he liked her just the same. She wondered what he would say about her if the poisoning took her and he had to teach someone else how to use her cloak.

Still with the visions of Rakdel in her head – the soaked cloth, the dripping green weapon – she made her way to the back of the store, where Khee and Seild were both sitting on a low bench in front of the door to Ganeth's workshop. The girl was reading to the beast, or thought she was. She had an upside down book in her hand, and was telling Khee a story from it.

"And then the orness uses her special machine that only she knows how to use, and she blows them all up. *Kala-booma!*" She spread her hands in the air.

Khee, if appearances didn't deceive, was curled up next to her, fast asleep.

At least he was until Seild saw Talia and bounced up, causing Khee to do the same. He uttered a startled roar and accidentally bared his teeth before he realized what was happening.

"What. You-? Ah…" Seild never seemed sure how to act around Talia when neither of them was on duty. She stopped and tried to put her thumbs over her eyes while still holding the book, at which point she put the corner of the book in her eye instead. "Ow!"

Talia could practically hear Khee laughing. Despite everything, she had to force herself not to do the same. Whatever could be said about the girl, she was one of the few creatures that could make her laugh in the middle of panic.

Talia's first instinct was to rush into Ganeth's lab and ask everything she could about what she'd seen. But first, she had to make sure Seild didn't see the panic rising in her. Very solemnly, she lowered herself down to a squat, waiting until Seild was done rubbing her injury. Her eye was red around the edges, but she didn't seem any worse for wear.

"How about when I'm not in my cloak, you can just call me Talia," she said. "And you can stop poking yourself in the eye with things."

"All right... Talia." The girl tried the name, and wrinkled her nose.

"How about Tal? Your mom calls me that sometimes," she said.

"Is she back?" The girl's face opened. So like her mother. While Talia could feel her own face closing, an erratic pulse growing in the corner of her jaw.

"Not yet. But soon, I bet. I saw some of the other greyes in the market earlier." *Dripping with something, afraid of being touched.*

"Speaking of which..." She wiggled her pack in Seild's direction. It was a ploy, and not a clever one, and she felt only a slight ping when Seild fell for it.

"You went to the market?"

"Oh? And why would someone such as yourself care about the market?"

A sudden shyness overtook the girl, who suddenly found a new interest in her feet. It didn't last; the smell of saltpetals was unmistakable as Talia pulled the bag from her pack. And remembered that she'd never replaced it. Skist. All she had were the crushed remnants. So much for her distraction.

"I'm sorry," she said. "They're all crushed."

"That's all right," the girl said. "Mom crushes them all

the time. Watch."

With practiced ease, Seild opened the bag with one hand, licked her finger, and then stuck her entire hand deep into the crumbs. "See? Khee can even eat them that way. Here, Khee!"

Khee shot Talia a glance, then stuck out the smallest portion of his tongues that he possibly could and allowed Seild to daintily press some of the crumbs to it. He rolled his tongues back into his mouth, said

no

so sharply that this time Talia did laugh. He sat on his rump, the edges of his wide mouth curled down, snorting out of his nose. Seild, who was busy sticking three wet and crumb-covered fingers in her mouth, didn't seem to care, or notice, that the beast didn't share her love of the treat.

"Please don't eat all of those in the next five minutes?" A useless plea but she had to make it. "I brought you something too, Khee." She tossed him the biggest piece of the jerky, which he caught, swallowed, and thanked her for in a single gesture of tooth and jaw.

"Ganeth? I'm coming in."

She waited for his answer before moving. Only once had she entered his workshop before he'd responded, and somehow she'd triggered something and a bunch of winged barbs had come flying at her face. Ganeth had called them off by blowing a weird scent out of a metal flower, but not before she'd felt their points whirring past her mouth, as if trying to find a way in.

"Come!" he said.

The door to Ganeth's workshop was made of sticky gel that you had to push your way through. She would have preferred to use her hex hand so she didn't have to touch it, but Ganeth wasn't sure it wouldn't gum up the electronics somehow. Her clothed elbow took the brunt of the push, but even then, she couldn't get through without it touching her skin. It wasn't squeamishness; she'd stuck her hands into lots of things, not the least of which was whatever was in the door that led to the clave. It was that the slick slide of it made her think of the vordcha, the rubbery squeal of their skin as they'd moved around her body. She could almost smell the chemical and copper of their devices melting into her blood.

She was sure if she told Ganeth, he'd replace the door with something else. But each time she tried to convince herself that it would get better. It didn't.

She didn't know what she expected to find, but it wasn't this. It was just Ganeth, his face planted behind a domed device. Not that seeing his face behind a device was that unusual. In fact, she probably saw him like that more often than any other way. But the fact that he was alone and there was no sign of Ardit and Rakdel deepened her confusion, and added to her growing sense of dread.

"Talia," Ganeth said, as she entered the room and shuddered off the feel of the gel. Ganeth's voice was warm, but he didn't look up. He did something and the dome on the device became translucent, so she could see his face through it, but the nature of it somehow showed his eyes as being much too large for his head. The effect was disconcerting, particularly when he was talking. "It's safe. I just need a few... moments... to..."

She knew better than to try to talk to him when he was focused. He'd do his best to respond, but it would end up being mostly nonsense. Words coming out of his mouth that had nothing to do with whatever was happening in his brain.

She watched him work instead. Ganeth was tall and broad, big all over, the kind of man you thought you'd be glad to have on your side in a fight. And while that was true enough, it wasn't for the reasons one would expect. He was, in fact, an utter abomination with a sword. Or an axe. Or, really, a blade or bow or weapon of any kind.

She'd been at the bookstore while Omuf-Rhi tried to give him a lesson once – and had suffered the consequences of that choice. Not only did Ganeth hate weapons, he wielded them as if he was throwing a live snake across the room. He'd nearly taken Talia's other arm off with a particularly errant swipe of his blade. While he'd been talking too vehemently with his hands, she was often quick to remind him. Not while he was actually trying to hit something.

What Ganeth *was* brilliant with were his devices. He didn't use them to fight – she thought he might be against fighting as part of his priesthood or something – but she was pretty sure that he could, and even would, if given the right incentive. If she was ever at war – a place she truly hoped to not be any time in the near future – he was the nonfighter she wanted at her side.

"Ganeth," she asked, unable to wait anymore. "I saw Ardit and Rakdel in the market. They've come back."

She waited to see what he said. Would he pretend he hadn't also seen them?

He blinked behind the device. One eye went bigger than the other. "They were early."

"They were… covered in something. Green. Moving…" She glanced over her shoulder at the door, making sure that Seild was still busy with her petals. "Like it was alive."

"Oh, yes," he said, his voice slightly muffled by the

device – she had no idea what he was doing back there. "I saw that."

She watched his eye grow smaller and bigger behind the device. He often said things that made no sense to her. Sometimes she could figure them out if she thought about it, but this one wasn't coming to her. She wondered if all Aeon Priests were like this, or just Ganeth. "You saw it? At the market?"

"No." Ganeth pulled himself from behind the device. His eyes were back to their normal size as he looked at her. "They were here. But I saw them earlier in the remote viewer. With the green... I thought it was venom, but now I am pretty sure it's a thinking acid of some kind. Sentient, not sapient." He tapped his eye, and then the device. Neither gesture meant anything to her.

She waited, shaking her head slightly.

"Ah," he said. "It might be easier to show you. Would you like to try it?"

"Not if it's going to make my eyes look like that."

"Your what look like what?" He shook his head. "Never mind, it doesn't matter. You can see what I saw and it will make sense. Come around the back. Stand where I was standing and put your eyes to the blank spaces in the back."

She did so, but had to crouch down a bit in order to make her eyes level with the places he pointed out. Inside the device, against a background of metal and synth, she could see a scene. At first, it was blurry and hard to make out – a couple of figures, a bunch of dark shapes that looked like trees or mountains.

"Ganeth, what...?"

And then the scene adjusted. Tightened and became

whole, as if her eyes had just started working correctly. She could see Isera, impossibly, as if she was standing just in front of her. She wielded a giant maul, the end of which was alight with green flames that sputtered and sparked with every swing.

In front of her, a giant yellow, pus-filled worm with several long necks opened its skin, and from a hundred, a thousand sudden mouths, spewed forth a liquid that drenched Isera's flame in seconds. Talia was sure it was the same liquid she'd seen on Ardit's blade in the marketplace.

Beside Isera, a greyes that she thought was Sarir – it was hard to tell through the helmet – was hacking at one of the creature's necks with a long sword. The neck opened under the blade, sending forth more of its insides, a liquid that seemed so hot it was boiling. Sarir fell to her knees, her mouth open. Although Talia couldn't hear her, she was sure the woman was howling.

Isera sidestepped, but barely – she was limping, dragging her left foot. One whole side of her face was covered in roiling green, and she had that eye closed, cocking her head in what seemed like an effort to give herself a better view of the creature.

Slowly, she raised one hand. Even through the device, Talia could see the cypher she wore on the inside of her palm. It pulsed out a white beam that opened up around the worm, capturing it in a ring of light. But it was clear that it wouldn't last long – already the creature's pus was eating through the material.

Talia couldn't stand to watch anymore. She pushed herself from the device. Her eyes felt scratchy and swollen. "Where are they, Ganeth? They're going to die. We have to help them."

"They're fine," he said. He had turned his attention to a large metal container and was poking at something inside it with a buzzing synthsteel rod. "I just looked them over."

It took her a moment to get his meaning. "Not Ardit and Rakdel. Isera. The others."

"Oh. They're fine, too. I already watched to the end."

She wanted to take the rod out of his hand and force him to give her his full attention, to answer all of her questions. Right. Now.

Instead, she said, "Explain." Then, remembering some of his past explanations, she added, "Explain it for *me*."

"It's not real," he said. "Or, rather, it is real. But it already happened."

"How? When?"

"I'm not sure… it's a recording, from the past."

"I don't understand," she said. Everything was blurred. Here was one place she thought she'd get answers and now she had too many answers and not enough questions. "How?"

"Well, there are these tiny particles in the air, everywhere around us, that we can't really see, called nano–"

"No," she said. His words weren't helping. She didn't know what he was talking about. She had to go to Isera. She had to do something. Maybe Ganeth was wrong. Maybe this wasn't the past. Maybe it was like what her visions were supposed to be. Maybe it hadn't happened yet and she could stop it.

"Those are the charn, aren't they?"

That did get his attention, for he carefully set the buzzing rod down and lifted his face. "What makes you think that?"

His expression was rarely readable, but now she could

see confusion and uncertainty in it. Maybe that's why she hadn't heard or read the word before. Maybe it was taboo, unspoken. Fears often were. "Aren't they?"

She was startled to hear him laugh, a sudden acrid sound that made her cheeks burn. "Those? No. No. They're... I don't know. Some type of worm, I imagine. Sure, they look dangerous. Well, they *are* dangerous. But nothing out of the ordinary. Just the type of thing that you and the greyes are positioned to protect us from. It's why all of this, all of you, exist."

Ganeth wasn't always the quickest to catch on to emotions, but he must have seen something in her face, because he quickly added, "I promise. I've watched the whole thing. They're fine. A few scratches, nothing out of the ordinary. They'll be on their way home soon."

"Do you promise me that they are not dead? Dying?" She couldn't get the tense right. It had happened, but was still happening, or maybe hadn't happened yet.

"They're not dead." He built a steeple from the entwine of his fingers. "I promise on the Sacred Chronicle of High Father Calaval."

She didn't know what that was, and she couldn't tell if she wanted the answer enough to ask twice. She couldn't shake that image of Isera, half blind. That creature. Its thousand mouths. Why hadn't she seen *that* in the poisoning?

The answer came as fast as the question: because she was a fraud. False.

"I want... I need... to watch the whole thing," she said.

He did something with the device, then nodded. She leaned in, pressed her eyes to the scene. She watched it all. Every swing and ache and grimace of pain. Every fall back and push forward. She watched every moment of her lie play out before her until she couldn't stand it anymore. And then she ran.

THE MARROW

Khee came with her. She didn't ask him to. She didn't even stop to say anything to Seild on her way out of Ganeth's door. But as she made her way across the city, she realized she could hear the mechbeast breathing beside her, keeping pace. In this latelight, his stripes looked paler than normal, almost cream colored. Like he was half shadow, half real.

At first, she didn't know why her feet took her to the Break. There were so other many places to run. To the tunnels. Out the front gate. Even back to her room. But none of them felt right. It wasn't until she stopped against the broken section of the wall that she realized what had drawn her. Here was the tiny hollow in the stones where she and Khee had lived when they'd first come to Enthait.

She knelt down to look into the darkness of it. It had seemed small then, but now she could see how small it really was. Not even a cave or a tunnel. Just a hollowed-out space big enough for two scrawny refugees.

"Remember this, Khee?" she asked.

yes

The sound was tinged with sadness, and some fear. She

wasn't surprised. The last time they'd stayed here had been bad. It was only a few weeks after she'd met Isera on the Green Road. Things had started to change after that. A little. Khee finally, finally gained some weight and began to explore the area around their hollow in the wall. Isera invited her to this ritual called taf, a kind of prayer combined with an herbed tea that grew colder as you drank it, until it was iced enough to sweat the glass in her hand. Talia had grown their stack of spoils for the leaving – shins, meat, a few containers, clothing, even a small square box that was supposed to explode if you threw it – into something that almost felt ready.

That last night here, she'd woken in the dark to a rare storm in the desert, the first one she'd seen since the snow at the blackweave. This one was not white, but black and blue. A crumbling thunder that roared through their hollowed cave as if to split it open, a blue light that rode down to the ground on thin, crackling legs and pushed the shadows back so that she could see the tightened pupils of Khee's eyes each time.

It wasn't the storm that had woken her. It was something else. Something was wrong.

It only took her moving awake to feel it. The top of her thigh thrummed so hard, the skin pulled so tight over whatever was festering in there, she thought it might split open. She put her hand to it, thinking to hold it all together with the press of finger and palm. The first touch made her voice echo the storm's scream.

Khee pushed into her back, a question without words.

"I'm all right." Her words through clenched teeth and spit couldn't have been reassuring. *Onas* she was not. She forced an inhale, then more words. "I'm all right."

Again. This time, gentler. Beneath the curious and careful press of her fingers, she could feel the heat, the foul press of skin. It was where she'd cut Khee's horn off. The wound she thought had healed – the skin *had* healed, but something inside had not.

She tried to roll up her pant leg, then to pull it up, found both impossible with the crush of pain and the single hand. She needed a knife, something sharp. She fumbled through her packed stuff, stunned to realize that in all her planning she had not thought to steal a weapon, that there was nothing there to cut the fabric.

"Can you rip it, Khee?" she asked.

hurt

"Yes," she said. As if he was waiting for something. "I'll scream."

yes

He too knew something of pain and waiting, for he slipped from behind her and dipped his head before any answer of hers could come. She heard, but didn't feel the clamp of his teeth over the fabric. Her thigh throbbed, thrummed, hot and then cold. Some of Khee's exhale, some of it her. He had a grip, but didn't move.

"Khee, what–?"

The crack of thunder drowned out her question, and in it, the scream that followed when Khee clamped down and pulled the fabric to the side. *Everything* jerked to the side, a pain that started at the wound and branched so hard that her toes curled and the side of her jaw throbbed.

The fabric tore, thank the gods it tore the first time, because she didn't think she could have done that again. She thought she would have fought Khee if he'd tried.

The words for *thank you* got tangled in her head, wouldn't make the passage to her mouth. The best she could do was to drop her head and pant gratefully against Khee's fur for a moment.

She twisted back to pull the fabric open between her fingers so she could see the wound in the next lightning strike and pain filled her head and the world was slipping into something black and grey and she heard the thunder again overhead, but the lightning never, ever came to split the dark.

How long later, she came awake on something less hard than rock floor, warmed by something both above and below. She flinched against the possibility of pain or noise or light, even before she remembered why. None came. Just the soft pale light that she'd come to associate with glowglobes and the sound of something moving around near her feet.

Not something. Someone. A thin figure in a brown apron. She watched through slitted eyes, calculated. Real? Not real? She vaguely remembered the acute thrum of her thigh, which was so absent now it almost created a space where it was missing. This was some kind of fever dream, she decided. She was still in the hollow of the wall, still festering, still dying.

A hand on her forehead, a human hand, a real hand. She pulled back so hard and sudden she heard her head smack off the firm surface beneath her. It took half a second for the pain that equaled the sound to show itself, sharp. At the same time, the wound in her thigh seemed to realize she was awake, and joined her, humming a high song of pain.

The hand went away.

"How are you feeling?" The voice was honeyed and soft, from far away.

She wanted to answer that voice, it sounded so nice. But she couldn't. There was nothing in her that didn't hurt and wasn't scared.

The voice went on as if it hadn't expected an answer. A second later, she realized it wasn't talking to her. There was someone else in the room. That someone else was answering.

"Like I got bit by a giant craqar beast with a million teeth."

"Seems about right."

Laughter, loud enough that it pulled her fully from the bad place. She opened her eyes. Beyond her feet, which were bare, two people were talking. Or, rather, one person – the thin one in the brown apron – and one something else. Big. Humanish. Covered in reddish-orange hair all over.

They both approached as she tried to sit up.

"How about not yet?" the aproned one said.

"How about yet." Talia tried to say it with a certain fervor and strength. It came out a jumbled mess of spit.

The laughter again.

"Stop," she tried. Better. An actual word.

"Sorry," the aproned one said. "I had to give you something for the pain. It's probably making you a little dizzy."

She sat part way up anyway, and the movement of the room made her want to vomit. She stayed it by closing her eyes for a moment. When it had eased enough that she thought it past, she pushed herself up with her left hand until she was nearly sitting fully, then slowly,

slowly laid back down.

Everything about the woman was thin except her cheekbones, which curved out of her face like the sides of a bowl. She wore a bright purple wrap around her head that brought warmth to her russet eyes. "Greyes Rakdel, chiurgeon and–"

"The best chiurgeon in the whole of Enthait." Spoken with such affection that the woman laughed, her cheeks dimpling. The one who'd spoken was tall and wide, and moved like someone carrying a lot more muscle than fat. He had six eyes, two of which regarded her carefully, while the other four, smaller and higher up on his head, seemed to be looking at the woman.

"Yes, thank you, Omuf-Rhi." She touched his arm in passing, a familiar gesture. She's done that a thousand times, Talia thought. More. "As I was saying…"

Her brain caught up to her in a sudden rush. How did she get here? What had happened to her leg? Where was–

"Where's Khee? Where's…" What did one call him to strangers? She realized she had no idea what kind of creature he truly was. "The creature I was with. Brownish. Big–"

"Teeth?" the man said. "Really, really big teeth?"

She nodded.

"He's fine. I can't say as much for myself." He held up his arm, which was wrapped in red strips, around and around. The fur near it was matted with something dark. "I don't know what you did for that creature, but he's the most loyal thing I've ever seen. I had to pretty much let him clamp on to my arm just so I could drag you here."

Khee, you fought for me?

"I'm sorry about your arm," she said. It sounded so

small, but it was all she had to offer.

He waved her apology away, but not impolitely. "I understand protecting the ones you love. We worked it out, your beast and I. I promised to try to save you, and he promised not to kill me. Well, he didn't actually promise. More just loosened his grip a little."

The two exchanged glances. Rakdel reached forward, gestured with a long, flat tool toward Talia's thigh. "May I?"

Talia hesitated, then nodded. The press of the metal was cold, but surprisingly not painful. She didn't know if that was because she was healing better there or because of the drugs Rakdel had given her.

"How did I get here?" Wherever here was.

Rakdel talked while she fiddled with the device, pressing it here and there along her leg. "Your creature's name is Khee?"

At Talia's nod, she continued, "Well, then, Khee came and found one of ours, and then pretty much dragged her back to wherever you were holed up. Wouldn't let up until you were here. Singleminded, that one."

That he was. A sweetness welled within her, an emotion she hadn't felt or wanted to feel in a long time. It was the drugs, she thought. Making her soft.

That was followed quickly by a sharper, jangled thought.

"One of ours?" she asked.

"I was going to say earlier, before I was interrupted..." Rakdel sent a quick glance at Omuf-Rhi, who laughed and held up his bandaged arm with a look of feigned pain.

"Ouch?" he said.

She merely shook her head at him. "Greyes Rakdel, chiurgeon and healer, in the service of Enthait, the orness, and the poison eater."

Talia had so many questions, but held her tongue. She'd learned from her interaction with Isera that while Enthait was too large of a city to know everyone, it wasn't a place that saw many strangers. People didn't cross the vast expanse of orange desert to come here. There was no reason to bring more attention to who or what she was. A stranger.

Rakdel removed the device from her thigh, shook it, and then put it to her ear for a moment. Whatever it told her, her face seemed pleased with the result.

"I won't lie to you," she said. "Your wound was very, very bad. So bad that I can't actually believe you're alive. The infection was…" She wrinkled her nose. "Let's just say that if your creature is single-minded, you are more so. Most wouldn't have survived that, not even if I'd taken the leg."

Rakdel allowed her glance to flow toward Talia's missing arm, the scarred flesh at the end that she normally kept wrapped in fabric, but which now rested, exposed, on her lap.

"Anyway, you should heal just fine," she said. "But it wouldn't hurt to stay here a few days, rest up. Eat something, maybe."

Talia shook her head, unable to speak for a moment, at the unexpected kindness that made the back of her throat hurt. She didn't have the room, or the money, for kindness.

"I can't. I don't even have a way to repay you for what you've already done," Talia said. "Nor…" it hurt to admit, "any skills for trade."

"You could take that creature of yours to the Keep,"

Omuf-Rhi said. "He'd kill half the animals in there in the first bout and you'd earn yourself some..." He faltered as he realized they were both looking at him, Rakdel with a fierce expression that pulled her skin even tighter over her cheekbones. Talia didn't know what her own face was doing, but she could feel a quick heat rising on the back of her neck.

"Sehwa," he said, holding up both hands, palms out, laughing. "I'm teasing. I'm teasing. Probably smarter for you to become the poison eater anyway, with that kind of resolve. You'd certainly outlast the last one."

"Out," Rakdel said. It was fierce, but that ferocity didn't quite cover up her attempt not to laugh. "Get out, before you say something that really makes me regret you."

Omuf-Rhi rolled his many eyes at Talia, as if to say, "Be on my side, yes?" but the response was not without a wry smile. "Well, poison eater or not," he said. "You can come and work in my store anytime. Repay me for these new holes in my arm. Protect me from thieves and the like."

The irony of that didn't escape her. Nor, she thought, him, for a moment later he lifted her pack up into her line of sight. "Here's everything from your... place. Except the creature, of course, who's outside. Which seems right, since he's currently the only one among us who doesn't actually need the medical attention of our city's greatest healer."

"Out," Rakdel said again. This time he went without further protest.

Rakdel picked something off the table next to her. "I don't know if you want this, but it came out of your leg, so it's yours to do with as you will. Sometimes it's important to know the things that try to kill us."

Talia held out her hand, let Rakdel drop the object softly into it. It was thin sliver of metal, no bigger than her thumb. A jagged, broken piece of blue-black blade. Talia fisted her hand around it, felt it cut her and was glad that the drugs had not dulled that pain at least.

Rakdel was looking her up and down, slowly. Talia tried not to squirm under the gaze, knowing everything she saw. Threadbare and torn pants, torn leg, missing arm, hair fallen from its wrap.

"You'll stay," she said finally. "A few days, at least. Khee too."

"No." She tried to get up, fell back. But she was nothing if not determined and she got herself up and out of the bed.

"You'll stay," Rakdel said, but she didn't move to stop her.

Out the door, and there in the room was Isera, asleep on a cot. She was still in her uniform, and in her sleep, she'd tossed one long arm over Khee, who was staring at her.

like.

Rakdel had been right – she'd stayed.

And now, she wondered if it had been the right thing to do. She half-crawled into the hole and found the stash of things, most of them as she'd left them. The food was, not surprisingly, torn into and destroyed. But the rest was there, still in the pack she'd stolen to keep it in. She slung it over her shoulder, and with Khee at her side, she climbed the broken and crumbling section of the wall.

From there, she could see down into the city on one side and down to the desert on the other. She'd come to Enthait from the south. She remembered little of the trip. Pieces. Ice and then forest and then this orange desert, eternal it seemed, where she had thought again and again that she would die. She didn't know what lay to the north or the west, and from here, it was near impossible to tell in the dark.

When she looked over the city, she *could* see most of the skars from here, even in the dark, their silhouettes shadowed against the blackening sky. The top of the long rectangular zaffre headquarters was barely visible in front of the clave, but the lights of the Eternal Market flickered with such strength that she wondered how far away you could see its spiral.

The wall was wide and she paced without paying mind to the structure beneath her feet. Khee trailed behind, sometimes stopping here and there to snuff at something moving inside the wall, but mostly keeping pace, quiet, waiting for something. Waiting for her.

She told herself she was getting perspective. But really what she was getting was even more confused. With each step, she felt the weight of what had happened to Isera and the others. No death, not this time, but injuries. And what of next time, when she sent them off into the world, unprepared for what was ahead of them? What happened when her lies got one of them killed?

"And there shall in Enthait be a weapon, so grand, so glorious, so powerful, it shall destroy all of the enemies and all of the beasts and all of the living and all of the dead and only the orness, the keeper of the aria, shall remain," she said out loud.

The line was from a dusty tome she'd found buried in a stack of Omuf-Rhi's books. She'd memorized it, kept it on her tongue like a seed every time she felt the vordcha coming for her, real or fake. She thought she'd wanted to be the poison eater, to see the danger coming, but then she'd read that and realized she'd been all wrong. She needed more than a long view of coming danger. She needed a weapon. A weapon so powerful it left nothing standing.

But at what cost? She knew that too, but had sidestepped the answer.

It had never been her plan to care about Enthait. About the people who moved and lived and loved inside its walls. She had become the poison eater not for them, but for herself.

The image of herself kneeling at Maeryl's side in the snow came unbidden, cold shivering up her spine, and the thing she'd forgotten in the poisondream, the word she'd whispered. *Vengeance.*

No, not for herself. For Maeryl. For Kanistl. For Anthleaon. For those who came after – the ones that the vordcha would turn into martyrs. And, yes, all right, maybe a little for herself.

She would not let go of that promise. But surely there was another way. She could run, let the vordcha track her to some other place, one where she could try to fulfill her promise without hope of succeeding. If she ran, the orness would find another poison eater, a true one. One that would take the poison and protect the city, protect the people, where she had failed.

But that was not a plan she could bear either; the city had not had a true poison eater since the orness. She didn't know how long that had been, but rumors said fifty years, sixty. More. The orness must be a hundred by now. Everyone else who had taken the poisons had died. Even Burrin, she thought, would die. For all she thought he hungered to be in her place, she could imagine only one reason that the orness would not appoint him the position. To protect him. To keep him from death.

She could go to the orness and tell her the truth, ask her to wield the aria against the vordcha. She couldn't imagine the orness believing her, not after she'd been lying to her, to the whole city, this whole time. Not that she knew how to find the orness anyway; she'd only ever seen her at the poisonings. Where did she live? How did she rule without being a presence in the city? She didn't know. She'd have to get to her through Burrin and that... that wasn't going to happen.

Do you promise to serve the city of Enthait? Do you promise to serve its people?

Yes.

Every choice she'd made here, selfish, fearful. She had stayed, telling herself it was different from running. But it was the same.

Will you run now? The question echoed her footsteps as she stepped along the wall. The city was silent here, exhaled no song, as if making room for the clang of her thoughts. *Yes. No. Either way, the losses seemed unbearable.*

The truth was she wasn't saving herself. She wasn't saving anyone. It was time for her to stop pretending to be something she was not. She was no hero, not to Khee or Maeryl or Isera or even to herself. Surely not to the city of Enthait.

Broken, one-armed, fallen coward.

Khee kept pace, silent, as she climbed off the wall and headed south across the city, until they were back in the room that she'd come to think of as *hers*, but which now seemed to belong wholly to someone else.

It wasn't until she'd hung the cloak on the hook and laid the hexed metal band on the table that she realized she'd made her decision. She had to leave Enthait. Allow the orness to choose the true poison eater. The thought felt heavy, as if the world itself was pulling her down, but also true, and there was a lightness in that.

She gathered the rest of her things into her pack. Not that she had much. A few more shins, some dried meats and fruit. The first set of clothes she'd bought here – long striped pants and a silverweave shirt that molded to her torso and provided a modicum of protection. She thought about leaving the blue-black split of metal, but in the end, she slipped it into the pocket of her pants, not minding the sharp edges through the fabric.

She stood before the seven silver marks on the wall. She touched each of the circles, surprised at how little emotion she had about them. She'd expected this to be the hard part.

"We have to leave, Khee," she said.

She could feel Khee's eyes on her before she turned. His stripes flickered brown-yellow and then settled back to brown. He fumbled for the word he wanted, a jumble of no understanding that rode through her.

"Try again?" she said.

This time it was direct and hollow-pointed and clear.

Softness?

His question jabbed her, fast and fisted, in the stomach. She could barely answer, couldn't bring her voice to rise more than a whisper. "No. No, Seild's not coming."

She knelt so that her face was level with his, and put her hand on the side of his head. He leaned into her, his breath warm on her wrist.

"You can stay, Khee," she said. "Stay with Seild. Stay with Isera."

stay

She felt his answer in her gut too, another punch, another knock of her breath against her teeth that forced an audible exhale from her. Yes, of course he would stay. What did she have to offer him? A life of running, a life of...

stay

he said again, and this time she understood he meant something else entirely. Not that he would stay, but that she should.

"I can't," she said. "I'm sorry."

She couldn't bear to hear and feel his next word, whatever it might be, and so she stepped out her door and onto the street without waiting for it. She would leave it to him to decide. Come or stay. It should be his choice. If he came with her, or he had something to say, she would know either way. But she couldn't take another gut punch. Not yet. Not while looking into his face.

Night had fallen while they'd been inside, but the moon was as full as she'd ever seen it, pale and luminescent. It seeped into every corner, chased out what few shadows remained until they stretched long and thin into the street. It was as if the day had come while she'd been gathering her things, if day was blue lit and powdered with stars. She blinked in the brightness of it.

So when the shadow, something blacker than shadow, moved forward into her line of sight, she raised her hand to her eyes as if to ward off a coming darkness.

"Talia," the darkness said. There was no formality, no address, but Talia recognized the voice at once.

"We should talk," the orness said.

Talia's whole life, she'd been good at avoiding things. It was what had gotten her this far. Scathed and broken, yes, but also alive.

For almost as long as she had been in the blackweave she had avoided, for example, the truth of how she came to be one of the Twelve Martyrs of the Forgotten Compass.

The vordcha stole me when I was young.

That was the story she had always told herself.

They stole me when I was young. She didn't know how young, exactly. Old enough to have spoken her first words – she could remember the shape of them on her tongue, even if she couldn't remember their sound. She saw the world at the height of other people's knees rather than their feet, but she got the sense that was a recent development. Old enough to have a name, a now-secret name that she only dared whisper, for fear of remembering.

There was only one lie in that story she told herself. A single word.

Stole.

Stole was the wrong word, but it was the one she always thought first, throwing it up like a shield to protect herself from the truth.

A better word, a truer word, was *given*. The monsters hadn't taken her. She'd been *given* to them.

An easy trade for a promise of safety and safekeeping. A promise barely heard over the better promise of more of the white fruit that split open around a blood-red pit. There was a memory she never looked at, of faces – her parents? She couldn't be sure, although the woman had eyes like hers – dipped into white flesh, smeared and dripping, gnawing as if the hunger would never end. Eyes glazed and unseeing. Unseeing her as they handed her over without questions, without concerns.

She refused to remember those blackened hands, the overlong fingers that hummed and crackled as they curled across her eyes, her mouth, her neck. The slick black skin. The acrid, rotting smell of her own breath as she sucked it in between the press of failing flesh.

Talia had always been good at avoiding things.

The orness was standing in front of her, and her first instinct was *run*.

"Don't," the orness said, as if she knew. Talia wondered if the orness knew, too, that she was planning to leave. Somehow. An impossibility – she hadn't spoken the words aloud, not to anyone but Khee – and still. There was timing and then there was *timing*.

She scanned the bright wide street, the narrow thin alley that led off it, dark as shadow. One of those might allow her to escape. Then Khee was behind her, pressing his body to the back of her knees. Cutting off her route to flee.

Traitor, she thought.

stay, came his answer. Soft as a purr in the base of her belly.

As far as Talia could tell, the orness carried no weapons. Talia saw no zaffre, no greyes. Dressed simply in a robe the color of a puddle reflecting night, black with constellations of stars across the sleeves, she was barely visible even in the bright light. Her hood was pulled up, hiding her hair. Her face was such a slippery thing. Like trying to grasp the very air with your eyes. Talia focused on the silver hoops that ran up the orness' right ear; they glowed faintly inside her hood and gave Talia's gaze something to hold on to.

The shifting shadow of the orness' face and outfit ached her eyes.

She was looking at the thing she'd hoped to become. And for a moment, she couldn't remember why she'd wanted it, needed it, so badly.

The orness' hands were palmed together, holding what at first looked like a very small version of the moon. Oblong and pale white, it seemed to give off its own light. An impossibility, but oddly she was growing used to those. Maybe impossibility just kept moving further out as you moved forward.

The orness saw her looking and opened her hands. "Moonfruit," she said. It rested on her palm so lightly it didn't actually seem to be touching the skin. "A gift, of sorts. They're quite rare."

"Why would you give me a gift?" Talia said.

"I get the sense that you are..." the orness tilted her head, like a shadow shifting, "thinking of traveling. I'd like to talk first."

"And then?"

The orness tossed the fruit from one hand to the other. It rose in a long arc, then fell lightly, slower than it should have, until it just barely rested on her opposite palm. "And then if you choose, you may..." She paused. "Choose."

"About what?" Khee wasn't letting loose the pressure on the back of her knees. She was pinned.

"It is a longer conversation than I'd like to have in the middle of the street at night," the orness said. "Come tomorrow, for taf. Bring the fruit. I'm a bit hard to find otherwise..." Her voice trailed away, sentence unfinished.

She tossed the fruit to Talia, a leisurely throw that slowed as it came toward her. Talia went to catch it with her hexed hand, realizing a moment too late that she'd left the band back in the room. The moonfruit sailed past, but so slowly that she had time to reach out with her true hand and pluck it from its endless descent.

When she looked up again, the shadow was gone, as if it had been nothing more than the poison dream.

There was no way she was staying, no way she was meeting the orness for taf. Sometimes the rituals here made her head spin, how everyone believed in them. All you had to do was look at Talia's own face, the supposed embodiment of the poison eater, and realize what kind of farce it all was.

She should have gone right out of the gates despite the orness' request, kept moving, kept her promise, but something was keeping her here. A mystery that she couldn't unravel. It was eating at her. Picking at her. Like she was picking at the moonfruit in her lap.

They were on the wall near the gate. She'd gotten this far toward leaving the city, but hadn't been able to make it any farther. Under the moon, the Tawn nearly glowed, a luminescent orange landscape that seemed like it might burst into flame at any moment.

"What does she want to talk about, Khee? What is all that…" She tried to mimic the orness' voice, but it came out all wrong somehow. Suddenly, she couldn't remember what her voice sounded like. "'And then if you choose, you may choose'? What does that even mean?"

He gave her no answer.

"Oh, now you're quiet, you traitor."

In her hand, the moonfruit wasn't weightless the way it had seemed in the orness' grasp. Instead, it was quite heavy for its size, clearly ripe. She used the blue-black blade to split the skin. It was tougher than she expected, leathery. It made her fight for it, and then she wished she hadn't. Beneath its pretty skin, the fruit smelled bad. Rank and raunchy. Musky. Far more animal than plant. Even Khee bared his teeth and shook his head when she held it to him.

"Some gift, Khee. Do you think she's trying to poison me?" She laughed at that, a black and unpleasant thing that she hated even as it came from her mouth. "Ah well, too late."

She ripped off a bit of the flesh, mostly for spite, and was surprised to find that its taste was beyond pleasant, perhaps one of the best things she'd eaten since she'd arrived. Sweet and cool, with something in it that made her cheeks buzz with pleasure.

"I still don't like her," she said around a mouthful of fruit. "Telling me to meet her, like a child."

Although spoken aloud her words did sound, even to herself, like a child. Like Seild in one of her rare moments of overtired pouting. But she didn't mean to be petulant. And she wasn't, in truth, angry at the orness. She barely knew the woman, beyond the rumors and the stories. Her ire was at herself, that she'd made a decision, a hard decision, the right decision. And yet it had been so weak that one small thing had thrown her off the path.

Not so small. She is the orness.

What did that even mean? To be the orness? Talia knew. She'd done her research. It meant to be the one with the power in her hands. The power to not just keep herself safe, but to destroy monsters. Monsters like the vordcha.

Perhaps the answer was to tell the orness the truth. To

ask for help. To *make* her help. For the city. That was her promise, her purpose, wasn't it? To help the city? How could she say no?

"Fine, Khee," she said, as if he'd just spent all this time convincing her. Which she supposed he had, in a way, if only by his silence. "I'll go talk to the orness. But she's not going to like it."

She bit down into the fruit and was surprised to find her teeth hit something solid. In the middle of the fruit, after she'd eaten it all, she found a pit. Tiny and metallic. In the shape of a star.

She looked down at the remaining pit, remembered the orness' words. *Bring the fruit. I'm a bit hard to find otherwise.*

"Skist," she muttered.

In the morning light, after a fitful sleep – this time her dream was not of the orness coming to close her eyes, but of the orness forcing them open, feeding her eyes full of the shine of moons and stars – Talia turned the star-shaped pit over and over in her hand. It was more ornate than she'd realized. Not just a pit, but something created, fashioned. A perfect, five-pronged star, the points sharp enough to break her skin with hardly any pressure. The entirety of its surface was covered over in symbols, letters that she didn't recognize, swirls. When she shook it, she heard something small rolling around inside.

She'd fallen asleep on the wall – not her first time, but certainly her first in a long time. This time she woke with an ache in her neck that wouldn't recede. *Gone soft.*

Her missing hand had more to say than usual. Sometimes she thought if she could just… she didn't know. Touch something with its memory or will her hand to come back, if only for a moment, it would do so and then she could say she was sorry for cutting it off, and it would forgive her and go quiet. As if it was just waiting on the other side of a door, and all she had to do was figure out how to open it.

Of course, she knew that wasn't true. Her hand and arm were just bone and metal now, a gristly remainder for someone else to find someday, buried in the dirt and soil alongside the blackweave.

From here, she could see the city, waking. It no longer sang, but those moving within its walls gave the morning a different sound. The loudest of the hawkers coming from the market – calls of fresh-baked pastries and morning fruits – mingled with the squawks and grunts of animals, the upstart of machinery. Groups of children gathered in clusters, on their way to one of the central schools where they would spend half the day learning basic skills and the other half training for their eventual zaffre tests. Zaffre milled about, too, in their blue uniforms, their colors slightly more muted, their outfits less detailed than those of the greyes.

For as busy as the city was, there was no movement from the direction where she'd sent Isera, Burrin, and the others. Come back, she willed. Come back and prove Ganeth true. But she couldn't will them to appear any more than she could will her arm back into being.

Far below, on the outer edge of the wall, Khee was walking along the strip called the vallum, sniffing into the cracks and crevices with his weirdly angular head. He wasn't made for that kind of hunting, she didn't think, and a second later, as if to prove her right, he lifted his wide face and opened his mouth to scent the air. His eyes were closed, and as he pushed his two long tongues out into the world, seeking for something she didn't know, she thought that he might be, at that moment, a picture of joy. Hard to know, but something in her shifted, the way it did when she watched him tumble with Seild, and it made her happy, if only for that moment, seeing him there.

He moved along the vallum, still scenting the air. The area was busy, filled with workers, as it often was in the days after the poisoning. It was weird to think that something that she did, that she was involved with, had such an impact. On the lives of those who bet on her. The lives of the zaffre who hunted down what she saw. Said she saw. The lives of these people, who bustled and built and planned against the creatures they believed she'd seen.

These were weapons, but weren't like the cyphers and artifacts that Ganeth and the zaffre used. And as far as she knew, the builders weren't part of the zaffre at all. Just people who believed that if the dangers got through the zaffre, it was best to be prepared, however they could. So they drove wooden stakes and wrapped sharpened sticks with wire and built traps out of discarded metal and synth. It gave the look a mismatched, junked feel, and yet from up here, there was a beauty in it. Or at least a comfort, in the long line of tools designed with a single purpose – the safety of the city.

There was a second row, farther out, called the deadly vallum. Not built here, but brought here. The remainder of every danger that had once threatened Enthait. The buried detonations. The shields and zappers, the electric devices. Each danger required a different type of device, something that was specifically designed to damage them. Over the years, the wall had become a long, wide row of devices, some working, some not. Some visible, some buried.

She'd heard the stories, like the ones the actors told to kids in the market. How, long ago, the creatures had come from the south and tried to devour the city, then little more than a village. How they'd nearly succeeded, taloned and coiled and mawed. The villagers had fought, but the creatures had shorn the village down to its barest numbers, only those who could run or hide. And then the orness had used her weapon and... *kala-booma!* as Seild would have said.

Each time a poison eater told of a coming danger, the Aeon Priests around the city went to work. They made their best protection – armor, weapons, maybe a barrier or a shield – and then placed them all along the deadly vallum. Well, not the Aeon Priests themselves. They were too valuable. Someone else with less experience and knowledge than they. It was something that no one ever spoke about. A backup in case the greyes failed. In case the danger came all the way to the city.

As she watched, a young man, lithe and quick on his feet, danced across the devices, coming to a stop on top of a long, thin triangle, balancing his feet on either side. He settled an orb on the triangle's very top, then positioned it, pointing it the way that the zaffre had gone. The way that she had sent them.

He saw her watching and gave her a wave and a quick grin. The gesture nearly knocked him off balance, and Talia held her breath until he caught it again and righted himself.

She hoped he wouldn't recognize her, and for a moment, she thought she was safe. But then he looked at Khee, walking the vallum, and back at her. At least in his precarious position, it meant he wasn't likely to try to honor her. But he did anyway, taking a moment to plant his feet more cleanly on the sides of the pyramid and then covering his eyes with his thumbs.

Oh, child, she thought. Do not fall. I have enough death on my hands already.

And he didn't, miracle of miracles. He wobbled, she raised one thumb to her eye in a gesture that was more "please pay attention to what you're doing" than anything formal. He went back to settling the device in its proper position on the top of the pyramid. Her exhale was loud enough that Khee glanced her way, and then left the path and began to walk back toward the wall where she sat.

In some way she did not understand, the vallum was protected. To walk from the city to the Tawn, you stayed on the path. But to walk from the Tawn to the city was another thing entirely. The path didn't appear. Not ever, as far as she could tell. You had to pick your way through the scattered debris, the treacherous piles of detonations and devices. She'd done it a few times and thought she'd made it because she was human, and could understand how human minds worked. But Khee seemed to have no problem either. What good, then, the vallum, if any beast could figure out how to walk across it?

But Khee was not any beast, was he?

No longer concerned that Khee wouldn't find his path, she returned her attention to the pit in her hand. She'd seen that pattern somewhere else, the loops and letters. She closed her eyes, sifted through the tumbling images in her brain, rejecting each one as it passed by without connecting.

Isera.

The zaffre.

The poison symbols.

The Eternal Market.

Books & Blades.

And then it came to her: the skars. All of the skars bore a pattern carved out of their tall shapes. She'd thought they were random, a sign of destruction or age, of wearing away. But now she wasn't so sure. Her fingers trembling, she turned the star over and over in her hands. Was it a key? A map? One of Ganeth's devices?

She stood just as Khee reached her. She held the star up to each of the skars, trying to match the symbols on the star with the ones on their sides. Nothing that she could see. They were similar, but nothing was a perfect match.

Khee was watching her curiously. "Thoughts?" she asked.

see

he said.

Oh, but he was maddening.

"Someday I hope you learn to talk in complete sentences," she said.

He stamped a foot on the wall, so clearly frustrated with her that she had to laugh. She lowered the star toward him. "Well, you figure it out then."

He snorted at her.

The star sang. It *sang*. Like the city sang. Wind through metal. An instrument. Of course. How had she not seen that?

"Do it again, Khee."

He did, and it did. A single, small note. But it was the city's note, its power undiminished by its size. Rain and blade.

But how did that help her find the orness? She lifted

the star to her own mouth, blew with more precision and length than she might have expected from Khee.

A moment later, she heard a soft low whistle in return. She stood there for a moment with the star in her hand, uncertain whether she'd actually just heard that sound.

She lifted the star to her mouth and tried again. Again, a few seconds later, a whistle back. Somewhere off to the northeast.

"Well done, Khee."

She didn't need words for the glow of satisfaction that he sent, a warmth that thrummed through her chest.

"Let's go." She hopped off the wall and began to follow a halting, discordant pattern through the city: stop, blow into the star, listen for the song. She was grateful that almost no one paid her any mind as she passed them; it was early enough in the day that people were about their own business. It was easier than she would have expected to follow the sound, as though the city was somehow helping her, delivering the song to her ears in a way that guided her.

In so doing, she arrived at a skar. She didn't know the name of this one – it was perhaps one of the most banal of them all. Fairly small, the top a bit broken off, its pattern less intricate than the rest. She should have studied up more on the patterns and the names. Too late now.

Keeping her distance, she walked around the square bottom of the skar, blowing into the star every so often, seeing if it would respond in a new way. When it was clear that was as far as the star was going to get her, she pulled her hood up and moved closer to the building.

Like so many skars, this one was a long curved blade made of some kind of metal set atop a square stone structure. The base alone was three times as wide as she was tall. She'd always assumed that the stone structures were solid – shoring up the tall blades. But now she wondered if that assumption had been correct.

No one seemed to be near. In fact, the entire area was weirdly deserted. There were buildings clustered around, but most of them looked long unused and cared for. They stood – nothing was broken or defaced, but they had the steady sad sag of buildings that no one cared for.

It was growing into late morning, the day already heated and windless, the sun nearly to full on its rise. Khee was settled into a sunless spot, stretched out and panting, eyes closed against the bright. She almost wished she could do the same.

Leaning in, she traced the walls. They were black stone, with a grey material packed between them. There didn't seem to be any doors or divides that she could see. No places for recessed buttons or keys. On the final wall, she noticed a pattern on the ground. Scuffs, maybe from footprints or something being dragged. She followed it to the wall, testing all of the elements with her fingers. Nothing.

She brought the star up against the stone. Still nothing. She was out of ideas.

Leaning in, she said, "Mihil." Please.

As her words moved through the star, the material, solid just moments before under her fingertips, became insubstantial. Her hand moved through it, almost easier than through air. She had to rock back on her heels to keep her balance, to keep herself from falling forward.

Steeling herself, she stuck her hand through again. The air on the other side was cold, and a little damp.

"I think I figured it out, Khee. I'll be right back."

He flopped his long tail, once, twice, but gave no other notice that he heard.

"Lazy beast."

stayed

came his smug response.

On the other hand, it was probably a good thing he wasn't human, with a voice box and the capacity for more than one word at a time. She didn't think she'd find him so amusing all the time.

She turned back toward the place where the wall had softened. She held her breath as she stepped through. She didn't know why. A sudden fear overwhelmed her that the material wasn't air or that it wouldn't allow her to breathe. And then she was through, into the dark, and there was nothing beneath her feet. She was falling, the sound of the star whistling as the air rushed by them both. She closed her eyes and tucked her body in on itself, bracing for the fall.

II. iisrad

SHADES

"Finally."

At the sound of the orness' voice, Talia opened her eyes. She was standing on a metal platform. She wasn't sure when she had stopped moving or how she had ended up here. All around her was green and green and green. Trees and flowers and herbs. The scent was one of clean dirt and lush growth, flowers and fruit. Walls rose up on either side of her, covered with pale green vines that twined up long poles and the sides of ladders.

She was under the Green Road.

She didn't say anything; she didn't trust her mouth to open. Her stomach was convinced she was still falling or going to fall or going to die. All, maybe.

Before her stood the orness, wrapped in a green outfit that hugged her perfectly. Much like the sky wrap she'd worn the night before, this too echoed the landscape, a dappled fabric, various shades of green. Unlike the other outfits Talia had seen her in, this showed the orness as she truly was. Lean and muscular, with a sense of ferocity in the width of her shoulders. She could see, then, Burrin in her. Or her in him.

Thick metal bracelets ran up her dark arms, from her wrists to her shoulders. Her fingers were covered in similar metals. Her skin was woven round and round with pale tattoos, shapes that echoed those of the pit, of the skars.

She wore no hood this time. Her ebony hair, the same color as her skin, was tightly braided strands that wound and wound around her head, reminding Talia of the nests she'd seen in the forest around the blackweave. The birdlike sensibility was furthered by the actual feathers wound in her hair. Her hair was feathers, or covered in feathers. No, wings. Her head was covered over in black wings, each stretched out as if to capture the very moment of leaving the ground.

Although nothing physical covered it, Talia still couldn't make out the orness' face. It was muddled and muted, pushed her gaze to the edges of it as if some unseen force was physically turning her head.

A boy, not much older than Seild, approached along the path that led off into the green, putting both fists to his eyes as he stopped. He was dressed in the greens of the forest. "The taf is ready, Orness." Without waiting for a response, he headed back the way he had come, and disappeared.

Talia, still mute, shook her head. She suddenly felt like Seild, manners forgotten. Whatever she thought about the orness, she needed to play the part of the poison eater. Needed the orness on her side. At least for now. Lifting her thumb to one eye, she began, "Moon meld you–"

"Mihil, no. None of that." The orness waved her hand. Gods, she sounded just like Talia, talking to Seild before the poisoning. "That's for *them*."

The way she said *them*, Talia understood she was talking about the citizens of Enthait.

"But we know better, don't we?" the orness said.

Talia didn't know what she knew, and so she didn't answer. She'd come here with no real plan, no weapon, no leverage. Only the faintest sense of what she wanted.

She found she was clutching the star so hard the points were digging into her flesh. She took a deep breath, forced herself to relax her fingers. She dropped the star into a pocket, cleared her throat.

"I would know your face, orness." Talia hadn't meant it to sound like a threat, and yet it hung in the air that way. The orness' posture tightened, every muscle seeming to pull in as she decided on her response. Her shoulders shook themselves out beneath her outfit, and she made a sound. It was, it took Talia a moment to realize, laughter. Rusted and resistant as an unused door, but laughter still.

"And I would know why you don't carry a weapon," the orness said. It was her opportunity to return the threat, and yet there wasn't one. Or it was so soft as to be invisible. A well-baited snare. Talia took it, sure of her ability to sidestep.

Who says I don't? was her first answer, and why don't you? was her second, but she swallowed them both back. If she wanted something out of this, she would have to give.

So, why not indeed?

"I forget," she said, momentarily surprised at her own honesty. "And I have Khee."

She often tried to forget that he, too, was a weapon. That he was built, created, twisted to be nothing but a weapon. One that had been sent to kill her. And yet had not. What did a weapon become when it chose to help rather than hurt?

"Ah," the orness said. "Your creature. My turn then."

The orness lifted a hand and did something to the shining loops that ran up her ear. A moment later, her face shimmered and rearranged itself. One red-hued eye came into focus, then swam away. The top of a mouth, painted the color of coal, disappeared and then returned. A thin dark snake slithered across the top of her nose, disappeared behind her ear.

Watching her face appear was like watching birds gather in preparation for flight. As soon as one feature settled in, another was off. It made Talia's eyes hurt, trying to see everything in one glance, to gather all of her features up in her gaze and force them together.

She wants you to get tired and give up. Focus.

She focused on one of the orness' eyes. Smaller than that, the black pupil in the middle, the way that a sliver of light caught itself in the shadow. That and that alone. She could feel the other pieces of the orness' face starting to click into place at the edges of her vision, their settling in nearly audible. She didn't allow herself to look at them. Forced her gaze to stare at nothing but that curved sliver of a moon. The moon's sliver widened until it seemed about to suck her into its light.

She was looking at the orness' face for a few moments before she even realized it. The woman in front of her was younger than she'd expected. How was she old enough to have Burrin as her son?

From the center of that unlined face, red irises shone with silvered pupils, sharp against the white of her eyes. A braided cord ran across the bridge of her nose, through her earrings, and trailed up into the hidden nest of her hair. Tiny charms hung from it, resting against her cheekbones. The whole thing bore Ganeth's aesthetic, and she wondered, not for the first time, how many layers there truly were to the man she thought of as something close to a friend.

The orness seemed to know that something had happened, that Talia could see her clearly for the first time, for she smiled. It was the kind of smile that made you feel so welcome you forgot the dangers all around. Serpent smile.

"Come," the orness – Talia didn't know what else to call her – beckoned and then stepped down a long winding path built of mossy rocks. "I'm far too ill and old to be standing here."

Talia felt like she'd been kicked in the pit of her stomach. Ill? Old? The woman who'd been standing in front of her, the one who was now leading the way quickly along a slippery, curving path, appeared in every way to be the exact opposite of those things. She wondered for a moment if she'd misheard. If those words had another meaning here, as so many did.

"Come," the orness said again, already far ahead. It was quickly becoming harder to see her, other than the shock of dark hair. Her outfit flowed and blended in among the plants with surprising ease.

Talia followed her down the path. Now that her body had stopped its downward fall, she could see and hear. She tried to take in the whole thing as she followed the orness, but there was too much. Far off, the trickle of water. More than a trickle, now that she listened to it. Beneath her feet, the mossy rocks were damp, as were the leaves she brushed against as she passed. Here and there, she spotted someone working, tending the plants or picking fruit. It wasn't as hot as she'd expected. In fact, at times it was oddly cool, despite the lack of breeze.

They made their way through what seemed like a maze of paths, and perhaps it was. Talia tried to keep it straight, to pay attention, but mostly she couldn't stop looking at the back of the orness.

"Here," the orness said finally, with a gesture.

It was a garden inside the garden. The walls were woven of trees, still living, braided together and bent inward to form a kind of egg-shaped room. Vines braided loosely across the top created the sense of a roof without blocking the light. At the door stood two tall zaffre. Bodyguards? Although she couldn't see the need for them down here. Unless there was another way in that she hadn't found yet. Which was entirely possible. Leave it to the orness to make her eat a fruit, blow in a pit, and find a secret nonexistent door while there was probably another real door in the city, one that people just walked in and out of.

The men stepped aside as they approached, touching their thumbs to their eyes.

Inside was a table, already set for taf. Two empty glasses and a small pot shaped like a leaf. Spoons, a knife sheathed in the tabletop, what looked like a bowl of honey that was glassine and amber, even a plate of sweet rolls with tiny yellow seeds on top. Beneath the flowers and the honey, Talia caught the scent of saltpetals, even though she didn't see them.

"Mihil," the orness gestured.

Talia sat. It was much hotter in here. Wetter too. She

couldn't get used to the sensation of the wet heat on her skin. It was damp enough that she felt like she was breathing in water. She brushed at her arms, even though she could see there was no visible water on her skin.

"It does take some getting used to," the orness said. Who didn't look like she was having any trouble getting used to it at all. "Supposedly, it is good for my health." Her voice showed just how very little stock she put in whoever had passed that information along.

The orness made a gesture with her hand, so small that Talia was surprised to see one of the men came forth and poured the tea into the glasses. They must just stand and watch her every move, every twitch. Talia didn't know how she could stand it, to be scrutinized so, at every moment. If she became the orness, she was glad that her stint would be short enough that she wouldn't have to do that part. Get the aria, kill the vordcha. So simple, and yet so hard.

She still didn't have a clue what she was going to say to the orness.

The orness picked up her full drink with both hands and nodded. Talia used a single hand, cupped it against the crook of her other elbow. She wondered if she would ever get used to this, the way the liquid went from hot to cold against her skin. She'd only taken the taf a few times, but by the time the recitation of the orison was completed and she could put the glass down, her palm often felt like ice, frozen to the glass. Thankfully, the orness' prayer was efficient, and plain to the point of banality. She blessed the city, asked for her citizens to be in good health, and slipped through the rest so fast that Talia had to scramble to echo her "Mihil, awos" at the end of it.

There was a moment of silence as they both took their first sip of the taf.

Now, Talia. Tell her the truth now. Tell her that you're not the true poison eater. Ask for her help. She felt the conversation slipping from her grasp. Or perhaps it had never been hers in the first place.

Talia opened her mouth to speak.

"Now…" The orness took a sip of her tea, eyeing Talia over the drink. "Tell me how long you've known that you were not the poison eater."

In the silence, bees hummed nearer, enticed by the table laden with sweets. One, striped gold and blue, fat and fuzzy, landed on the edge of the taf pot, whipping its wings. A brown and silver spider dropped down on an invisible thread, plucked the bee tight against its abdomen, and lifted itself back into the air.

Talia was too stunned to lie. So she did the very thing she'd planned to do, even if she hadn't planned to do it quite this way. She told the truth.

"Since the very first one." The words had no taste on her tongue, and she was surprised at the ease of them.

The orness sipped her tea. She barely moved, and yet gave every indication that she had just leaned in. "How?"

"Because I saw nothing." Talia shook her head. Put the glass carefully on the table. It was so cold the water had beaded up all along it, making it slippery to the touch. "Nothing about Enthait anyway. Just my own memories."

"And yet you survived."

"Yet," Talia said. She hadn't known just what she would find here, with the orness. An adversary, likely. A full-out enemy perhaps. Not a friend. And yet, she was falling somewhere in between. Like someone who thought to be all of those things, but didn't quite know what any of them meant.

"And you continue to survive."

It was not a question, but it was spoken like one. A single word rippling beneath it. *Why?*

Talia found herself answering as if it had been asked out loud. "I don't know."

Liar.

Not Khee's voice in her chest, from so far away. But one she knew just the same. The vordcha's mech had changed her – something residual, something lasting. Even after she'd removed it all from her body, her body knew what it had carried. Had adapted, altered, reshaped itself into something more, or less, than human.

The orness raised her cup, but didn't drink from it. "Are you so sure?"

For this, Talia had no answer she wanted to give. It seemed the longer they sat there, the more the orness' face was changing. Her eyes were not as crimson as Talia had first thought. More reddish-brown, the color of sun-burnished wood. Her skin was more lined than it had seemed at first glance, echoes of lives etched at the sides of her mouth, the corners of her eyes, the center of her brow. A trick of the light. But a dazzling one.

"Do you know how this all works?" the orness asked. She waved a single hand around her, enveloping the garden, the table, the city above, even Talia. One of the zaffre stepped forward at the gesture, and she stopped him with a stay of her finger. He settled back to his post near the doorway, unmoving.

"Yes," Talia said, even though she wasn't sure what

this the orness meant.

"You're a bad liar." Talia felt her brow lift involuntarily at that. Just *how much* did the orness know, or suspect? "I am surprised that Greyes Isera has not seen through you. Nor her daughter. They must be truly enamored of you."

Her cheeks, already warm with the heat, flared and pulsed.

"Don't look so surprised," the orness said. "I know everything that happens in Enthait's walls. It's my job."

Not everything, Talia thought. But then she wasn't so sure.

"Why am I here?"

"Because you do not yet understand." Everything the orness said seemed to have a thread of something else carefully woven beneath, something she wasn't saying. Talia kept trying to pluck those threads out, but it was like catching spider strands against the wind.

"Here." The orness put her finger out to lean it against the pot. Another bee had landed on the rim, fanning its wings. Now it stepped from the pot to her skin, where it stopped on the tip of her finger to clean its feet. "Everything has a role to play. This bee, even.

"You, it seems, were planning to leave Enthait, planning to pass *your* role to someone else." She wagged her finger. The bee hissed, a low buzzing whine, but didn't dislodge.

The orness waved the bee off her finger with a sharp snap of her hand. It fell for a brief second before its wings whirred, and then it lazily caught itself and lifted off into the air. Then, abruptly, its wings stopped and it began to fall.

"It stung me," she said simply. "As it was supposed to. And then it died. Also as it was supposed to.

"Now," the orness continued, as she flicked the small dead body off the table. She wiped her hands on one of the folded cloths beside the pitcher. "Tell me: what do you know of your role?"

"I know you chose me to be the poison eater over your own son. And that you didn't teach me anything." She didn't know why she suddenly felt the need to lash out. Perhaps because the orness had implied she was a bee, and if a bee's job was to sting, then she would do so.

"The Eye didn't expect you to live," the orness said matter-of-factly. "Thus, I didn't either. What else do you know?"

"I know that the Eye makes poisons. Which are supposed to connect me... connect the poison eater... to the datasphere, some machine or something in the sky, which can see the future or danger or something." She was still fuzzy on that part. She assumed true poison eaters had a better sense of how it worked. If the machine actually talked to them.

"And," Talia took a deep breath, dove in with all she had. "I know you have a weapon. Something dangerous. Something only you can use."

"The aria," the orness said. "You can say its name."

"I want that device. The aria," Talia said. "I need it."

The orness' laugh was as bitter as a nyryn petal. It made Talia's skin itch. "Then you had better get on with being the orness, hadn't you?"

The orness twisted her lips to the side, saying nothing. She was laughing at her. Toying with her like one of her guards, one of her bees.

"I want to ask a different question," Talia said. She felt like she'd been taking lessons from Isera in *onas*. At least in the "hides nothing" part. She wasn't anywhere even close to seeing all. "How did you know? That I knew I was false?"

The orness glanced up at the edge of the garden. For the first time, Talia noticed the air was swarming with the mirrored orbs. There were no lights here, and the things seemed lost, unmoored. One wafted through the air between the two of them, landing briefly on the table before it lifted back up, rising toward the makeshift ceiling.

Something in the orness' demeanor changed. She leaned back, and Talia could see that even her arms seemed older, more worn. Veins rivered up the backs of her hands. The ripples in her knuckles were deeper. More illusions. More deception. Was it so that Talia would feel sorry for her, give her the upper hand somehow? Not likely. She didn't understand the orness' game – not yet – but she would. And until then, there was no softness.

The orness sucked air in through her teeth. It was the sound of wind over old bone. It was the sound of disappointment. "That is the wrong question," she said. "But the answer is that I always know. I knew from the moment you were chosen."

Talia let that slide over her, through her. The orness had known from the beginning, and had let her keep putting herself in danger, putting the city in danger. To what end? And at what cost?

"I asked how you knew," she said.

"Oh," the orness said. Talia expected her to laugh, and when she didn't this time, it was somehow worse than when she did. "You *don't* know how it works. Not at all. I knew because there is no such thing as the true poison eater. There never was, never will be. The poison eater is a lie. A lie told by the city to itself, carried by the voices all around it, buoyed by belief."

Every time Talia thought she had all of this figured out, and every time, it slipped through her fingers. Like water. No, thinner. Like poison dreams. She took another sip of the tea so she didn't have to reply, and it caught in her throat, choking her.

If there was no true poison eater, then there was no true orness. And that meant there was no device. No aria. Everything she had worked for, had nearly died for, did not exist.

Wait. Be silent. Be still. It was the mantra of her sisters, hiding in the shadows when the vordcha had slumped down into the blackweave and begun to wail for them.

If she could just keep herself steady, maybe the orness would tell her everything she needed to know. Of course, there was a chance that she was telling her all of this only because she was planning to kill her. Talia hadn't ruled it out. She thought of her blue-black blade back in the room, regretted her choices.

"Usually, the chosen don't figure it out," the orness said. "Or, rather, by the time they're beginning to figure it out, they're already dead. And we're on to the next one. Belief. It keeps the system healthy. Like your heart. You believe it keeps pumping, and so it pumps." She squeezed her fist. "Pumping."

Talia was no chiurgeon, but she didn't think that was how it worked.

"Why did you choose me? I'm not from here. I have no belief."

The orness looked pained at that. The first real emotion Talia had seen from her, and it was no more than the push of her lips tight. Half a heartbeat. So easily missed. But it gave her hope.

"What I can't figure out is how you're surviving the poisons," the orness went on, as if Talia had not asked. "Each time, I think, 'this is the one where you go down,' and yet. Here you are."

"Here I am," Talia said, because the orness had paused long enough that she had to say something.

"So tell me your secret," the orness said. "I know how *I* survived, and the one before me. Are you just going on rote instinct and faith? Is Ganeth helping you? Plays both sides, that one." She touched the charm devices that lined her face, smirking beneath them. "But I'm guessing you know that already by now. How we love our Aeon Priest."

Talia forced her trembling hand around her glass, waiting until it stilled before she attempted to pick the drink off the table. She sipped the tea, letting its frost flow over her tongue, a clean palate for the words she needed to speak.

Because she had no answer to the questions the orness had left lying on the table between them twice now, she asked instead.

"If it's false, why not fake the poison? Make it so that people don't have to die."

"Because no one can carry that all the way to the tenth poison. How long can you carry that secret? That what you do is false? Everything about it is a lie?"

Oh, you have no idea, Talia thought. And right there, the power shifted. Just a bit.

"How long can you keep sending the ones you care about out into danger for no reason?" the orness asked, and the power shifted back like fickle wind. She waved away another bee. "Do you think you won't go up there right now and spread that news if I don't stop you?"

The orness did mean to try to kill her, then. There was a sudden, aching relief in that. They would fight, and Talia would be free. One way or another.

"You did," Talia said. "You carried it."

"Yes," the orness mused. "Yes, I did."

"So you just…" Talia made sure she had the words she wanted. "Just want me to keep pretending, keep taking the poison, keep sending out the greyes…" Your son. Your only son. "Until I die? Why would I do that? I don't care about your city."

"Isn't that what you've been doing?" A smug sip, lips tight to the glass, watching her.

"There is no aria." It wasn't a question, but resignation. All she'd worked for, lost. She would go away, leave or take Khee as he chose, find a new way to fulfill her promise to Maeryl.

"There are still those you care for who live within these walls."

Isera. Oh, such a stinging hatred for this woman. It rose in her and made her nose prickle on the edges, her eyes water. *Wait. Be silent. Be still.*

She waited. She was silent. She was still.

"There have only been a few times when the Eye has chosen one so young," the orness said at last. She spoke so softly it was hard for Talia to parse whether she was saying *I* or *the Eye*.

"So vulnerable. They never make it through the first poisoning. Such a shame."

Talia thought of Khee saying *Softness*, and her chest filled with heat. Another failure to see what was coming. Not the poison eater's this time. But her own.

"I'll take her away." Even as she said it, knowing how it sounded. Futile. Grasping. She was only just now beginning to understand the power the orness held. And, more importantly, all the ways in which she would choose to use that power.

"We all have a role," the orness said. "It is up to each of us to decide whether to fulfill that role. Or whether to allow that role to be given to someone else."

Silence. Not even the bees. Above them, the city went on and on. She wondered if it was singing.

"How did *you* survive the poisons?" Talia tried to add a bit of coy, a bit of reverence. Not too much. The orness was smart – she could see that part of her in Burrin as well. A change too sudden, and she would laugh that bitter laugh and Talia would learn nothing.

The orness glanced at the globules floating nearby – there were two large ones and a small one, hanging in the air. She beckoned to her guards. Both came toward the table, quick strides.

"Could you bring us some more sweet breads?" she said, although neither of them had touched the rolls. As the guards left, their movement caught the globules, swirling them away through the air. Quickly, the orness leaned in. For one half second, her entire visage changed. She was everything she'd said she was. Old. Ill. Her eyes were half-blind with white, the seams in her face deep and heavy. Her cheeks gaunt. Her hair had thinned, gone an off yellow.

"I didn't," she said simply. Honestly. Even her voice was different. Exhausted. "Don't eat the tenth one."

And then she leaned back and a moment later, she was as she'd been. Red-eyed. Vibrant. Her hair raven and swirling around her head.

She was trying to tell Talia something, but it was in some deep code that she couldn't read.

Talia was still trying to figure it out when the guards returned. As they placed the basket of unnecessary breads on the table, the orness pulled a long knife out of the slit in the table where it had been sheathed. She opened one of the sweet rolls with just the metal tip, spreading the bread on a small silver plate. She didn't eat it. Merely folded it back over on itself with tight fingers, as if trying to undo the break.

"I will do as you ask, but when the poison takes me, you will not choose her." She needed to have one thing to keep hold of.

The orness nodded, almost imperceptible.

"Not good enough," Talia said. "Promise it."

"I am the orness."

Talia pushed her chair back, scraping it across the ground, wishing it made more noise than the soft whoosh of dirt. "No, you're not. Not anymore. Not to me. Promise it on this city you profess to love so dearly."

"The moon shall meld me," the woman before her said as she steepled her fingers together. "And I shall shine."

A few of the silver orbs returned, sliding through the air with directness. The old woman ticked her head to the side, looking so much like a predator listening to prey that Talia had to quell her startled response. After a moment, she nodded, and turned those burnished eyes up to meet Talia's own.

"The greyes have returned."

The greyes came home – Isera came home – and Talia missed it. She was being escorted out of the heat and green by the same boy who'd announced the taf. He was light on his feet through the maze. She was ashamed to admit she had a hard time not gasping for breath as she strode after him.

"How do people get in and out? The workers? The orness?" she asked, but he was already far ahead of her and every word gave her a little less air. So she quieted and tried to meet his stride and soon he was opening a door for her in the wall that she hadn't even seen and she was stepping out into the tunnels.

She stood, silent and lost in the blackness, yelling all the swear words she'd ever learned until she was pretty sure she'd used up her quota of angry words for the rest of her whole life. Then she breathed in the darkness until she felt like she could walk again.

At first, she tried to find her way through the tunnels by logic. Guessing she had entered somewhere along the western curve of the Green Road and going left each time to see if it would bring her to somewhere near the gate where the greyes would enter.

But then she missed a turn and gave up, and just started walking. Instinct would lead her out somewhere. It was the best she could hope for. She'd never, not once, run into someone else in the tunnels, so finding a guide out was hopeless.

She was filled to overflowing with all that the orness

had laid on her. The orness' words were buzzing around in her brain like bees, and she needed to settle some of them down so she could think. She should have asked so many things. Usually she was decent with people, but for whatever reason, the orness set her on edge and she hadn't asked anything more.

Some of what the orness said had seemed true. To the bone, to the core. And other parts? Less so. But she couldn't yet tell the difference. It couldn't all be true, because that made no sense. What she did know was mostly what she didn't know.

Either way, she couldn't leave Enthait now.

You could. The voice sounded, oddly, like Maeryl's. For a moment, it was a relief to be given that permission. To hear someone else – even if that someone was dead – say that she was not bound here. That she had a choice. Not like the orness had implied, but a real and true choice.

The problem was that both of her choices involved *stay*.

It took her a long time to find her way out of the tunnels. By the time she emerged, it was so far into the night that even the noise of the Eternal Market was dimmed. The moon too, waning. The sweat of the green had coated her skin in saltsea, and the night air froze it into thin rivulets. Somewhere, an entire day had slipped by without her. How long since she'd slept? Days. Two? Three? She didn't even recognize what part of the city she was in, whether from lack of knowing or from exhaustion, she couldn't say.

Every bone in her body pointed her toward Isera's, but she could not. The orness' words swam through her body like a pill filled with poison. She dared not be in Isera's presence, dared not look at her in those mismatched eyes. If she was going to keep this secret, she had to keep it herself. At least for a little while. At least until she could wrap it up inside a casing that Isera would not see through. Another lie to stack on top of all the lies.

Talia knew that it would come, when Isera finally saw through her, into her. She also knew that part of the reason she hadn't so far was because of whatever it was she felt for Talia. Since that first day, she'd never used the mechanics in her grey eye to study Talia's face when she talked. It was only a matter of time – *It's my job to see true.* But now, there was so much more at stake. She couldn't risk it.

With no small amount of shame, she hailed a cart pulled by a tall, fidgeting aneen, gave an address as close to the clave as she could without giving herself away, and was in such sound sleep by the time they arrived that the driver had to wake her with a near-vicious shake. She had no idea how long he'd been doing so, but it was clear from his face that he'd begun to think she might be dead.

"Sehwa," she mumbled as she dropped the last of her shins into his outstretched hand.

Her room was as she'd left it. Cloak on its hook. Hexed armband. Blue-black blade. Seven silver circles.

But no Khee.

She was alone. And so she slept and did not dream of the orness coming to take away her sight.

In the morning, the city was throwing a party. It often did, when the greyes came home.

She and Khee skirted as much of it as they could. He'd been waiting outside the door that morning and she didn't want to admit to either of them how happy she'd been to see him. Now, as they walked, he leaned into her through the crowded parts. It was a comfort that she welcomed.

Everywhere vendors were plying those who walked by with free samples, fresh fruit, baked goods, hunks of meat long cooked over herbed flames. She took the ones for Khee, but couldn't bring herself to eat. The city itself did not sing today, but the people did. The sounds of live music flowed through the streets, some of it beautiful and haunting, other bits of it wild and full of energy. It made for a jangled discordance that seemed right somehow. It matched the jaggedness of her thoughts. Even her outfit felt confused – she wore the hexed armband, but not the arm. The poison eater cloak, but turned inside out. Her blue-black blade was tucked into a pocket.

"Khee, did you see Isera yesterday?" It helped to say her name out loud. She was so afraid that Isera would take one look at her and would know everything. But it was a risk she was going to have to take.

see.

The word conveyed a sense of comfort and softness, whether he meant it to or not.

"We'll go see her," she said. "But I have to do one quick thing first."

Softness?

She hesitated to answer, because she knew it wasn't going to be something Khee wanted to hear. But Khee was perhaps the only living creature she'd never lied to, and she wouldn't start now. Not over this.

"Omuf-Rhi," she said.

Khee yawned, showing his teeth. A little girl passed by, half-eaten meat dangling off a stick, and she squealed when she saw his mouth. Likely she thought the beast coming toward her meant to have her food for himself, but Talia knew Khee well enough to know that he was just expressing his discomfort.

"We'll make it quick," she promised.

Omuf-Rhi's store Books & Blades was aptly named. Tucked inside a clay brick building with an open roof, the very center held a round fenced ring for teaching fighting lessons. Everywhere else was books, scrolls, maps, sheaves, anything that could be written on. Piles, shelves, piles that eventually formed shelves. There was order, but it was nearly incomprehensible to anyone but Omuf-Rhi, and possibly even to him.

A week or so after Rakdel had pulled the blue-black blade from her leg, Talia had made her way carefully – her thigh not-so-gently reminding her of its condition with every step – to Books & Blades to see about Omuf-Rhi's offer of a job. "Take a left at the Moon Skar and keep on going almost to the wall. You can't miss me."

She had carried a fist filled with the blue-black blade but empty of expectations. A not-small part of her hoped that the haired creature called Omuf-Rhi had forgotten her. That she could go back to her singular goal of preparing to run.

As soon as she walked in, she discovered that he was not someone who easily forgot things.

"Hello, future champion of the Keep. Hello, future poison eater!"

He was the first one to give her the moniker *poison eater*, long before it became true.

no.

Khee had stopped at that, sat down on his haunches, and wouldn't go any farther. It was clear from the start that Omuf-Rhi liked Khee more than Khee liked him. And no amount of jerky or even ground meat was going to remedy that.

"I know it's nothing personal," Omuf-Rhi said each time Khee took whatever was offered and then promptly snubbed him. "Although I'm the one who should be mad, being the one with a new set of teeth marks in my arm and all."

"Why don't you ever say you're sorry to him?" she'd asked Khee once. He'd blinked at her without responding. Hours later, a small word had sidled up to her sideways, scared and tentative.

shame.

She'd put her hand softly on Khee's head and let him keep taking the treats that Omuf-Rhi offered without bringing it up again.

What she and Khee created in the silences, Omuf-Rhi filled in with words. He talked. A lot. It didn't take long before she discovered far more about him than she ever wanted to know. He loved Rakdel. He thought she loved him back, but she never said it. He was something called a lattimor. And the purple wing-shaped patch across his back was actually where his brain lived. That last one wasn't quite right, but despite him describing it to her multiple times in myriad different ways, she was still a little muddy on how it worked.

Talia didn't mind listening – everything he said was interesting enough, but her favorite times were when he left her to read while he taught fighting lessons in the circle. Mostly, it seemed to be young people whose parents were willing to pay well to mold their children in hopes for the zaffre. Which was a good thing, because the entire time she'd been there, she hadn't seen him sell more than a dozen books.

She, on the other hand, read as many as she could fit in, especially in those early days. She wasn't particular, and she read sporadically, picking up and putting down as her interest waxed and waned. She'd learned to read from her sisters, many of whom had come to the vordcha older than her, and who had more time in the world before the blackweave and the martyrdom. She wasn't quick, but her speed had improved each day.

By then, she had rented a room nearby – at Isera's suggestion. The room was tiny, on the top floor of a three-story building. Hot, and full of insects that crawled and buzzed, and seemed to come in through windows and out of the very walls.

good

Khee had said when she'd showed it to him, and truly it was. Way better than the blackweave, way better than the sticky, tarry webs crisscrossed too loose, too high up, so that she always felt like she would fall through it to the ground. Which wasn't ground, but yet another weave, another wall to keep them in. Better even than the wall-hole they'd been tucked into not so long ago.

"Temporary," she'd said. The word held less conviction than it would have had a week before, and she didn't yet know how she felt about that.

So many moons ago. Long enough that when she walked into the shop this morning, and Omuf-Rhi said, "Hello, poison eater!" it wasn't a joke between them anymore. It was truth and serious. She was grateful that he didn't lift his thumbs from the thin blade he was sharpening across his knees.

There was no one in the place, which wasn't unusual

for this time of day. Or, really, ever.

"Where's your beast?" Omuf-Rhi asked.

Talia glanced over her shoulder. Khee had been next to her the whole way, and now he wasn't. A second glance showed him just outside, resting on his haunches, watching through the open door.

"How's Rakdel?" she asked.

He seemed surprised at her question. To set him at ease, she lifted one shoulder in a soft shrug. "I heard they ran into something in the Tawn."

"She's fine," he said. "She's with Isera." Pointed.

"I didn't come to work today," she said. "I need information." If she was going to lie to Isera – and she was, she realized as she stood there – then she needed some truths to do it with. If there was any place to find those truths, it was here.

"Help yourself," he said.

She started toward the section where history lived, then stopped and turned.

"I've been thinking," she said.

He waited.

"I don't have a weapon." Her words were stilted. She was bad at asking.

He didn't really have eyebrows, but he lifted one of the furrowed ridges above his eyes.

"I should," she said. "I think."

He must have sensed her mood, for on any other day, he would have given her far more information about weapons than she needed or wanted. How they were made, what was best for what, why the materials mattered. Today, he said, of the blade across his lap, "I have this one."

It was red-handled, the blade of burnished turquoise. "I

would borrow it," she said. "If I may."

"You can keep it," he said. "If you're willing to work for a bit today while you gather your information. Rakdel's been tending to the…" He faltered, paused, as if he wasn't sure what he'd been going to say. She got the sense he was being careful, an odd moment for someone who usually seemed to talk first, regret after. He left the thought and finished with, "I'd like to take her some food."

She nodded assent, and he set the blade on the top of the wall that surrounded the training ring.

How long she stood before the weapon without touching it, she didn't know. Long enough that the sun coming through the building's roof shifted her shadow in front of her.

Finally she put her hand on the red hilt, wrapped her fingers around it. It was warm from the sun, and smelled of sharpening oil and the stuffing of the practice targets.

Why do you never carry a weapon?

She thought she'd answered the orness true. But as her palm met the red leather, as she lifted it and tested the heft of the weapon in her hand and saw how easy it would be to let it go and watch it fall, she knew. *Oh, Maeryl. Oh, sisters. I am sorry.*

She spent a bit of time reacquainting herself with a blade. She tried her hexed hand – her former weapon hand – but it didn't grasp the hilt the way she'd hoped. It took her a while to get comfortable with wielding a weapon in her left hand. But she worked at the training targets until she was sweating and stuck with dust. By the end, she could slip the blade in and out of the sheath she'd borrowed from Omuf-Rhi's training stock with accuracy and something akin to speed. Like with stealing – not that she did that anymore – she wasn't sure she'd ever be great at it, but she at least felt like she could handle herself.

When she was done, she splashed her face and took a long drink from the water reserve next to the ring. She couldn't put it off any longer. Anymore and she would have been avoiding what she'd come to do.

Omuf-Rhi kept saying he had a perfect system for organizing the books, but if it was true, she'd never deciphered it, beyond a general sense of theme. She'd looked for the tome of history from which she'd memorized the line about the device, but couldn't find it. Either it had been accidentally relegated to some unknown area of the store or someone had purchased it.

A thin, black book called *The Ten Poisons* caught her eye. It seemed to be a medical notebook of sorts, full of details about poisons, far more than ten. Handwritten notations in various colors of ink filled the edges of the pages. At the very back, a chapter called *Eating Poison.*

She read it with a roughness in her gut. It was, she thought, similar if not identical to what she'd read before. She found the line she'd memorized, but also much of it that she had forgotten or perhaps just hadn't seen the first time.

The winged beasts of metal and mist shall arrive in great numbers to darken the skies. And there shall in Enthait be a weapon, so grand, so glorious, so powerful, it shall destroy all of the enemies and all of the beasts and all of the living and all of the dead and only the orness, the keeper of the aria, shall remain. And the orness shall know the song of the aria, so that she may sing it free upon the city.

The winged beasts of metal and mist? The song of the aria? The phrases rolled around in her brain, painful as a pebble, but she couldn't make sense of it. The entire thing read like a prophecy of the future, but also like a retelling of the past. Which was it? Or was it both?

She read the rest of the book, looking for more about the winged beasts or the device, but there was little else there that seemed useful.

It was evening before Omuf-Rhi returned. She was bent over one of the last books in her pile, Khee at her side. An unnamed tome – there were a surprising number of books that bore no title – which appeared to capture the history, not of Enthait, but of a city that rose into the sky and rested on nothing but air. It seemed to have been located where Enthait now stood, but the map inside the front cover wasn't clear enough to tell her for certain. Other than that, her search hadn't turned up as much as she'd hoped.

"How's Rakdel holding up?" she asked, when she sensed Omuf-Rhi's shadow at her back. It was the safest thing she could ask.

She closed her book with her finger between its pages. Piled up the three she wanted to take with her. She didn't think he'd mind. Or even notice, as exhausted as he looked. There were no shadows under his eyes, but she'd noticed that when he grew tired, the hair along his arms seemed to flatten and she could see the shape on his back fluttering slightly.

He ran a hand over the books she'd piled up, but didn't say anything about them. "You should go and see her."

He didn't mean Rakdel.

"Yes," she lied. She wasn't ready. She hadn't found anything she needed. "As soon as I finish these."

He gave her a look and opened his mouth, as if to say

something. He let it go and let her go.

Khee rose, stretched and padded out ahead of her, not even giving Omuf-Rhi so much as a glance before he left.

She stepped to the door, stopped at the threshold between light and shadow. "Khee's sorry," she said.

"I know."

WARD

In the end, she hadn't lied after all. She did as Omuf-Rhi had suggested and went to see her. Or tried to.

She couldn't not. The war within her that the orness had started – lie about everything she was and keep up the farce, or tell the truth and put everyone in danger – was waging in her head, and she couldn't tell what was right and what was wrong anymore. Her fear of being found out, of disappointing Isera, had fallen away in the last few hours, replaced by a deeper, greater fear. That Isera was dead or dying and that she had stayed away, not to protect Isera, but because she was, would always be, the one who dropped her weapon and ran away.

No. With a sudden deep need, she nearly ran toward Isera's, Khee easily keeping pace beside her. Her new blade banged against her hip, comforting in its novelty.

Ardit and Rynz were standing in front of Isera's door. Not just standing. Guarding. Waiting. It was in the stance, the loose hand, the way they weren't talking as they stood, one on either side of the entrance. They both had the air of someone expecting people to be going in and out. All except one.

Talia drew up short when she saw them, but she was already in the street, already in eyesight. Khee, less aware, kept running a step or two after she did.

Rynz saw them first. He ducked his chin to the side, gave his head a small shake. His fingers tapped the flickerstick at his side. A warning. For her? She thought so.

She hissed at Khee, who caught on fast and pulled back. A moment later, they were both tucked into the shadows between the houses, invisible from the greyes' vantage point.

For one single heartbeat, relief flooded through her, cool and sweet. She'd tried. She'd run, but toward and not away. It wasn't her own cowardice, but something beyond her control, that kept her from seeing Isera. She'd done everything she could.

That thought, and the sensation of relief, didn't even last long enough for her to believe it.

"Skist," she muttered, as Khee nudged her hand with his wide snout.

They'd have to find a different way.

The wall above Isera's house was high and flat. Talia squatted on it, watching the path to the house. Since they'd sneaked here – coming the long way around from the north so they were less likely to be seen – the zaffre had been coming and going. Khee panted next to her, his tail occasionally thumping against the stones.

The moon was coming up to full. Whatever the seasons here, this one stretched out long days of light. It was still warm, though, even into the night, and she was grateful for the quiet breeze that sometimes made it from somewhere across the desert to cool her skin.

She'd picked a place on the wall where they could see Isera's house, but just barely. Or she could. She actually had no idea what Khee's eyesight was like. As a predator, it was probably pretty good. As a predator who'd been enhanced by the vordcha, she was sure it was far better than that.

She was about to ask him, when she saw two more people come toward the house. She didn't think they could see her from there, but she lowered herself down toward the wall anyway. One of them wore a brown apron. Rakdel. She was pulling a metal container much like the one the Painter used, except she knew this one wasn't filled with pain and sorrow, but with medical supplies. No, no, no. Ganeth had promised.

The orness saying, *How we love our Aeon Priest...*

Talia's heart was a wild thing.

"Khee, please go and see." She was hoping that no one would look at him sideways, as often as he was seen in Seild's company. Maybe they'd let him in if he was by himself. "Just let me know if she's all right, yes? If the chiurgeon says anything..."

There was no word attached to his response – or if there was, it wasn't one she understood – just a general sense of confusion that pinged around inside her like an insect looking for a landing place.

"Right..." She didn't want that feeling again. She would do a better job with her words in the future. Of course, he wouldn't know what a chiurgeon was. "Rakdel."

He didn't say anything, but he eyed her a long moment, as if to say, *you're not fooling anyone*, and then he went as she requested, making his way carefully down the wall and disappearing from sight.

A moment later, he reported back with a quick
wait.

So she did. She crouched on the balls of her feet, watching the street in front of Isera's house for a sign of anyone else coming or going. There was nothing. A man came swiftly down the street, a shining sword in hand as she watched, but he seemed to be headed elsewhere, and didn't stop or slow down at Isera's house.

You promised, Ganeth. You promised she was all right.

And then she thought of the orness' face charms. *How we love our Aeon Priests.*

And you believed him.

She could handle Khee's voice inside her and that other voice – familiar, but one whose name she hadn't yet spoken, whose face she had not yet looked at – but not the orness' mocking tone. "Get out," she said aloud, but even in doing so, she knew the orness was right.

Sooner or later, she was going to have to decide: did she trust Ganeth or not? She had trusted him, but the orness' words had put a crack in that. Which wasn't right, because she trusted the orness less than she trusted anyone. And yet. And yet.

Rakdel came out of the house, wiping her hands on her apron. Talia stood and took a step forward; Rakdel would give her answers. Rakdel would tell her the truth.

The sudden hook at the back of her legs caught her completely by surprise. She let out a small, involuntary yelp – not at the pain, which hadn't yet had time to sink in – but at the shock of being swept off her feet. Her body's instinct was to tumble into a rollaway, but this high up and with this thin a ledge, she wasn't sure she wouldn't fall right off the wall.

Instead, she let herself go down on her back, flatten to the stone. It was risky, but if she had any chance of coming out of this, she needed to be able to see her attacker. She landed hard, her back instantly pinging in protest, the air whooshing out of her lungs in such a hard rush that she was instantly dizzy. Her hexed arm hit the wall with a sharp crack.

"Burrin," she breathed. So he did know how to softstep with those shoes when he needed to. Good to know. If a little belated.

He stood above her, the end of one of his long sticks pointing at her chest. His face was reddened in a big splash above his cheek. The kind of mark a spew of acid might make if you weren't expecting it enough to sidestep. The creatures had gotten him too, then. Seeing him like that did little to appease her fears.

He stood tall before her. His sepia skin was near-black beneath the eyes and his blues were dusted and dirtied.

"You are no poison eater." Each word accented with a poke of his stick – not hard enough to do her damage, but hard enough that she flinched each time. Burrin did not thumb his mouth after he spoke, as most would if they were making an accusation. She didn't know if it was because he thought it was beneath him or because he was once again proving that he needn't follow rituals. And, truly, he didn't need to. Every word was honed with an edge that made it clear that he was accusing her of being a liar.

Oh, you have no idea.

She tried to bring her knees up toward her chest, both to protect herself and to see how badly she might be hurt. A little stiff, but she thought it was just an impact blow.

She began to push herself off the wall, but he leaned into his stick. She felt the sharp shape of it through her shirt.

"Stay down," he said.

"Burrin–"

"No. Stay down. Stop talking," he said. "You don't get to talk right now. I've seen you. I know that you have this ability to... make people believe your stories, to tell them what they want to hear, or what you want them to hear. And they just believe you. You did it to me. To the orness." She found it interesting that he never spoke about her as his mother, but always as the orness. Was he following ritual, or was there something else there? Burrin took his stick away from her chest long enough to point it down toward the house where she'd sent Khee. "To Isera."

She'd never heard him say so many words in a single space before. The crack against her back still made it hard to breathe and something from the wall was digging into her hip, but she found words anyway.

"Tell me what you know," she said. An offering, on the table. Allies.

He came back with anger. "I know you lied. The charn is made up, a child's tale for warning away children. But I was willing to go and see because... I don't know why. Because I am a child of this city. Because I believed. Instead, you sent us into an ambush. Why?" Another jab with his stick.

"I didn't..." she started. But she had, hadn't she? "Burrin, my vision was wrong. But it was not deliberate."

"I don't believe you. Get up," he said. He stepped away and pushed his fist into his chest. An invitation. No, a demand.

She did not accept. She would not fight him. Not like this.

"Get. Up. I don't care if the orness did choose you." The end of his weapon grew slightly less controlled each time. No, not less controlled. She didn't think there was a moment that he was not completely in control. The pressure was increasing in careful increments. If she was going to keep him from sticking that right through her chest, she needed to get him to back down.

She curled her true hand into a fist, pumped it against her chest once. Agreed to his fight. At least then there were rules. He had to let her get up, find her weapon.

She rose, clumsily, using her true hand to push her forward, trying to buy time. She gripped the red-handled blade, surprised at how grateful she was to have it tucked at her side.

"I don't yet know why we're fighting," she said and she heard the fear in her voice give way to resolve. "But after I beat you, I will ask."

She sounded more confident than she felt, but if she was honest with herself, she'd kind of been aching for a fight. Of course, she'd worked a lot of that out against the training dummy, dulling the need somewhat. But still. Burrin. For some reason, there'd always been that tension between them. She twirled the blade between her fingers. The movement was still a little stiff, but it got better the second time around.

Burrin adjusted the grip, flexing and tightening each finger over the pole, one at a time. "I will not kill you," he said.

It was not a statement meant to placate. It was, she thought, the smartest thing he could have uttered. For a moment, she saw everything that made him the true leader of the zaffre, a good leader. Even in his anger, he was smart and he was sure. He knew that she would never beat him in this kind of hand-to-hand. She was a fine fighter when her life depended on it, but he had just made sure she knew that her life did not depend on it. And so she would pull her punches, and she would lose.

Burrin lifted his long pole. "But I may hurt you very badly."

"Like Isera is hurt very badly?" she said. It was a risk, but it turned out to be a worthwhile one. For the mention of her name seemed to momentarily stop him. *Skist. That meant she really was–*

Burrin's pause was a ploy. She realized it a moment too late, and he was on her with the side of his stick, a sharp slap against her side that clenched her teeth against her breath. She swore under her exhale.

She looked away, hoping his gaze would follow. She didn't know if it did, but she stepped forward and underhanded her new knife so the pommel caught him in the jaw.

He was ready for her, missing most of the impact with a cant of his head. His eyes went hard and when he came for her again, it was with a quick thrust of his elbow. She'd had her eyes on his weapon, and completely missed the jab coming. It was followed by a low kick to the side of her knee. The joint buckled, spilling her back to the ground.

When she went down this time, it really did knock the breath from her. She heard something crack in her back, like a dry twig over a knee. The world spun, went black and gray. Already, her hand ached, so unused to holding a weapon.

Burrin was faster, stronger, and better trained than she was. She had to decide quickly whether to fight him or stay down. Every instinct told her to stay where she was, to let him have this one.

In the end, she pushed herself up, not to antagonize him or meet him as she might have once, but because she could tell that he needed badly to beat someone. And it might as well be her. She didn't know who else he had at his disposal. She would give him a fair fight, even though he would win, and then she would find out what she could.

She rushed him, raising her knife in her true hand just as she fisted her hex hand, coming in with both. He moved away from the blade right into her punch in the side, as she'd hoped. She'd never hit anything with her hex hand before, and was surprised that she felt nothing; it completely absorbed the impact of the hit. So much so that she wasn't sure how hard she'd landed her blow until he oofed air out and covered his ribs with his arm.

She stepped back, out of the way, but the length of Burrin's weapon caught her against the side of the head, just above her neck, so hard that she saw light in her eyes. For just a moment, she was sure she was blinded, that she'd stumble forth and fall from the wall.

But then her vision returned, and Burrin was moving in on her. His pole still pointed at her, his face a grimace of trial and pain.

She changed her mind – she wasn't going to let him beat her. On instinct, she shoved her knee against the inside of his thigh, along the muscle, and felt a moment of pleasure as his eyes went wide. He went down on a half knee, groaning. The hit had been indirect – she'd intended it to be – and he wasn't down for very long.

He narrowed his eyes at her as he pushed himself halfway to stand. "Is *this* what we're doing?" he asked. "You fight dirty."

She felt a little bad as his jawline clenched. It passed.

"You started this, but didn't tell me how to win. I lay that on you."

They were not poison eater and leader of the zaffre now. Something else, something new. She didn't know if she liked it or hated it.

They were both panting. The back of Talia's head was pounding so hard she could feel the pressure in her teeth. She gingerly reached up to touch the curve of her head just above her spine and wasn't surprised that her fingers came away smeared with blood.

"Maybe we should have a conversation instead," she said.

Burrin's lip was swelling, and fast. He sucked on it, as if to cool it and dispel the pain. "This *is* a conversation," he said. She could tell by the way his words were slightly blurred together that it hurt him to speak. "Beating you is the best... kind of conversation."

"Cachosa." It was a word she'd heard Seild get in trouble for using. She didn't know exactly what it meant, but she knew it was negative. She liked the way it fit into her mouth, and she liked the way it made her feel when she said it to Burrin.

His laughter was so sudden that she caught her breath. "Did Seild teach you that word?" he asked.

She nodded. "Should I even ask what it means?"

"No," he said. "But please say it to me at the end of every fight we ever have."

"Does that mean that this one is over?"

He hesitated a long time before he gave a curt nod. "For now."

"Good," she said. "Because I've never killed anyone before, and I don't think I want my first kill to be you. I want it to be special."

Burrin started laughing at that, so hard he started to cough. "Really, you've never?" he asked.

"Never," she said. "But I guess this also means that there will be more fights, so perhaps I'll get my chance."

In the silence, except for their quiet huffs of breath, they stood on the wall and looked out over the city. From here, you could almost see the entire thing. It was easy to forget the size of it when you were inside it every day.

In comparison to the stretch of the city, she felt like she and Burrin were closer than they had been. She could have reached out and touched his hand.

"Burrin," she said. She was thinking about everything the orness had told her and about why he'd wanted to fight her. "Have none of the other poison eaters ever been wrong?"

He wiped a bit of blood from his lip. "Often," he said. "More often than not."

"Then why…" She spread her hands between them. His lip. Her back. Their breath. "Why all this? Or did you beat all of them up every time they were wrong?"

"You know why," he said.

But she didn't.

"I already told you," he said. She expected his eyes to be hard when he said it. Angry. Instead they softened. His whole face did.

She had to shake her head, hope that he would give her more.

He cast his gaze, a slow, exaggerated movement, toward Isera's house.

Oh, she had misunderstood so much.

"No," he said when he saw her face. "It's not like that between us. Not anymore. But it was. Six years or so ago."

"Oh," she said again, as she began to understand. So many pieces fell into place. Why he mistrusted her. Why Isera had always acted like Burrin couldn't know about them. It wasn't because he was leader of the zaffre; it was because she was protecting him. But of course he knew. He was smart and he paid attention.

And six years ago was a long...

Another click, a door opening.

"Oh, Seild..." she said. "Seild is..."

He didn't have to say yes, and so he didn't.

And your mother is a cold bitch with a blackfruit pit for a heart.

"Seild doesn't know, does she?" She thought of the way the girl had stiffened around him.

Burrin shook his head, one movement. "And she won't. The orness can never know she has a granddaughter."

So he did know his mother a bit then. More than she'd thought, but not as much as he probably should. *I'd bet ten shins and one of those sticks you carry that the orness is fully aware of the girl's lineage.*

His words had carried a question.

"I'll keep your secret," she said. No hesitation. It wasn't a lie. She would never tell the orness. She didn't have to. "And hers. You may trust me."

"I don't trust you. Not even this much." He pinched his fingers together so that they were touching, tight, no space or light between. "But I think that Seild needs you, and

Isera too, and as much as I might want to sometimes, I won't take that from them."

She felt obligated to give him something in return.

"You're right, you know," she said.

He glanced at her without turning his head. In the falling light, his face was half lit, his sharp features filled with shadow.

"I'm false," she said. "I'm not the true poison eater."

He put a palm to his cheek, wiggled his jaw beneath it with a wince of pain. "You are right more often than most. I've seen enough of them to know."

He wasn't telling an untruth. She'd come up with something each time, sure that she was making them up in her own brain. But had she been? There had always been something there, something beyond her. Had the poison been planting things the whole time? She felt like she couldn't be sure of anything anymore. Everything felt like it was half lie, half truth and not only could she not figure out which one something was, she couldn't always tell one half from the other.

She opened her mouth to try to convince him otherwise. Once she'd gotten some of it out there, she had a sudden, desperate need to say the whole thing. To have someone believe her, to know her.

But he spoke before she could. "It's my fault. I'm the one who read your vision. I'm the one who said 'charn.' Even though I knew it wasn't, couldn't be. I'm not angry with you. I'm angry with myself."

It was a bigger admission than her own, somehow. And she let it sit there for a moment, trying to figure out how to handle it. The bones in her spine whispered angrily, and she stretched to alleviate the discomfort.

"My back says you have a funny way of showing that," she said finally.

"I'm sorry I hit you," he said.

"I'm sorry I kneed you."

"I don't think you are," he said. But his tone was light.

"Are we friends now?" she asked.

"No," he said.

Burrin pushed his weapon back into the holder at his back. For a moment she thought he might extend his hand to help her up, but he merely looked at her for a moment longer.

"Go see Isera," he said. "Since I can feel your worry from here."

An hour ago, she would not have believed his gesture to be a kindness. Now, she nodded, so grateful that tears pricked the corners of her eyes.

She wondered how much he knew that he wasn't saying. About her, about the poison eater, the orness, all of it. Did he know everything? She didn't think so. There were layers of secrets, down and down. She thought Burrin had scratched beneath the very first one, but that was as far as he was willing to go.

Burrin, too, was layered. She wondered if she'd even begun to make a dent in his shell.

He wiped his hands over his outfit, slapping away the dirt, and then began to carefully make his way down the path at the far side of the wall.

"Burrin," she called after him.

He stopped, but didn't turn.

"Is that why you've made Seild afraid of you?" She saw his neck tighten, his spine pull up to stack him taller. He didn't give her an answer. He didn't have to. She understood well enough pushing things away from you to try to keep them safe.

"Go see her," he said. "Unless you want to fight me again, sooner than later."

Talia knelt there a moment longer, willing her breath to slow. Something was definitely wrong in her back, along the sides of her spine, from the tightening she felt inside each breath. When she lifted her hexed arm, she had a hard time making the fingers flex. They were stiff and slow-moving, as if they were near frozen.

Pulling herself up to sitting required quick, short breaths to ease the pain and her good hand to the ground, to help her fold. Oddly, she hadn't heard anything from Khee – not even an update for *wait* – and she couldn't see Isera's house from this position, so she carefully pulled herself up to a crouch, and then to a stand.

From here, she couldn't make out anyone coming or going. She had no idea if they were inside the house still, or out.

"Khee, what is happening down there?"

Still Khee was silent.

It was time to go down and see for herself.

The guards were gone from the front entrance. Rakdel opened the door at her knock. Her brown apron was splattered and dirty, the swirls of her knuckles filled with red.

"Poison Eater." She sounded tired, but not surprised to see her.

"I just need to know if she's all right," Talia said. Her back hurt, her head hurt, her heart hurt. Each word was like an abrasion to those wounds.

"Come in," she said. "She'll be fine. You, however..."
That look that only Rakdel could give her. Appraising,
wordlessly requesting some action from her.

Talia looked back pointedly at the bloodied apron. "Will
she?"

"Affah," Rakdel said. "Some healing to do, but nothing
out of the ordinary for her position."

The front room was full of people. It was the first time
she'd been here when it wasn't just her and Isera. She
hadn't realized how small the space was, and how the two
of them had taken up so little of it.

Members of the zaffre and others she didn't know
stood around, talking. Khee. Rynz. Ganeth, bent over a
tall portable workspace, muttering to himself as he fiddled
with something small and round. Seild, her face resting on
the top of the workstation, watched whatever Ganeth was
doing with a quiet intensity. He said something, low, and
the girl shifted, then held out a long, thin wire tool to him
across the table.

And Isera, oh, Isera. Standing with her back to Talia,
but standing. Alive. If she wasn't already short of breath
before, she would have been at that moment. It was one
thing to tell yourself you believed, and another to see your
belief standing in front of you.

Talia exhaled, then groaned softly as her back shifted,
sending a ping of pain down through her hips. Damn
Burrin and his need to be an avenger.

Isera turned at the sound, all smile and lit-up face. "Tal–
" She caught herself just in time. "Finwa, Poison Eater...
oh, forget it. Everyone knows. I'm too tired and bad at
pretending that I'm not glad you're here."

Talia couldn't speak or move or even feel the pain in

her spine. It wasn't what Isera had said. Any other time that alone would have knocked her flat. It was how Isera looked. Not her uniform, torn and stained. Not her arm, bandaged around the elbow in a swatch of red cloth.

But her face.

Her grey eye was gone.

Instead, a hole in the side of her face. Folds of skin at the back of the hollow, surrounded by long dark lashes, top and bottom. In the very center, a glowing worm twisted and thrashed.

Like a poison dream had slipped from its cage and lumbered here, waiting until the right moment to show itself. Look what horrors you've wrought. *Liar. False.*

Her knees twisted, went numb. Everything swam. She staggered, but she would not, did not, fall. But she retched, remembering something she couldn't place, her hand over her mouth.

Nearly everyone in the room was looking at them. Some blatantly. Others sideways. Only Ganeth and Seild seemed captivated by their work.

"Ah," Isera said, and covered the hollow with her fist. "I forgot... I must look... It's only temporary. Ganeth is..." She fell silent, twisted her lips. Her loss for words shook Talia almost as much as her missing eye.

In truth, Talia couldn't have cared how it looked, other than the fear and guilt it brought with it. She shook the dream off with a fierceness that was hard won and stepped close to Isera. Not a worm, she thought as she neared her. More like a living root.

Isera was watching her, her expression all question: what choice do you make now, Poison Eater, with my face ravaged and my vision halved?

"I..." Talia started, and then her throat closed, tight and choking, before she could finish.

Her cheeks burned from guilt. And shame at her reaction. She would not have Isera think that the loss of an eye mattered to her. That she was a hypocrite.

She tried again. "No," she said. "Not that. I don't care about that." She put her hand toward the side of Isera's face, slow, waited to see her nod before her palm landed and pressed. "What happened? I'm so sorry."

"There were creatures," Isera said. "Not the charn. Something else." She didn't sense blame in Isera's voice, but she felt it anyway. She always did. Always would.

"I saw them," Talia said. "I saw them in Ganeth's device. I saw you get hurt. I'm sorry."

"It's really nothing," Isera said. And she seemed to believe it, which made the tightness in Talia's spine loosen just a little. "It happens from time to time. Ganeth's going to grow me a new one. Or rather, I'm going to grow myself a new one."

"Almost ready," Ganeth said. A small ticking followed his voice, and then he said, "Seild, grab that."

Seild suddenly seemed to realize Talia was there. "Tal, we're making an eye egg!"

Isera touched the back of Talia's hand. "Ganeth needs to put me in incubation for a short while. Just until it grows back."

Something must have shown in Talia's face, because Isera reached out and touched the corner of her mouth. "Don't worry. I've done this before," she said. "But if you ever wanted to lie to me about anything..." She pointed to the missing eye. "...now is the time."

It took Talia a moment to realize she was teasing, but

still the words dug with sharp little barbs. Tooth and claw.

"We're ready," Ganeth said.

"Hurry, hurry," Seild said. "It's dripping."

Isera leaned in and touched Talia's forehead with her own. "See you soon, Poison Eater," she said. "Keep an eye on the wild one." Talia didn't know if she meant Khee or Seild. Both, perhaps.

The rest of the greyes and zaffre and strangers said, nearly in unison, "Moon meld you, Greyes Isera." Talia echoed it, half a word late, but wanted desperately to believe that her words would matter.

She watched as Isera and Ganeth headed toward the back of the house, Ganeth cradling a tiny grey orb in his cupped hands.

So many things they hadn't told each other.

The curtain closed behind them. The room went quiet in the slow, falling way of emptying spaces. Seild came up to her and took her true hand inside her tiny one. Talia looked at her and for the first time, she could see Burrin in her. And the orness too.

But it was Isera's mismatched eyes that were staring back at her, asking all of the questions she had no answers for.

"Come, let me have a look at you," Rakdel said, when the room had mostly cleared. The zaffre and the others had left. Seild and Khee had walked quietly, somberly, into the yard, as if they were not child and beast, but two adults with important things to discuss. It hurt her heart, to watch them go.

Khee hadn't said a word to her since he'd left her on the wall. She wanted to call after them. But Khee would talk when he was ready. She could do nothing but wait.

Talia tried to wave Rakdel away, to distract her by asking, "Are you all right? You looked bad in the market yesterday?" But the chiurgeon just laughed and aimed her toward a chair.

"Have you forgotten who I am? Sit. Sit and I won't even ask you who punched you." She looked at the side of Talia's neck. "...who punched you with a big stick that seems an awful lot like a big stick I'm familiar with."

Talia said nothing. Burrin's pain was a private thing. He'd only brought it to her because he'd had nowhere else to go.

Rakdel touched here, there. Pulled things out of her box and used them to look at or feel at the parts of Talia's body that hurt and then put them back in. True to her word, she did not ask Talia how she'd come by her wounds.

Finally, she sat back on her heels.

"Do you want the whole list or just the ones I think you should do something about?"

"That," Talia said. Her breath had gotten shorter and tighter as she sat there, and now she hitched up her spine, trying to make more room in her lungs. It didn't help that she kept looking toward the back of the house, as if she expected Isera to come back any second. Every time she swung her head around, her spine shifted in a broken, uneven way. "That second one."

"I think you might have cracked a rib, you've gotten yourself a good jab to the head, and you've got some kind of injury in your back that I can't figure out. Not a broken bone, but a broken... something." She leaned in, feeling along Talia's back as she spoke, down the carved pattern on either side of her spine. Talia had forgotten, as Rakdel was touching her, about the scar until this very moment. She resisted the urge to push the chiurgeon's hands away in… shame? Fear? She wasn't sure.

"Right. There," Rakdel was saying. "Can you feel it?"

No. But then yes. Out of all the pain she felt back there, a new one bloomed at the touch, sharp and bladed. It took what little remained of her breath.

Ganeth came out from the back room, wiping down a small square object with a cloth. "She's in," he said, as he settled it into place on the workbench and started folding it up. "Four days, probably, for it to root fully. I'll come back tomorrow and check."

"Ganeth, will you…" Rakdel motioned him over. "What do you make of her back?" Before Talia could even open her mouth to protest, Rakdel said, "Healer's curiosity. Humor me."

She did, despite her instinct not to. Ganeth's fingers were softer than Rakdel's, the skin, not the touch. He made tiny, sure movements across her back. Precise movements of hands used to working with things much smaller, more delicate, than the human spine.

Something passed between Ganeth and Rakdel. A look that was beyond her.

"That's what I thought too," Rakdel said. "Did you know you have some kind of metal in your back? Embedded or–"

"Implanted, I think," Ganeth said. "Interwoven in your spine."

No. No. No. Her mouth went bitter and dry, all at once. She'd cut off her hand. Her scalp. Khee's horns. All of it gone. Only for this. Her stomach, which had not fully recovered from Burrin, from Isera, roiled and threatened to turn over yet again.

No. She would not, could not admit that all of her planning, her loss, the pain she'd taken and given, was for so little. Mostly, she felt stupid. Of course the vordcha did not make a brand upon their martyrs just to brand them. Of course her spine was laced with their tech. How could she have been so stupid? So blind?

The vordcha would use it to track her. Certainly, they already were. They would come for her. For all of them. And the weapon she'd thought she had – the orness, the device – it was all a lie.

"The mech is broken," Ganeth said. "In two places. That might not be a new break though. It's hard to tell. I'm not sure what it does, but we could try to fix it."

"Or take it out," Rakdel said. "Are you in much pain?"

Talia thought about her response very carefully before she made it.

How are you surviving the poisons? the orness had asked her.

She hadn't answered, but she'd known. Or thought she'd known. But, oh, the truth was slippery and oily and much, much worse. Maybe it wasn't some residual effect of the mech that was saving her from death. Maybe it was the mech still buried beneath her skin. If so, that meant the very thing that was saving her was also drawing the vordcha to her, to all of them.

Now it was broken.

"No, no pain," she lied. "I feel fine. But do you think you could look at this?" She pulled off her hexed armband and passed it over to Ganeth. "I think I punched the wrong thing with it."

•••

The days that followed took on a short-breath routine. First, check in on Isera and Seild.

Isera was fully encased in a cocoon of soft, pellucid synth. Ganeth called it a symbiotic sheath. At first glance, she appeared as if she were sleeping, her one visible eye moving behind her lid in rapid, strained movements and her lips clasped tight. The other eye, the one that Seild had called the eye egg, was covered with a mass of yellow goo that undulated, as if it was alive. Maybe it was.

It never got easy to see her like that. Not even the fact that everyone else seemed to treat this as normal, as common as taking taf or eating dinner, helped her overcome the quick beat of her heart as she looked down at her, wrapped and unconscious on the bed.

Seild was spending time – too much time, likely – sitting in her mother's room. Sometimes she "read," other times she slept. Sometimes, the scariest times, she sat there, picking at the design in the bedspread, pulling the same thread again and again. Talia tried to get her to come with her to Books & Blades or the Eternal Market or anywhere she wanted to go, but the girl refused in a way that was so adult, so undercarried with all of her fear and loss, that Talia couldn't bear to force her.

Often Khee stayed with Seild too. He hadn't talked to Talia since the day of the fight, and he seemed to be spending more and more time with the girl. Talia told herself that she wasn't jealous; she just missed him. She allowed herself to feel that hurt, the confusion and unfinish of it. She thought that if he could just tell her why he was silent, she would handle it better. But of course, to do that, he would have to speak to her.

To keep her mind off Khee, Isera, Seild, she spent her

time trying to solve the problem of being the poison eater. She kept running it over and over in her mind, tugging at it the way Seild was tugging at her mother's bedspread: if she stopped being the poison eater, the orness would take Seild as the next one. But if it was the vordcha's mech keeping her alive, would it do so while it was broken? And would fixing it call the vordcha down upon them?

She went back to the base of the skar twice, trying to find her way back in, to talk to the orness, but the door wouldn't open for her again. And the orness never came for her, even though she walked the top of the walls at night, looking for the glow of a moonfruit or the shadow that was darker than shadows ought to be.

She walked by Ganeth's shop at least once a day, but never went in. The orness' words, true or not, had planted a seed of doubt in her mind about him. She never was good at trust, and she knew the orness' words overlapped with her early reaction to him – so like the vordcha – in a way that wasn't useful, but even that was not enough to convince her to step inside, to call out his name, to ask him for help.

Most days, she spent her time at Books & Blades, where she paged through what felt like endless piles of books looking for answers that she didn't find. In addition to the obvious – how do I survive this? How does everyone survive this? – she was looking for answers about what was real, what was not. Who was the orness? What was the truth of the poison eater? Of the aria?

Each day, she told herself that it would be the day she would find something useful in the books. A clear and perfect explanation of what was true and what was false.

And each day, she left the store, having gained a little more knowledge, but not enough. Never enough.

The moon was already shifting, moving into its next phase. It wouldn't be long before it was time for another poisoning. She'd hoped to have a better understanding of it, to have a *plan* for surviving it before that happened. But time was slipping away, and her ideas were dwindling faster than her understanding was growing.

It was three days before the next poisoning when she again headed to Omuf-Rhi's shop. Khee was with her, silent but close enough that she could feel his heat against her leg.

When they arrived, Omuf-Rhi was reading, so engrossed in his book that he didn't hear her enter the shop. She found that in the silence, she missed his echoing hello. Rather than bother him, she buried herself in the store's dusty stacks.

She watched him read, his head down, flipping through the pages far faster than she could. It would have taken her half a day, more, to make it through the pages he'd completed just while she stood there watching.

He was an enigma to her in many ways, flowing between a self that could spend hours training with a weapon, and then the next day, be so engrossed in learning from words that he didn't even hear someone talking to him. Most she had known had one thing, and one thing only, to their passion.

You don't have to do everything alone, Talia. You ran once. But that doesn't mean you will always run. Trust yourself to trust others.

It was so hard.

"Omuf-Rhi," she said, as she stepped up closer to him.

Where the glow lights hit his body, his hair was tawny, almost golden. "Are you from here? From Enthait?"

"No," he murmured, not stopping in his reading.

"Where did you come from?" she asked.

He lifted his head and she wondered yet again what set of eyes he saw her with, or if it was all of them.

"A place called Seshar, far, far to the west."

"Do they have an orness there? A poison eater?"

"No," he said. "Although they have other stories, other myths."

Stories and myths, he said. Not histories. Not futures. Stories and myths. As in things that were not always true.

She considered for a moment, trying to figure out what she wanted to ask. Khee sat on his haunches next to her. He'd started coming inside in the last week or so, even if Omuf-Rhi was there.

"Did you bring all of these with you? From the... Seshar." The *sh* in the middle was hard to get her tongue out of the way for.

"My mother was also a bookseller," he said. There was nothing else forthcoming, which was unusual. He'd been quiet lately, and she wondered if there were things on his mind or if there was another reason.

She picked up a book near her hand. *The Wonders of Our World: The Steadfast and Beyond.* Naind Oreni. Another, smaller. *Verses of the Hidden Realms.* Books and books. She'd never work her way through all of them. Not even with her improved reading skills.

"Have you read all of these books?"

"Most," he said.

"And do you remember them all?"

Omuf-Rhi carried a set of very thin silver blades in a

pouch on his belt that he tucked into whatever books he was reading; he did so with one now, closing the cover so softly she didn't hear it.

"Most." There was a question in his voice.

She did her best to answer it, without actually doing so. The orness had said that she saw the whole city. Whether or not that was true, she didn't know. What she did know was that everything she asked out loud about her, about the poisoning, it felt like a risk. The question was: was that a risk worth taking? After a moment's uncertainty, she decided that it was.

She moved in closer, leaned her elbows on the counter.

"What do all of these books say of the orness? How old she is? When she came to power?"

He shrugged. "They don't."

She waited, to see if there was more. It was infuriating, sometimes, how much he talked when she didn't need him to, and how little he did when she wanted information from him. "Why do you think that is?" she prodded.

He considered for a long moment. There was a plate of dried fruit and meat at his elbow, and he reached for a handful, then pushed the dish toward her. "I think because the orness is a tale for the telling, not for the reading."

"What's the difference?" She took one of the pieces of meat, tossed it to Khee. He snapped it out of the air and then grinned, both of his tongues lolling to the side. Sometimes, she supposed, you didn't need language to communicate with each other.

"One is immutable and so you write it down," Omuf-Rhi said. "Because it can stay the same forever. The other needs to be malleable, to have the option to change with the world, and the world's needs."

"Or the city and the city's needs," she said.

He stopped chewing for a moment. "Yes, I suppose so."

"Do you believe?"

"In you?" There was a layer of tease in his words that brought back the image of him on the night they'd met, his arm wrapped and bleeding. You couldn't even see the teeth marks any longer.

"In me," she said. "In the orness, in some unknown danger called the charn, in her weapon. The whole thing." She felt herself walking on a thin, unsteady path, dangerous on all sides. *Careful, child.*

"I believe that the city needs to believe." He spread his hands. "Beyond that, I don't know."

"No one ever asks," she said. "Whether it's worth it? All these deaths? Trying to find the true poison eater? The orness?"

"If they believe it is the way it must be, who would question it?"

"So..." She was doing her best to think through everything that was moving around in her brain. "So if the poison eater was a lie..." Too late she realized her mistake, having spoken it aloud, but there was nowhere else to go. "*If,*" she emphasized. "Would that mean the orness was also? And the aria? And would it matter, if the city believed in it?"

"Do you think you're a lie?" he asked.

Skist. That wasn't the part of the weave she was hoping he'd pluck out. But of course he would.

"No," she said quickly. Weirdly, it felt true. Perfect. The orness had her so spun around that she couldn't tell her own lies from truths anymore.

"But the aria..." She tried to bring him back. "Does

that seem true? Real?"

"That seems like a question for Ganeth," he said. "He knows far more about devices than I do."

Yes. But she kept thinking about what the orness had said. *We love our Aeon Priest.* She trusted Ganeth with many things that mattered to her, but with this, she couldn't know. It wasn't that she questioned his loyalty, but rather the strength of his ability to say no to the orness' requests.

"I'd ask you where all this is coming from," Omuf-Rhi said. "But I like to think that I know you well enough by now to know that you won't tell me."

"Ask me again tomorrow," she said, as she headed toward the stack of books where she'd last left off. "And I just might."

On the day Isera was supposed to leave incubation – a word that Talia would never get used to – she met Ganeth leaving Isera's just as she was arriving. She knew it was weird that she trusted Ganeth with Isera, her health, her eye, her everything, but not with her own concerns. She tried not to let her confusion show when she talked to him.

"How's the hand?" he asked, as he caught a glimpse of it.

Ganeth had fixed her hexed arm. When he returned it, it bore a new blue in its hexes, and a new section. A piece of tubing connected to the elbow of it. "For punching," he said. "You'll want to test it out before you get into more fights, though."

She lifted it, and flexed it into a fist for him. "Fightworthy," she said. It was true. When she couldn't sit and stare at books anymore, she often took a turn in the fighting ring.

Mostly with her blade, but she'd found that the new fist was useful and damaging against the practice dummies. And weirdly satisfying.

"How's Isera?" she asked.

Silence. Everyone was so silent these days. She had never been one to want people to talk to her, but now she wished just one person would open themselves like a book and give her all of the answers she needed.

"It's not healing as well as I might have expected," he said. As he talked, he fiddled with a green-hued device that looked almost like an insect. It folded and unfolded its legs. It was similar to something she'd seen Seild playing with not that long ago. "It's possible I didn't allow the eye to germinate enough before I implanted it. She wanted me to hurry."

He didn't say Isera's name, mostly talked about things Talia didn't understand. She let him. She knew he was talking about her, even when he wasn't.

"There's an infection. Staying in the symbiotic sheath for longer means a greater chance of survival. But stay too long and the sheath can become parasitic instead of symbiotic. Rakdel and I will have to watch it closely."

She was hearing words that she could only hope had other meanings than the ones she knew. Was this the orness' doing? Had she put Ganeth up to this, giving him orders to do something to Isera?

But his actions told her otherwise. He was stroking the device in his hand with his thumb, shaking his head a bit. He was worried for Isera, just as she was. Whatever he did for the orness, this was different.

"What does that mean?" she asked, finally. "In me terms."

"I promise to do my best." He was speaking slowly, fiddling with his device, and she could tell he was thinking through the words before he said them. "But she is in bad shape."

She reached out blindly, searching for something, anything to grasp and finally found the edge of the doorway. She would have fallen but for Khee, pressing his whole weight at the back of her knees.

"I haven't told Seild," he said. He looked away from the device at her, and she saw a rare flicker of emotion in his gaze. "I think she's... Maybe you could talk to her. I'm not very good at it, I don't think."

"I will," she said. Promising something she had no idea how to do.

There was no change in Isera or the sheath that she could see, standing beside the bed, looking down at her. She could hear the sound of Isera's teeth grinding in short, sharp clicks, the exhale of her breath through the material, her own shallow inhales.

"Finwa, Greyes Isera," she said. She didn't touch her. She was afraid that touching her skin and feeling, instead, the weird texture of the synth was more than she could bear. But she talked to her sometimes. About what she was reading. Or things that Seild had said or done. Nothing about the orness. Nothing about the poison eater.

"Ganeth says she can't hear you," Seild had said once, plucking at the blanket between each word. Probably true. But maybe that was why she did it.

As she stood there, she heard a yell coming from outside. It was Seild, she was sure of it. Coming from out back. She ran through the house, fumbling with the back door, unable to get it to open at first, making it worse with her panic.

There, Seild was down on her knees in the red sand. She appeared to be headbutting Khee with a loud fighting cry. A second later, Khee rolled over and pinned her under his side, which elicited another shout from the girl. It was like watching a bout of saglo wrestling between two wild things that didn't know the rules.

"What, moon meld me, are you doing?" Talia asked.

Both creatures scrambled up, panting. Seild's grin showed a layer of red – it took Talia a moment to realize that it wasn't blood that filled her mouth and coated her teeth, but sand. Her hair – two long braids that she'd clearly attempted to do herself – was also filled with sand. A long red ribbon was woven raggedly between the hairs and trailed down her back.

For some reason, the brown stripes in Khee's fur had attracted more sand than the rest of him, giving the impression, for just a moment, that he was streaked with blood. Then he shook himself, sending a cloud of sand into the air that quickly fell and covered them both in a dusting of red.

"Hello, Tal!" Seild said. She ran forward and wrapped her arms around Talia's waist. Since their talk at Ganeth's so long ago, the girl had taken her words to heart. Calling her Tal, forgoing the rituals. Perhaps a little too much, Talia thought, for her own good. But now was not the time for that.

"Hello, Seild. Please tell me you're not planning to headbutt me in the stomach like you did Khee. I'd hate to have to sit on you."

The girl giggled, letting go, leaving faint clouds of red all along the front of Talia's pants and shirt. "No. His Softness is teaching me how to fight!" Talia waited for the pang of mirth from Khee that often followed Seild calling him that, and felt the absence of it like a hunger when it didn't come.

"Is he?" She glanced at Khee, who looked at her with his usual unreadable gaze. "And why is that?"

Seild cocked her head for a moment, as if listening to something. "He says I'm not safe."

Well, that answered that question. If she'd had any remaining doubts that Khee and Seild were able to talk, they were gone now.

"Because of your mom?" Talia said. "She's going to get better."

She bit down on her tongue, but too late. The words were out there, settling into the dust around her feet. *Oh, Talia. Will you never stop taking the road of lies?*

But Seild didn't seem to be listening to her. She had her chin on her chest, her brows pulled down. "No, because of the..." She twisted her lips, and squinted one eye closed before shaking her head. "I don't know. I can't really understand what he's saying."

Talia looked at Khee for an explanation, but of course, she got nothing.

"May I show you my moves?" Seild asked a moment later. "I'm getting very good. I can't wait to show my mom."

She lowered her voice, leaned in, as if to tell a secret. "Did you know my mom's coming back today? With her new eye egg?" She tapped the side of her own grey eye. Not for the first time, Talia wondered when she'd gotten it. Was she just a baby the first time they'd put her in that encasement? Did she remember it? Was it the orness' doing? Or something else?

"I bet you are getting very good," Talia said. "Perhaps later, though. I'd like to talk to Khee alone for a moment."

As the girl's face fell, she quickly added, "Official poison eater business. Otherwise, you know I'd let you stay. Maybe you could make us the taf today? I don't know how, and it's nearly time."

"I'm not old enough," Seild said. She kicked the sand. Puffs of dust swirled up around her already coated boots.

"I know," Talia said. "But you already know how to do it, don't you?"

At the girl's nod, Talia said, "Then just this one time, all right? It will be our secret."

"I like secrets," Seild said.

"Me too." *Not really. Not anymore.* They were heavy stones.

When Seild was gone into the house, Talia stepped over to Khee. She went down on her knees in front of him. It was a gesture reminiscent of when they'd found each other, and she made it purposefully, as an offering.

She thought about also touching her thumbs to her eyes, but that was a now ritual, not a then ritual, and it didn't seem right. Instead, she bowed her head slightly, her arms resting on her thighs.

"Khee? What's happened? Why won't you talk to me anymore?"

She felt the silence, heavy and gutted in her chest, a hollow that had been empty for so long she barely remembered what it felt like to be full.

Unexpectedly, Khee lowered himself to his knees too, then all the way down. He laid his head in Talia's lap. The heat and weight of him, the unexpected kindness, made her eyes sting with tears. She wiped them away quickly, roughly, with the back of her hand so they wouldn't fall onto his fur.

She'd been thinking he'd rejected her. That she'd done something wrong. But as he looked up at her, his blue gaze inscrutable, but not unkind, she realized she'd been wrong.

He'd been talking to her the whole time, she just hadn't been able to hear him. What had happened?

"Oh, Khee," she said. "I miss you."

She put her hand in his fur, ran her fingers along the brown stripes. At her touch, they flared yellow, and she remembered the promises they'd made each other in the snow.

"I don't understand what's happened," she said. "But I will find a way to fix it. I have a feeling we're going to need each other."

As if he agreed, he closed his eyes and sighed, a low, slow exhale that even she could understand.

By the time Talia got into the house, Seild was nearly done making the taf. The entire front room smelled of sweet fruit, a scent that reminded her of sitting in the orness' garden room.

Talia wiped her face with the back of her hand, then brushed the sand from both her and Khee. It was obvious from the little trail of red across the floor that Seild had not done the same.

"Seild," she said, as the girl stirred the drink.

Oh, all the things that came out of her mouth and she could not find this one.

"Your mom needs more time with her... eye egg. To..." She didn't have the words that Ganeth would have had about how it worked, what was happening inside there. Not that those words would have helped much. "To come back to us," she finished.

Seild didn't cry or react as Talia had expected. She stretched up on her toes to open a cupboard, bringing out two cups. One of them was Seild's small red cup, with two handles and a small opening, clearly designed for someone who was as reckless with things as a small child could be. The other was a beautiful green one, etched with flowers and birds, that Isera had given Talia when they'd taken taf together. Talia had thanked her and started to put it in her pack after, but Isera had put her hand on her arm, saying, "You can leave it here if you like. Something tells me that you don't take taf very often in your tiny room beneath the clave."

She hadn't, of course, the kitchen or the supplies for such a thing in her room. Not to mention someone to share the ritual with – unless Khee counted, and she couldn't imagine that meat eater trying something that, while it had the color of blood, did not have any of its essence. She'd said yes, and left the cup here. It was the first small movement toward what they might become, and the memory of it made her eyes sting at the corners.

Enough crying for now. Later, when you're not in front of the child.

"I can't reach my mom's," Seild said. Her voice broke a little on each word until the last one was little more than a sob. "But I suppose..." She didn't finish. *But I suppose it doesn't matter.*

All right, maybe a little crying.

Instead, she forced a soft smile. "We'll take the taf into your mom's room," Talia said. "I bet the smell will make her feel better."

She waited for Seild's small nod, and then reached into the cupboard to take the cup that Isera favored – a pale bowl with no handles, the mottled gray-white of storm clouds.

Talia helped Seild pour the taf. That small opening may have been perfect for Seild to drink from, but it was not perfect for pouring into. Talia splashed it hot across her hands, muttering a low curse that caused Seild to put her hands over her mouth and start giggling. It was a sound Talia recognized. Not pure laughter, but laughter born of worry.

"Oh, you think that's funny, do you?" she teased.

Eyes wide, Seild shook her head, tried to still her laughter. It erupted from behind her hands, though, until her body was shaking so hard from trying to hold it in that Talia thought she might crack apart. *I would spill and swear a thousand times, child, to see you laugh like that.*

The thought was unexpected and sharp as a thorn. *What will you do if Isera dies?*

She wasn't dying. She wasn't. This was just a complication. *Everyone dies.*

She pushed the rest of the thought away by pushing the cup full of taf into Seild's hand. Taking the other two cups, she followed the girl into Isera's room.

Isera was where she'd left her. Perfectly still, except for the slow push of her breath as her chest rose and fell. Of course she was. Only in Talia's hopes would she have gotten out of bed, or even sat up, thanking them for the drink and asking how their day had been.

Talia set the cup on the table next to the bed while Seild carefully climbed backward up on to the bed to sit next to her mother.

"May I say the orison?" Seild was very quiet, nearly as still as her mother, her tiny hands through both handles and wrapped carefully around her cup.

Talia dipped her head to hide her surprise. Saying the orison was typically done by the highest ranked in the room. "You may."

"Moon meld iisrad, shades..." Seild started, faltered. Talia could see her blinking hard, trying to stem the tears that fell anyway. Talia wanted to reach for her, but stayed her hand. She thought this was something Seild needed to do alone. Khee, who was curled in the doorway, lifted his head and looked between the two of them, but didn't leave his post. Seild swallowed, started again. "Moon meld ebeli, memories cleave the marrow. I would ask you for..."

Her bottom lip trembled, and she looked up at Talia with an expression full of pain and fear and confusion. "I don't know... I don't know what I want to ask for. I thought I did, but... I just want her to be all right."

"Then ask for that," Talia said.

"It's not selfish?"

"It's not selfish."

As if she knew she wouldn't make it through the whole thing again, she started at the end this time. "I would ask you for a thing that matters most to me. It is no small thing..."

She sounded like such an adult, already a zaffre, already the head of the house, already leading the orison. The sound of it, so serious and pained, was so unlike her usual light chatter that Talia's throat closed. Someday, she might well be a greyes. Or more – leader of Enthait. Not like the orness, but like herself, in her own way, which might be full of secrets, but would not be full of lies.

Seild paused, long enough to exhale a small, shaky breath. "Awos, I would ask you that Greyes Isera Alhemor – my mom and friend to Poison Eater Tal…" She looked at Talia, panic in her eyes.

"That's fine," Talia said. She had taken no last name, even though it was customary to do so here. Perhaps it was something to think about in the future.

"…Poison Eater Talia – that she heal and be well again." Seild's voice dropped to barely a whisper, so low that if Talia hadn't been sitting right beside her, she wouldn't have heard it. "Bring her back to us, to me and Tal. Finwa, awos. Mihil, awos."

"Mihil, awos," Talia echoed. Together, they drank.

Talia barely sipped hers. It tasted as the poison always did. Bitter, blackened lies.

Seild was looking at her mother. She settled her cup carefully on her lap so that she could take one hand off it to touch the shell that coated her mother.

"It has to work, right? The poisons always promise to protect us."

The stab in the heart nearly doubled Talia over. She couldn't breathe. It was all she could do to stay upright, to keep her cup clenched in her fist. Her stomach flooded with ice, as if she'd drunk the entire cup of taf in a single swallow. Everything in her body told her to tell the truth for once, not to get the girl's hopes up. This wasn't a secret, it was a lie, and she didn't need to keep telling it.

"I'm sure of it," she said.

YOUR EYES

For the first time, Seild was not her escort during the poisoning.

It was one of the other greyes, a man named Athmor. She'd heard others call him Ath, but that had seemed the kind of distinction reserved for people who knew him far better than she did. Or who wanted to know him better than she did.

Athmor was slow of speech, rigorous in h is rituals, leaving her longing for Seild's quick impatience with the process. He'd seemed a little leery of Khee when he'd first entered her room, and she'd hoped that might speed up the formalities, but no such luck. She stood before him, fiddling with the blue-black blade tucked under her armband, for what seemed like hours while he recited each of the proper poisons.

While her instinct was to blame the orness for the change of events, she thought it more likely to do with the fact that Isera was still in incubation. Last time she'd crossed paths with Rakdel – her on her way in, Talia on her way out – the chiurgeon tried to explain to Talia everything that had gone wrong, in far too much detail, and even though she was trying to help, she never actually did. Ganeth wasn't much better. Mostly, he just shook his head and handed her something. Last time, it was a metal triangle that chirped and whirred, but didn't seem to do anything else. She supposed it was his way of offering comfort. Or it was entirely possible that he was just handing her something because he didn't know what else to do with himself.

She understood the feeling. There was a blackness stealing over her that she didn't know how to shake. She slept little at night, often falling asleep over a book midday, waking into the glare, gasping fetid air, the linger of ebony fingers oozing across her face.

To top it off, Seild was angry at her. Well, angry at the world. Talia just happened to be the direction in which the girl's emotions were aimed. And her aim was never off. "It's your fault that my mom is like this. Yours." And there was no way for Seild to know, and so it was just fear and anger, but it was so close to the truth that Talia almost couldn't stand to hear it. But she did – she listened, and when Seild's small fists and fierce headbutts found her, Talia let them come. Seild was the only reason she was standing here now, listening to Athmor drone on and on, giving the poisons power and name they didn't deserve.

She rubbed her fingers together; her thumb was still wet from the ink. Eighth circle, eighth moon, eighth poison. And still she had no plan, no hope, no idea whether this would be the poisoning that killed her. Even if she lived, there would be no Isera after, no Scarlet Sisk. Whatever the outcome, she just wanted to be done with it.

"Poison Eater?" Athmor was finished, standing before her with his thumbs over his eyes. She got the sense he hadn't been talking for a while now; long enough that he'd worked up the courage to nudge her gently. Not a chastisement – she hadn't let him hang that long, but a query nonetheless.

She nodded. "Apologies. I am ready."

The tunnel. The door. Talia went through the process, barely paying attention. Her gaze was inward, toward the shadowed blackness.

Inside the clave, almost everything as it always was. The crowd. The symbols. The greyes standing on each. The orness. It was hard not to see her face now, even beneath her hood. Talia had seen what was beneath Ganeth's device, and there was no way to cover that back up.

Even Burrin was the same. The alert stance. If Seild were here, would she still draw in her breath, afraid? But Seild was not here, and Talia saw Burrin now as he was. Not an ally, not yet, but perhaps not an enemy either.

Only Isera was missing. The empty light shining up through the floor into the nothing that was her absence.

Talia didn't know what she'd expected, but certainly she'd thought *something* else would have changed. But it was the same roar of the crowds, the zaffre in their places, the orness' face still obscured. Even though she knew what she looked like beneath that device, she couldn't find a single feature in the frame of her memory, not even with her standing here, right in front of her.

Everything was the same. Everything except her. Now she knew how false it was. Not just her. But the whole thing. Only the poison was real, only the deaths. A part of her wanted to stand in the middle of the clave and shout out the truth. *You all believe in a farce, a lie! This will not protect you.*

But she didn't. Coward or savior, she didn't know. She was who she was.

And the crowd wouldn't have heard her or cared. Their chants were rising up into the domed roof, feet stamping along the floors, fists to the walls.

There was a new intimacy in the press of the orness' thumbs. Not from something that the orness was doing differently, but from their shared knowledge. A thing that Talia carried in her brain like a seed, a tiny place from which knowledge and understanding began to grow. And darkness, there was darkness there too. A hidden, secret desire. Not vengeance. Something deeper. An unjustness that this woman had the power to hold a whole city in captivity, in falsity.

Except I know something you don't, she thought. *I know that somehow, some way, I am going to bring you down.*

It was the first moment that she believed she might live through this poisoning. What had changed between her room and here? She didn't know. But suddenly she knew: this poisoning would not kill her. And that knowledge bought her time and hope. Two things she desperately needed.

Talia felt the power balance between her and the orness begin to shift just slightly. It was almost as if the orness felt it too, for her thumbs pressed a bit harder to Talia's eyes, turning so that the edges of her nails dug into the folds of her eyelids. *That is the wrong place to start*, Talia thought, just as the sharpness receded and she could see again.

"Do you promise to serve the city of Enthait?" the orness asked. "Do you promise to serve its people?"

"I do," Talia said. And she thought it might be true.

"You may begin."

Talia knelt before the device. She could feel the eyes at her back. The crowds, betting their lives and shins on something that had never existed. Setting their hopes on her, that she would keep them safe. Even more false than she'd thought.

She reached in, touched something hard and sharp. When she pulled it out, it was a purple crystal, squares stacked together, nearly as long as her pinky. Nearly as big around. It smelled of flowers falling open in the heat, but the angles, the length of it... Her throat was already tightening at the thought of trying to swallow such a thing.

The crowd chanted as she held the poison in her palm. "Iisrad! Iisrad! Poison Eater!"

She put the poison on her tongue. It turned into liquid so quickly she nearly choked it back out. Hot sweet spray that rose up the back of her throat into her nose. She coughed, once, a single, sharp bark.

I forgot to say Finwa, she thought. *I forgot to say I'm sorry. I am going to die after all.* And then the poison took her and she went down.

THE POISONING – IISRAD

Cathaliaste, the last of the Twelve Martyrs, stripped herself down, step by step. The sky fell, and she fell. The snow stopped and she stopped. Day broke and she went on, the mechbeast at her side.

Everything of her old life fell away.

The vordcha – their slick, black-oiled bodies glowing red through their skins. The shavings they'd made of their orifices before they'd gathered them back together into puckered and pinched overlays. The scent of their bodies in the blackweave, rot and rut and pus. The needles and injectors and metal weavings they pulled from themselves. Memories. Humanity. She saw them as oil and claw, their fleshless mouths that ripped and tore.

Her sisters, their white-cloaked bodies flowing red through the icing snow. Before that, the moments they'd stolen from the vordcha. Even in the screaming, there was strength.

She thought she had pulled every bit of the vordcha's metal from her, tugging the thin wires of their memory out of her veins, the black stink coated with her blood.

What she couldn't pull out, she'd cut off. Her arm and the bits of her scalp that she'd carved off with nothing more than a thin blade and the grip of her teeth over tongue to keep her still. They lived in her no more. She was sure of it.

She could feel the blue-black shard of Maeryl's blade in its nest inside her thigh. It rested, sheltered in her muscle, the sharpness cutting her away little by little with each step.

The last to go was her name and her title, given to her by the vordcha, its power over her broken into two and then to three, stripped of its ranking, whittled to its core. She would reforge it anew in the wind and the walking. Herself too.

Talia.

She tried the name on like new clothing and the sound of it ripped the seams of the world.

"Talia," she said out loud. It wasn't perfect, but it was better. It was something more like her, anyway. Less like the creatures she'd come from.

Khee

said the creature at her side.

Talia was sure she would never get used to the creature's sudden need to say something. Not an unwelcome intrusion, but an unexpected one nevertheless.

"Khee," she said. To show she had heard.

The creature said nothing.

They moved, far and long. As straight a line as they could, their only sense of direction *away*. They ate little, slept less. The wind and ice hammered them or didn't, and it mattered little. It was as if they both knew that there were only two outcomes: stop for something, anything, and the vordcha would come for them. Keep pressing forward and hope it was far enough.

In days, they were both delirious, hungry. Hydrated, at least, scoop after scoop of snow that was so thick and rugged it was almost like food. She tugged the hardest pieces she could find from the ground, passed it over her teeth and dreamt of meat.

"What do you think they are, Khee? Human? No. Monsters."

Khee answered, words that made sounds into the sky, lined up and then fluttered away like wings. Words that she knew, but the order was off. The letters and lines shimmered, as if she were trying to read them underwater. Or pass them through a sieve that drained away their meaning.

He seemed to know she wasn't understanding it, but didn't have the means or the will to elucidate further.

After a time, the snow softened. Here and there, berries or bugs. Khee's leg was healing, although he limped still. Her arm was, on the other hand, worse. Festering and red, a constant tickling ache, as though she was being burrowed into, stung by a hundred tiny insects. She was hot and then cold, and then hot again, and still she walked. Or was half carried, a stumbling body at Khee's shoulder.

In that way, they passed out of snow and ice into the green of a forest and beyond, to an orange heat that shimmered like a living thing. She felt it against her cheeks in a moment when she was already aching and fevered, and she fell. Not because she needed to, but because she chose. She couldn't hold herself up anymore. And for what? For the constant dream of being found again, of being hunted and brought low by the vordcha. No. She would go here, in the sand.

She could feel Khee watching her. Waiting.

"No," she said. But she was saying it to all the ones who weren't there. Maeryl. Her other sisters. The vordcha. Even the other mechbeasts who'd charged and tumbled and fought her. Her own fear. Her fallen knife, fallen life.

Eventually the sun went down and she rose up. She wasn't well, not in the least. She wouldn't survive this trip across the orange sands, she didn't think. But she owed it to Khee to keep him company, to protect him from being alone for as long as she could.

"We're safe here," she lied. Each word fell from her tongue like a worm, like a root, squirming to the ground. She squished each one, before they could crawl back to the blackweave. Traitors. Spies.

The shadows that walked at night kept her up, creeping on the edge of her vision. Maeryl, with her fingers broken and bloody, sat on the dunes beside her. A bird with triangles for wings flapped on her shoulders, pecked out one of her eyes and drew it, long-rooted, away from her face with its bill.

Seeing her there, Talia understood that this was not true. Not the real, not the memory. Something wholly different. Something with purpose.

The space between them shrank until they were touching, thigh to thigh. Every breath layered in reek and rot. Something squelched through the fabric, bubbled wet against the side of Talia's leg.

"I didn't recognize you at first," Maeryl said. "I couldn't find you in the blackweave."

Her voice was metal and Talia realized her mouth was too. Teeth and tongue and the black hole of her throat. Her face was covered in metal bandages that shone with red from the inside. The braids of her hair were black serpents tied off with their own pink tongues and the blacks of her eyes were spiders that fluttered their legs like lashes.

Her eyes bulged through the bandages, became vermillion buds that bloomed open into pink insides.

"You're dead," Talia said.

"You're saying the obvious," Maeryl said. "Say something different."

She was petting Khee with gloved hands. Gloves that *were* hands. Carved from someone else's body and sewn to her arms at the elbows. They billowed, fabric or synth or skin. Inside them, things small and black shifted and scuttled.

The thing that wasn't Maeryl flicked a hand and ran it down Khee's back. Except it wasn't Khee, not really. It was Khee gone inside out, the red of his flesh a raw and ruddy skin. Sutures, puckered and pink, ran along the lines of his shoulders. The creature shifted, and something inside went the other way, broken and bulging. His four eyes were unseeing, white and thick, running with mucus. His snout lifted – the entirety of it nothing more than three rows of long, skeletal fingers that came together like teeth. Sharpened at the ends. He sniffed the air and blood spattered from the holes in his bones.

like

Or maybe it was

look

the creature said in something that had once been Khee's voice but now was bitter acid in the bowl of her stomach. Talia put her hand over her mouth, trying not to retch.

At her feet, a tree sprouted, slithered up her leg. Blackened and broken at the trunk. The branches darkened with a thousand wings. Each opened its mouth and sang. Knifeblade. Flesh. Spattered storm. The bones of her spine ached with the tremble and caw. Her body snapped, bent backward, up on itself, until she was head and feet touching.

"Why are you here?" she asked with a mouth that no longer worked.

"You know," the thing that was Maeryl and not Maeryl said.

I don't! The words fell from her mouth, into the awaiting beaks below. Fought over. Snapped up before she could reach to save them.

The thing that was Maeryl and not Maeryl held up its cuffed hands filled with milky blood. Each of those hands was Talia's, the skin rotted away to bone and metal. The fingers traced a shape upon a table made of whitened wood. Letters. Then words. Shimmering and white.

Around them, the blackweave grew. It pulsed like a living, breathing thing. A door opened, releasing shadows into the world. Shadows that shaped, hardened, became fleshless mouths that skitched and snapped. Slick black fingers lengthening to reach across space and time, wrap around her throat.

"Beware the salt," the fingers said.

Laughter bubbled from the open sores in Maeryl's face, even as her mouth split into two, unhinged into screaming.

"Charncharncharn," the thing burbled as it tilted its fists. Rain poured down, drowned their feet with bone-white wet. "The sea is coming for you, sister. Fix the break."

She woke, gasping. This time she knew, without question, what was real. It all was. The poisoning and this, her body, the bed, the Painter, standing over her. The charn. The orness. Even herself. All of it.

She *was* the poison eater.

And she was dying.

Not in the blackhang of poisoned memory. In the real.

All those times before had been nothing – echoed aches of pain, a misremembered leaving. This was death in her everything, the very things that made up the weave of her body. She felt them failing, one by one, the cloak of her skin turning inside out.

She coughed into the space of her missing fist, and the air came away from her mouth bloodied and flecked with white.

Beware the salt.

There was no more air, no more breath. None of the things she needed to make words. The poison had taken it all, filled her with its deadly multiplicities, spores that sprouted and grew into the hollow spaces inside her.

"Painter," she tried.

The Painter was already unpacking his paints, perfecting his colors. She could smell them, acrid and dry as mothdust.

"Help me," she said.

"I was not made for succor," he said, "but beauty."

He held the tip of his fingers, brushed and colored, to her eye. The color was right. It always was. The light slanted through the mekalan, shifting the letters across her face.

THE MOON DID MELD US AND WE DID SHINE

"You shall be beautiful upon the wall," he said.

The weave of her body turned again, inside out, the pain of a thousand bee stings beneath her skin. Tearing down the length of her spine. Her vision slid, left her with shadows of shadows. She was nothing left but the bones of her lies. Bleached and broken, a tangled skein.

I couldn't find you in the blackweave, Maeryl had said.

The sea is coming for you, sister. Fix the break.

The mech in her spine. Broken. Khee couldn't talk to her. The vordcha couldn't find her. They wouldn't come for her.

They were all safe. The city, Khee, the others. She had done as the orness asked. She would die as the poison eater. No one would know that she wasn't true.

The poison made her promises in whispers and slantlight. Strokes of comfort across her skin. *One more turn, inside out, and then we'll be done, us and you. All eternity upon the wall.*

She was dying. And she was almost alone. And that was her penance and her poison and her place.

No.

You promised.

Softness?

Coming through the poisoned sweetness, echoing into the hollows left behind. Khee's voice and her voice and Maeryl's and the orness' and Isera's and even Burrin's. Hope and promise and vengeance and something else. That thing she hadn't had a name for. Not in the poisondream, not in the blackweave, not until this very moment.

She hated the words, fought them. She should have cast them out from her as she cast out Khee. Made silence. Just her and the drift of silence now. That's how it should have ended. If she hadn't been a coward. If she hadn't run.

Live.

Shut up. Shut up. Shut up.

But they wouldn't. And under their sound, the poison's

soft tongue grew rough, ripping away at her flesh. It became the long, burnt-scent hand across her mouth. Clackteeth tearing sutures open, that black slick slide of mech between the soft places of her body. Maeryl going dull after, losing days and space and time.

She reached out with a hand that did not exist, and that hand became the thing it wanted to become and it was hexed and light and it grasped the Painter's sleeve.

"I need..." she said. What did she need? So many things. But first. "Ganeth. And Rakdel. Burrin." There were more names, more things she needed, but she couldn't say them.

"I cannot," the Painter said. He was uncoiling the wiring from his device, slow blue loops of metal that hurt her eyes to listen to. "It is my duty to shine you eternal."

"I am not..." Oh, it hurt her to say it, in so many ways. "I am not dead yet."

"Yet," he echoed, and it sounded like he said it a hundred times, a thousand.

"Next time. Next time I promise you can have me."

The sleeve slid from her hand, the light blanking away, the hand turning back to air, back to nothingness.

Burrin was standing over her. How long? Her mouth had nothing in it. Not air, not words. She was shaking. From him? From her own body? It was hard to focus. Her tongue moved like meat long dead.

"Like it better when I can hear you coming," she said.

"We are not that," he said, but his voice carried no conviction. "Not friends."

"Dying."

His expression said nothing that she could read. But his words said everything. "I know."

He thought she'd asked him here to say goodbye.

It might have made her laugh, if she'd been capable of laughing.

"No," she said. "Ganeth. Rakdel. Need them to fix me. Tell them my spine. They'll know." She could feel the poison slinking into her marrow, fighting at the edges of her eyes. "I have to go away now. Mihil, hurry."

She had no idea if he would do as she asked. And she couldn't find the right word to keep herself in the world a moment longer. The blackness took her like a dark ocean and finally she drowned.

Light. Sound. Rakdel's fingers against her neck. She fought the swim, lashed out with her hand and voice even after she knew what was happening, unable to stop herself, waiting for her body to catch up to her mind.

"Thank you," she whispered to Burrin. "Thank you thank you thank you." But she didn't know if she said it aloud, if he could hear her.

Rakdel's hand came back to her, at her shoulder. "We're going to help you turn over," she said.

"I can." But she couldn't, not fully, and it took the four of them – Rakdel and Ganeth and Burrin and herself – to get her face down. Even so, she was panting, spittle-ridden. She soaked the sheet red with her exhales.

A moment later, Khee's fur was under her fingers. She closed them, tight, across the softness.

"I'm going to give you something," Rakdel said. "For the pain."

"No." She couldn't be out of it. Couldn't be drowsy. She needed to be here, to be present. To see if it worked. If she was going to fight through this, she was going to fight through it.

"There's going to be a lot of pain," Rakdel said.

The sound coming from her throat was a bark. "I know." She wasn't a masochist. Pain didn't interest her in that way. She was so many levels deep in pain that there was nowhere more to go. She could handle it. She needed to handle it. "Don't dawdle."

Before this, she'd forgotten pain. Living in Enthait *had* softened her, some.

She made it through the first cuts, the way she could feel the skin open across her back, but when she felt the first tug of the mech in her body, she howled. Pushed the sound through the fabric into the air and it was the song of every pain she'd ever carried. Hers. Maeryl's. Her sisters'. Khee's. All of them. Every break and slice and agony came back to her in a rush, and she breathed them out with the force of her whole voice.

Khee pressed against her, a weight that meant something even in her red-black bruise of anguish.

She felt someone's fingers – Ganeth's, likely, for he'd been smooth and sure up to that point – falter, and she broke the clench of her teeth apart to inhale. "Go," she said. "Keep going."

Ganeth and Rakdel talked above her as they worked. About the mech. But even after her wails had quieted to sobs and sniffles, she couldn't understand their words. She could hear Burrin, pacing, metal steps, steady, sure, around the room.

Finally, the numbness came, and with it, a new understanding. She would not run. Somehow she knew that to be true, in a way she never had before. She would not run again. No matter how the end came, she would stand strong. She would fight with Khee at her side. And whoever else joined her. She would fight.

Words came through the haze at her. Ganeth's voice. "I think it's fixed."

Rakdel's voice. "How will we know?"

And, a moment later, as if in answer, as she hadn't even dared to hope,

like.

She would have jumped off the cot and buried her face in Khee's stripes, if not for the fact that Ganeth's hands were still at her back. Closing her up. She could feel the tug of her skin, the shifting of the mech beneath it. Pain, but also a tingling satisfaction as he pulled each stitch tight.

When she *could* sit, she pressed her hand to the side of Khee's face, savored the weight of his head, the intensity of his gaze. "Welcome back," she said.

yes.

She could tell they all had questions, but she didn't have the strength to answer them. She didn't even have answers. "Can I talk to Burrin for a moment?" she asked.

When they were gone, all except Khee, who she couldn't bear to let go of – her fingers were still curled in his fur – she said, "Burrin, something's coming." It was her turn to skip the formalities.

"Something always is."

"No," she said. Her throat was raw, and her voice came through shards of glass. "Something real."

He glanced away from the mekalan at her. She didn't look at him. He touched a painted face. Then another. She waited for Burrin to make his next move. The eyes of the dead, watching her. Eternal. Eternity.

Burrin waited, one beat, two, and then looked back

over the painted faces.

"What are you saying?"

"Burrin, I think…"

She thought of Maeryl – because now in the after, she could tell it *was* Maeryl in the poison dream. Not the Maeryl she had known, but Maeryl in the only way she could find to connect.

And Khee too. Khee telling her to look. And she had.

Winged creatures of metal and mist.

How had she not known? How had she not put that together? The deliberate slicing away of memories. The vordcha weren't the only ones.

"The charn are coming," she said.

Burrin snorted softly. Disbelief. She didn't blame him.

"I saw them in the poisoning. It's a long story, but they're coming… they're coming because of me."

She'd expected him to call her a liar. Or perhaps to laugh. He was looking intently at her face.

"These are the moments when Isera is sorely missed," he said. So many layers in that, Burrin peeling one back for her, if only for a moment.

"Do you believe you are the poison eater?" he asked.

The question caught her so off-guard that she answered honestly. "Yes."

Oh. Oh.

"Good," he said. He looked out over the mekalan. The light came through and cast his face in colors. "Because I think you are too. Isera thinks you are. Seild and Khee think you are. You are the only one who does not believe."

The orness. The orness did not believe. The orness had told her so. *The poison eater is a lie.* But what if it wasn't? What if the orness was wrong? Or a liar herself?

She had a million things to say and not a single thing to say.

"What do you need?" Burrin asked.

"I need..." What did she need? She was so surprised by his question that she couldn't think of the answer at first.

The vordcha felt most real after the poisonings, Talia realized. Why? Because of the memories. That was the thing about memories. You had to look at them, didn't you? Revisit them? In order to keep them alive. The vordcha had pushed their memories into their martyrs so they didn't have to keep them.

But they didn't understand that all they had to do was not look at them again. Keep them locked up, in cages, and pretend.

She needed the opposite. She needed to tell the story to someone. She needed to keep those memories, that fear, alive. And the only person she could share it with was the one person she was afraid to.

"I need to wait until Isera has healed," she said, and was surprised her voice showed no signs that she didn't know if Isera *would* heal. "And then I need to tell you a story. All of you. Ganeth, Rakdel, Omuf-Rhi."

She could see him trying to decide whether to ask more questions, trying to decide whether to say yes. She only had part of a plan forming in her mind, but she had enough to know that she didn't think she could do this without him.

"Do you trust me, Burrin?"

"Not even a little bit," he said. But when he held his fingers up, there was just enough space to see the light between them.

•••

A few days after the poisoning, Seild's prayer worked. Or Ganeth's mechskills did. Or Rakdel's healing. Talia wasn't entirely convinced they weren't all the same thing. When you said a prayer and science answered, wasn't that exactly what you'd asked for?

"Everything should be normal now," Ganeth said, although it was clear as he sprayed the sheath with a mister and the entire thing dissolved instantly that he had a different idea of normal than she did. Ganeth had suggested she send Seild and Khee off in the world for a bit, just in case things went poorly. She'd done so, but not without a sense of worry at his words.

Her concern was not lessened as she looked down at Isera, silent, still, her breathing shallow, her eye still slathered in pulsing goo.

The goo came off with a soft sucking sound. Beneath it, Isera's grey eye was wide open. It blinked twice, contracted with the noise of wings, and then closed.

"I have to get this back into the tank before it dies," Ganeth said of the goo, which was seeping out over his palm with soft undulations. "Surprising how often I use it."

Talia didn't even want to think about that. She could barely get the sucking sound of it leaving Isera's face out of her mind. "I'll stay with her," she said.

He hesitated. "Rakdel will come soon."

She nodded. "It's all right," she said. "I can do this."

She sat on the side of the bed carefully. The movement shifted the scars across her back, tightened her skin. But not as bad as before. She was healing.

Shortly after Ganeth left, Isera came to. She tried to sit up, groaning softly. It was like watching someone come awake after a long night of too much drinking. Or perhaps much like what the Painter saw after a poisoning.

"No," Talia said. She put her hand on Isera's arm. The contact jolted her; had it been so long since they'd touched? "Not yet."

For a moment, Isera's face looked foggy as if she couldn't remember what had happened to her or where she was, but quickly her expression cleared.

"Talia," she said, and fell back against the pillows. She looked as healthy as Talia had ever seen her. The blue in her hair brought out flecks of navy in her new eye. "Seild?"

"Good. Off with Khee," she said. "Probably giving him fighting lessons."

At Isera's look of confusion, she shook her head. "Everything is fine. Ganeth was just here. He chided me for sitting on the side of your bed, lest I shake you too hard. But I'm doing it anyway."

Isera laughed, soundless, her nose wrinkling up. Talia kept going. "Can you imagine if I'd told him that I let Seild or Khee come and say hello while you were in there? I think he would have challenged me to a round of saglo. Although, let's be honest, he wouldn't have won."

Still laughing, Isera put her hand over her grey eye. Talia could hear it whir, adjusting. Talia tried not to imagine what she would see, sitting there. Were her old lies something visible, like a cloud around her?

"For someone who doesn't seem to care much about anything that's not made of mech, Ganeth can be funny like that," Isera was saying. "How his emotions come through. When I got my head ripped open by a ravage bear a few years back, he yelled at me the entire time that

Rakdel was stitching me up."

Talia didn't want to think about Isera and a giant bear either, claws and skin, but now the image wouldn't leave her.

"Ganeth says you're doing great," she said. "That you were lucky."

Lucky. Except not really, because it was some kind of horrible unluck that she was stuck with a woman whose lies had put her in harm's way. No. That was a place in her head she wasn't willing to go. Not again. This one wasn't her fault. Not entirely.

"I feel lucky," Isera said. That half-smile, crooked. "And I can see you, your whole self, with both of my eyes, which is lovely."

What can you see?

It's my job to see true.

Part of her wanted Isera to call her out, to say, "I see everything," so she could come fully clean. But Isera didn't. And that, no matter what Talia wanted, was better anyway. She had to do it herself. She was almost ready. She could feel it building in her. No more lies. She needed just a few days, a few perfect days with Isera before she broke everything to pieces with truth.

"I do believe you've gone soft while you were in there, Greyes Isera," she said.

"Not soft. Starving. Dirty. Surprisingly tired. Is this what it's like when you eat the poison?"

She didn't know, but it seemed close. "Probably. Similar," Talia said. She didn't mention that she'd almost died. She was sure Isera would hear it soon enough.

"Do you wake up wanting me as much as I woke up wanting you?" Isera asked.

"Probably. Similar." But now she was teasing, and it showed in her words.

"Then you should kiss me so that we can find out."

She did, and they did. It turned out the answer was yes.

III. onysa

THESE TONGUES

For a few perfect days, while Isera recovered, they fell into a routine. A slowlife of little more than flirting with Saric over saltpetals, watching Seild and Khee playfight in the yard, playing a few rounds of switchfall, a game that Talia was horrible at, but which she kept winning anyway because Isera had no poker face. Burrin and Ganeth came to visit, some of the others, for dinner or taf.

Isera's eye grew stronger each day. By the end of the week, she'd be back in uniform.

To Talia, it felt like a beautiful day when you could see the storm just off the horizon. It wouldn't, couldn't, last, but she was refusing to look at the proof. Not yet, she kept thinking. Not yet. Just one more day. One more day before she had to tell Isera the truth. One more day before she had to step down that path of ending everything.

That day came sooner than she expected. She and Khee were walking through the moonmarket, ostensibly in search of a pastry Isera liked. Something called ternes. But it was more than that. Talia wanted, needed, to touch the city with some inner part of her. To hear it and feel it around her. To connect with it. Eyes and hands and heart. Sometimes she expected it to give her some kind of clue as to what she was doing. After all, it was the city she was supposed to be protecting. But other than its occasional song, she found the city to be silent on the matter.

Khee pressed in beside her and she found herself reaching out to touch his fur periodically. He moved into her touch, and each time she was comforted.

If the Eternal Market was where the goods lived, then the smaller, more hidden moonmarket was where the secrets lived. Here, the crowd was furtive, silent, heads down and hands in the shadows. Keeping to themselves. There was something hidden in every pocket, every transaction, every face. The roads here were split and scarred, broken down the middle, making it easy to lose one's footing, and it gave people a perfect excuse to keep their gaze on the ground.

Permanent stalls were rare here. Each person was their own store, carrying their supplies in boxes, or their hands, or small hovering carts. There were no saltpetals here, no frivolities, no music. Food, weapons, addictives, here and there clothing designed not for fashion but for furtiveness.

A woman in an ornate wheeled chair rolled by, pushing herself over a sharp ridge in the road with a grunt. The brim of her tall, wide hat was covered with long sticks, each of which gave off a small blue glow and the scent of lemony incense.

Talia found a food vendor by smell, bought him out of the dried jerky that hung in long strips from the pole he carried over his shoulder. She threw a piece to Khee, and tucked the rest into her bag for later.

"Ternes?" she asked of the other food vendors as they

went by. Most shook their heads. But one, a young man wrapped in a too-big coat topped off by a wide belt, nodded. He pulled open one of the sacks hanging at his waist, brought out a synth bag of yellow buns covered with some kind of seeds.

"Two shins," he said. "For the whole of them."

She was pretty sure they were stolen. Likely from one of the vendors in the Eternal Market. But they looked fresh baked, so maybe not. Plus, he was scrawny. Even his fingers holding the bag didn't have enough fat on them, the knuckles concave in their swirls. She gave him three and nodded her thanks.

"This is going to be good, Khee," she said. The words sounded like lies before she even said them. "I still don't know what's going on, exactly, but I'm figuring it out. And I have ternes. Whatever they are."

The bag smelled good, a bit savory, a bit sweet, so they couldn't be all bad.

On the way out of the market, they passed an old man on the corner, his back curving like a letter, who wore a banner across his chest. She caught something of it out of the corner of her eye as she went by, like a snatch of a dream. She circled back.

He reached out to her, blindly, his hands grasping.

"What is that you wear?" she asked him.

The man straightened himself so that he stood almost upright – she could tell it pained him – and showed her the painted fabric upon his chest. For a moment, she thought she'd been mistaken, that it wasn't a banner, but one of Angha's blankets.

But no, it was just her face on the fabric that had make her think that. Her face, painted on the banner. Blue eyes.

Blue cloak. The artist had taken liberties – lengthened her nose, removed the red streaks from her hair, but it was easily her.

And above her face, in bold silver letters: CROSA.

Careful.

In the bottom corner, it bore the mark of the orness. An etched star.

She put a hand on the man's shoulder, acknowledging that she'd seen enough. He lowered himself back down gratefully.

Bending her knees so that she might be at his eye level, she asked, "Where did you get that banner? Who asked you to wear it?"

"They paid me six shins." As he answered, she caught his eyes in the moon sliver – covered white, unseeing orbs.

"Do you know who?"

He shook his head and touched the edge of the fabric. "What does it say?" he asked.

It says I'm in trouble.

"Finwa," she said. "You can take it off now," and tucked her remaining few shins into his fist.

No one else would see that banner, she knew. It was a message for her. From the orness. She was watching, waiting, for Talia to make her move.

Talia knew she should be scared. But if anything, the orness' not-so-subtle message awoke an anger in her. Born from a sense of justice, or perhaps fear, she found that she grew more angry, rather than less. She couldn't remember the last time her blood sang in her ears the way it did when she'd seen her face on that banner.

CROSA.

She spat the word out. She'd be damned if she was going to be careful now. She still didn't have a handle on what exactly the orness' game was, but she would figure it out, and when she did... she didn't know yet. But she would figure that out too.

What she didn't want was for her anger to pull her from the bigger, more important danger: the vordcha. Sometimes, tucked as she was into this city, inside these walls, they seemed so far away, so unreal, that she had a hard time keeping them at the forefront of her mind. The details were fading. Slippery as snow.

The orness was a monster, yes. But she wasn't a monster like the vordcha. She was just here, now, and that made her scarier and bigger than she deserved to be. It was time to tell Isera the truth, all of it.

The silver spiral on Isera's door both beckoned and turned away. But Talia had had her fill of turning away. She would leave this choice in Isera's hands. It was possible she would want no part of it.

Isera poured them drinks – a fizzy thing that went up Talia's nose, but was more savory than sweet. If she wasn't thinking on other things, she would have taken the time to realize how much she enjoyed it on her tongue.

But she needed her tongue for other things now, and so she only took a sip before setting her glass back on the table.

"I don't know where to start," she said. There was so much to the story. What mattered, what did she need to keep alive? The horror, the fear. She needed to hear how dangerous, how inhuman they were, even if from her own mouth so she would not forget. So that when they came, she was not unready.

"Start with you," Isera said. And it made sense to her, and so she did. Talia told her the thing she'd never told anyone, barely even herself, about being given over to the monsters. Although, of course, she hadn't known then that they were monsters, so perhaps those who had given her away hadn't known either.

lies.

Khee was right. She'd known everything they were the first time she'd seen them. Even at her age.

She backtracked, picked up the thread she'd dropped when she'd told that lie, and went forward. She told of the implants and mech the vordcha had slid inside their veins. How it gave her memories and emotions that weren't hers. She told Isera of Maeryl, and their escape plan. How she'd run, fallen, craven. And returned, only to fall again.

It came out in a rush. Not a story, then. Not like the ones she'd woven for her sisters, for Burrin. This was how the truth sounded. Broken and tattered.

She even told her part in the lie. How she'd believed she wasn't the true poison eater, but had told no one. She skipped over the orness, Seild, the device, kept it on her tongue. Seeds for later.

Through it, Isera sat, quiet.

"I'm done," Talia said. She was. Spent. Exhausted. Unsure that she had accomplished what she'd set out to do. The vordcha seemed both more and less real now that she'd talked about them. Scarier, but also she was just so tired.

"Can I ask questions?" Isera asked.

Talia nodded. Of course. Her hand was shaking, and she wrapped it around the glass to keep her fingers still.

"Are they human?"

Talia searched for the answer she wanted, knowing the near impossibility of trying to describe something that was both human and inhuman. Something that for so long had been her only understanding of the world. She had forgotten what small life she'd been allowed to live before the blackweave, and that made everything the vordcha did seem normal. At least, it had until Maeryl. Maeryl, who had come to the vordcha so much later than the rest of them. Maeryl, who'd remembered the ocean and her family and her love and even her language before the vordcha had begun to take it away.

"They were trying their best not to be human," she said. "Maybe they were once. But I don't think so."

"What will they do, when they come?"

"Destroy everything," she said. "Except me. Possibly Khee. They'll take us. Make us what we were. Something worse." She didn't want to think about that part. They would not kill her. They would take her, back to that place, fill her full of metal and mech. She would die here, by her own hand, before she allowed that.

She didn't say what she knew in her heart. That they would also take Seild and maybe others. Their mechbeasts and martyrs were dead. It was possible they were already searching, filling the blackweave with new ones. More than possible. Probable. In fact, she thought that might be why they hadn't come for her yet. They were rebuilding an army. So that when they did come, she could not say no.

"I'm sorry I lied to you," Talia said.

Isera shook her head, and Talia could feel her heart, the way it unmoored and began to plummet through her insides.

"No," Isera said. "I told you once it's my job to see true. That isn't the same as seeing the truth. Sometimes, the truest things must be shrouded in lies to keep them safe." Talia thought of Burrin, of Seild, of the orness. Had the orness told her something false to protect something true?

"I don't know how to stop them," Talia said.

Isera leaned forward, put both of her hands on Talia's real arm. "We'll find a way."

And in that moment, beneath the fierce mismatched gaze, Talia felt hope begin to bloom. And something else too. Something that made her nerves spark and sing. Not the city's knife-edge song, but something fresh and clean and new.

As soon as she told Isera, it felt like time was running out. She didn't know why, but she could feel it in her blood, in the mech in her back, in the way Khee's stripes started flaring random colors at all times of day. Seild giggled and clapped her hands each time she saw it, but Khee was less thrilled, sharp-toothed and growly, pacing and sending wordless questions to her.

She didn't think the vordcha were coming yet. But they would be soon. Not just for her and Khee. They would not pick and choose. They would destroy every bit of the city, everything inside it, if they could. She'd known that for a long time, even if she was only beginning to come to terms with it.

She needed to find out when and how. She needed to do another poisoning. And she needed to do it now. But first, she had a promise to keep. A story to tell.

If there had been a way to tell Ganeth ahead of time that she was coming, she would have. She knew he had devices, ways to communicate with others from far away (how we love our Aeon Priests), but he'd never given her one. And so she ran.

Flat out, ungainly, huffing breath. Grateful there were no crowds to weave around. Grateful for the way in which her clothing shifted with her and did not get in the way. Even grateful for the jostled pain in her spine, for it reminded her, each step, what she was running for. Khee in such a long, flat-out run that he sometimes got ahead of her, had to circle back.

She hit the door of Ganeth's shop still running, and caught her cloak on the doorframe. The fabric wouldn't tear and it wouldn't come loose and so she stood in the doorway like a child, yelling Ganeth's name while she yanked at it.

He was dressed in the giant yellow suit that she'd first seen him in. It disappeared as he pushed a button and came forward.

"I need..." she started, still stuck in the doorway.

Ganeth shook his head, eyeing her cloak with a wince.

She gave the fabric another yank, and it came loose from whatever outcropping had held it, nearly sending her tumbling into Ganeth's questioning form.

"You've ripped the–"

"Please, Ganeth," she said.

Ganeth took her wrist. A steadying. She nodded in thanks, but also in surprise. Had he ever touched her before, in a gesture not related to a device? She didn't think so.

"I need you to get..." Each word a panted breath. And here she'd thought Khee was growing complacent and out of shape in the city. "To gather the others. It's time."

He didn't ask for what. She knew then that Burrin had told him. Prepared him. *Moon meld you, Burrin.*

"I have message capsules somewhere around here," he said. Which made no sense to her, but she'd run too far and too fast and couldn't ask another question yet.

He rummaged along the shelves nearby, pulling things out, putting them back, muttering. "Here," he said, as he held up four synth capsules, each nearly as long as her hand. "Just record your message, and then say a description of the person. It will find them."

She took one. She'd expected it to feel odd – cold where it should be hot, squishy where it seemed solid – but it was just an ordinary capsule. Off-white synth. Heavy for its size. "Just talk?" she asked. "No button or…?"

"Just talk," he said.

She did Isera's first, a little embarrassed to know that Ganeth was standing there as she described her. When she was done with it, she looked up. "Now what?"

"Now it…" He started, and then the capsule disappeared from her hand. Her hand, still clutching its shape, suddenly empty. "Now it does that," he finished.

By the time she finished all four of them, she was already used to the sensation of weight leaving with such suddenness.

"It shouldn't take too long for them to be delivered," Ganeth said. To the question she was about to ask he said, "Finwa, of course I'll meet you there."

Unable to run anymore – the jostle had awoken something in her back – she and Khee walked to the Sisk, where she hoped the others were waiting. She had so much to tell them. And to ask of them. There was every chance they would turn their backs on her. And they had every right to. It was dangerous. More so than she could have even explained.

Her back was sore, but manageable. Rakdel had given her gel to ease the pain, but she hadn't used it. Now she wished she had.

"Khee," she said as she walked. "I think..." It was tentative, barely an idea. "I think the orness lied to me. About me being false. About the poison eater being false."

Or did Talia just want and need that to be true? Because she had made all this plan and because she needed a weapon, and so would build one out of belief, just as the citizens of Enthait built theirs. From nothing more than stories and dreams and plays for children.

Stories were not nothing. But they were not real either.

And no. There was something else.

She picked her way over the uneven flagstones of the street. They were nearly to the bar and she slowed her steps, needing to figure out one more thing before she went in.

"The orness wants me to believe it's false, but yet... she wants me to keep taking the poisons."

why

Khee nudged.

"If I knew that," she said.

She could tell Khee was trying to lead her toward something, something she needed to see. But it was like the orness' face behind her device. Too slippery to grab hold of with her vision. She was grasping at shadows, at snatches of song. Nothing tangible enough to make it stay.

"I'm going to keep talking and you keep asking questions

until I get this right."

He exposed his rows of teeth in a long yawn, then stretched at her feet, but kept pace with her. Tacit agreement. And a bit of poking fun. He clearly thought that her speed at sorting things was not up to proper pace.

"Is she trying to kill me? No, I don't think so. She's a monster, but she's a monster with a plan. And I think that plan involves me staying alive. Not because she cares about me, but because she cares about Enthait. In fact..." She wasn't sure of this. She waited to see how it sounded coming out of her mouth before she took a stance. "I think she wants me to become the orness."

Khee didn't disagree. He just said,

and.

"There is always an *and*," Talia said. "But I don't know it. I don't."

Her back felt raw, stung each time her cloak moved over it. Rather than let it distract her, she sank into it, into the pain.

"And..." she tried again. Waiting to see what would come to her tongue. "The orness is old. Older than that visage she wears."

She'd reached the end of the road, could see the bar's soft light from where she stood.

"And when she's no longer the orness, she's going to... what? Spend time playing grandmother to Seild? 'Hey child, I know you're my granddaughter, but guess what? I threatened to have you killed.'"

no.

"You're right, that's a little harsh. She didn't threaten to kill her. Just to stick her full of poison while she said a finwa over her."

no.

"That's not a question." Her voice came out harsher than she meant it to.

Khee stopped at the door to the Sisk, looking at her. Waiting patiently for her to understand… what?

"What is it, Khee? Why lie? What is she trying to protect? And from whom?"

Sometimes, the truest things must be shrouded in lies to keep them safe.

Oh.

"I'm not the bee, am I?" she said. "She was trying to tell me, even then. And I missed it, completely. The whole thing."

She had to sit down in front of the door, butt to the rough layers of cobblestones, head resting against the hard wall behind her.

"The orness is the one who's dying," she said.

yes.

"And it's all my fault."

The Sisk was quiet in the way that only public places can be quiet. A low murmur that, she hoped, would drown out their conversation. She didn't know how the orness knew things – it was one of the things she meant to ask Ganeth tonight – but she needed her not to know about this. If that was even possible.

Ziralyt gave her a nod as she entered, and she paused a moment, to see if there were any other signals he had for her. Instead, he came forth and clasped her shoulders, dropped his head to hers in greeting.

"Moon meld you, Poison Eater. It's been a long time. Your friends are in the back."

We are not friends, Burrin had said. And yet she wondered. She'd had sisters and captors and lovers. Enemies. Allies. Were she and Khee friends? Any of them? Maybe. No matter, there was a chance they wouldn't be after what she was about to tell them. But she thought they might still help her anyway.

"And you, Ziralyt," she said. "Will you bring us drinks? Something strong. And something for Khee if you have it."

He nodded, cast a quick glance at Khee, who bared his teeth in a playful way. Or at least, *she* knew it was playful. Probably to everyone else it just looked like he wanted to eat them. "Affah."

The goldglam was there again, dancing to a much smaller crowd. Dressed in reds and oranges, a burnt sunset swirling round and round. Hair wrapped up and up and tinted gray-white, so like storm clouds that Talia nearly expected rain to begin falling as she walked by.

Everyone had come. Part of her wanted to stop a moment, to sink into that, but she was afraid that if she stopped, she would not go forward again.

They all sat round the table, a tension in their shoulders. Isera had changed into a grey outfit, something that seemed to flow over her when she moved. She played her fingers over and over the rim of her glass, endless circles.

Burrin, still dressed in his zaffre uniform, had leaned his sticks against the wall and was waiting, his hands folded. Ganeth was at the end of the table. It felt like the first time she'd ever seen him sitting, and it reminded her of how wide he was, how much room he took up. And yet, he worked with such small, small things. Rakdel had come and, she was happy to see, Omuf-Rhi.

They were talking, here and there, but mostly quiet. As soon as they saw her, they made room. Khee laid himself under the table at her feet, sighing loudly enough to make them all laugh. It was strained but it broke the tension, softened their faces around the table.

Everyone waited, silent. She fidgeted with her hexed hand. Ziralyt came back with drinks – a clear bottle filled with honeyed liquid, and glasses. He knelt under the table and gave Khee something she couldn't see, but a moment later, she felt Khee's teeth crunching something hard against her feet.

Burrin poured. When all the glasses were full, she lifted hers and the others followed.

"Moon meld us and mold us and keep us from harm," she said.

"And we shall shine," the others said.

She took a sip, held back the cough that came with the burn. Something strong, she'd said. And Ziralyt had certainly obliged.

She waited until everyone had drunk.

"I need to tell you a story," she said. Unlike all of the other stories she'd told – to her sisters, to the zaffre, to herself – this one needed to be true. As true as she could make it. After her experience telling part of it to Isera, she thought that she could make it pretty damn true. But not without help. "This is going to be hard to tell and hard to hear," she said. "And so I ask of you to listen and wait to the end. Because more than anything, I am a coward, still."

She felt the prick of tears at the corners of her eyes, startling in their urgency, and forced them back. "...and if you give me any reason to pause, any at all, I will fall."

They were quiet and still, and she took that as a yes, and
so she told them everything. She started with the parts
that Isera had already heard. The vordcha. Her sisters and
their attempted escape. How she had run, craven, fallen –
Isera touched her hand at that, and Talia both felt like she
didn't deserve the kindness and felt like she needed it so
badly she could not have turned it away.

And then she told the parts that hurt to say. How she
had come to Enthait and lied to all of them, in order to
keep herself safe, in order to have control of the device
that could destroy the vordcha, but that could destroy of
them as well.

Isera had moved her hands back to hold her drink,
almost protectively, at that. Talia did not blame her. She
knew the risks she was putting on the table.

She'd told it true, and each bit of the story was like a
stone that she was setting aside. By the time she was done,
she was both empty and heavier than she'd ever been.

The only thing she hadn't told them yet was what the
orness had told her. It wasn't that she was afraid or even
that she was following the orness' wishes–

threat

Khee said from under the table.

You weren't even there, beast, she thought, though not
unkindly.

She took a sip of her drink, could see, out of the corner
of her eye, flashes of the glam, who'd stopped dancing and
was now sitting at a table nearby with a handsome young
couple. They were laughing, and she allowed herself a
moment to envy them. They weren't much younger than
she, but how different their life seemed. To have spent it
all under the promise of safety here in Enthait. Real or

otherwise. Did she want to take that from them? No.

No, she would keep that part from all of them. For now. Because she wasn't sure if the orness had lied, and she almost thought she understood why. But it wasn't all altruistic. There was that other part too. To make her plan work, she needed them to believe – not just in her, but in the orness, in the device, as well. And telling the orness' story would cast a question over all of them. Was it fair to ask it of them, to join her when she wasn't telling them everything? Was it fair to tell them everything and then expect them to still join her? She didn't know.

Monster.

This voice was neither Khee's nor Maeryl's. It was all hers.

Not as much as her.

Comparing yourself to a worse monster does not make you not one.

Fair.

"I know the vordcha are coming. But I don't know when or how. The only way for me to know is to do another poisoning. Now, not later."

She stopped, breathed. She didn't have any words left. She was pretty sure she'd used them all up. Her throat felt raw, and she took a sip of her drink, hoping to ease it, but it was scratchy and made her cough instead.

The silence stretched.

"What do you need us to do?" Burrin. Who hadn't taken a drink beyond that first toast.

It wasn't what she'd expected. "Don't you have questions?"

"That wasn't a question?"

"I mean…" She swept her hands at all of them. "About

the rest of it. The things I just told you."

They looked at each other, side eyes, expressions that she almost caught. Even now, she knew the language, she knew the stories, and still she was the outsider. Even Ganeth seemed to understand what was happening better than she did.

Finally, it was Isera that spoke. "She speaks true."

"Your eye?" Burrin asked.

"No," she said. "I don't need it."

Burrin looked at Ganeth, who nodded.

"Then yes," Burrin said, "I do have a question. It is: what do you need us to do?"

She would have hugged him, if that was a thing. But she didn't think it was. At least not with Burrin. She supposed she could invite him to a fight and kick him in the groin again, but that didn't seem like the kind of thank you she wanted to give.

She could only duck her head, her cheeks flushed, and mutter, "Thank you" into her glass.

"First, I need answers. Ganeth, how does the Eye work? How does it find the dangers?" she asked. Then wished she hadn't, for she couldn't follow his explanation. It was *datasphere* and *nanotech* and *the numenera* and she gave up after the first minute and hoped it didn't matter. She got the gist of it at least.

"And the orness' device, the aria?"

"Same thing, I imagine," he said. "I've never seen it."

The surprise must have shown on her face, because he lifted a brow at her in question. "You didn't make it," she said, flatly. Starting to understand the length of things.

"I didn't make the Eye either. I just understand it better, because I've seen it. I have no idea what the aria is. They're both far older than I am. Some say they're from the before city."

"The one in the clouds," she said.

He looked surprised, but nodded. She noticed Omuf-Rhi drinking his shot, and grinning a bit, almost as if he were proud of her.

"Do we know what the aria looks like? Maybe like the Eye? Only bigger?"

Ganeth pressed his lips together in thought. "It isn't always true that the more powerful a thing, the larger the size. But I would guess... something powerful enough to do that kind of damage would need to be bigger. Bigger than the Eye. Not certainly. But likely."

"I don't..." It was Omuf-Rhi, speaking for the first time. "I don't understand how the charn and the vordcha connect. Are they the same creatures?"

"I wish they were," she said. "And I didn't understand the connection either. Not for the longest time. The poisoning was telling me. I just couldn't see it."

Out of all the things she'd said, this was the one she dreaded speaking aloud the most. Because until she said it, it was just a wild belief that lived in her head. One that she could deny. Saying it made it real. An undeniable possibility. She *was* the poison eater. She *had* seen the danger and had pretended she hadn't.

She closed her eyes, found that memory deep beneath her skin and called it up. Sifting through it was like sifting through glass shards. No one cut deeply, but all together, a thousand tiny pains.

"I think the charn are creatures that we, the sisters, thought of as the swarm." Just saying the word made her shiver through snow and blood. "Like a scouting party.

They sting with this kind of…" She shivered remembering it. "Numbing venom."

Burrin leaned in, his arms long on the table. "You're telling me that the charn, the creatures that fill our tales, that created this entire thing…" He circled an arm at her. Meaning: the poison eater, the orness, the aria. "That's just their *scouting party*?" The phrase was full of incredulity.

"I wish I could say no. But yes." She felt Khee's warmth against her feet beneath the table. "And then they'll send creatures like Khee."

She reconsidered, in no small part due to Khee butting her in the leg with his head. "No, not at all like Khee. They're all different, modified somehow. I think they start with different kinds of creatures. And then they build them for war, for killing. Not just killing. For…" She stopped, trying to find the right word. The extra teeth, the barbed claws, the skin pulling away slowly. What words for that? "For killing," she finished lamely.

"And then the vordcha will come?" Isera's eyes flickered in the pale light.

"I think so," Talia said. Then changed it to a more confident, "yes."

"Why didn't these vordcha come before?" Omuf-Rhi asked. "The stories don't tell of anything after the charn."

She'd been thinking about that herself.

"I think the first time, they were just scouting. Looking for new martyrs. But the orness, the city, fended off their charn and the vordcha decided Enthait wasn't worth it." Talia thought of all the ways and places her sisters had been chosen – small towns, traveling parties, out alone. Few came from large cities. Maeryl, but she'd been on the sea by herself when she'd been taken.

"Then…" Omuf-Rhi continued, "why will the vordcha come now?"

She tasted her answer on her tongue before she gave it, bitter and sour. "Because of me. They'll come because of me."

"I guess we'd better figure out how to stop them, then," Burrin said.

"Wait. Before you say that, you do understand that this is all my fault, right?" she pressed. "I am bringing these creatures here."

"You're telling us the obvious," Burrin said and, for a moment, it was Maeryl's voice coming from his mouth, and she shuddered, hard enough to splash her drink. She cupped the glass with her hexed hand, brought it back under control.

"Then I'll say the other, which is even more obvious: if we try this plan, it could destroy the city. Not just me. All of us. We might not get out in time. We might not take out the vordcha. We might…" her voice trailed away. She was suddenly, deeply, tired.

"You forget. It's your job to see the dangers, Poison Eater," Burrin said. "It's our job to stop them."

The plan they came up with was easy. No. Easy was very much the wrong word. It was simple. Which, as far as Talia was concerned, was the best kind of plan.

Burrin and Isera asked questions about strategy, about the vordcha, about the way they fought and thought.

"Let's say that it's true – the myriad, the charn – are just the first wave," Burrin said. "That's taken care of."

Talia started to say, "It is?" but closed her mouth. Of course, he thought it was. She hadn't told him about the orness, about the possibility that the device might not even exist.

How can you believe in you, and not believe in her? She didn't know.

Before he could ask it, Burrin went on with his plan-making. "So, then the... what do you call them?"

"Mechbeasts."

"Mechbeasts. The vallum will help with those, Ganeth?"

Ganeth was doodling something on a piece of paper. From where Talia sat, it looked like a belt with a number of weird devices hanging off it.

"Yes," he said. "It's well-stocked – it's been ages since something made its way to the actual city walls. We'll have the leavers do more."

Leavers. That must be the name for those who worked the vallum's non-mechanical protections. It was a good name.

"You really think the vordcha will come?" Burrin asked.

"I don't know," she admitted. "I have always assumed so. They seemed like they would. But not until we are beaten down. Not until they know we will be cowed and... easy."

Isera sucked in her breath, then tried to cover it with an exhale, as though she'd just been breathing normally.

Burrin was pulling out the device that held his map and Talia didn't think he'd noticed Isera's response, but he paused in his own gesture for a moment before flattening the map.

"From the south?" he asked.

Talia nodded, watched the city unfold across the table. She pointed to the place, beyond the map, where she thought she had come from.

"The vordcha won't come until the day. They don't..."

She wasn't sure what word she was looking for. It wasn't "sleep." They didn't seem to sleep, ever, but they stayed indoors, in the shade. "They burrow. Cocoon. I don't have a word for it. They won't expose themselves at night unless they have to."

"Is that a weakness, something we can exploit?"

"I don't think so. It's not a weakness. Maybe a preference." She wasn't sure.

Ganeth had stopped drawing and was tapping a small cylinder. She'd thought he'd stopped listening. But then she realized he was recording something.

"Do they breathe like humans?" Ganeth asked.

"As opposed to…?"

"I mean, do they have lungs, mouths? In and out of some body part?"

"I don't… I don't know."

yes.

"Khee says yes." How Khee knew that, she had no idea. But she trusted him.

"I could create some weapons that create traitorous nanoparticles. Disperse it as a gas of some kind. Something that only affected them."

Talia just shook her head. "I don't understand any of that, but I trust you. I trust all of you. You do those things. I will convince the orness to perform the poisoning ahead of time."

Maybe it wasn't the best plan, but it was the only one they had.

Getting to the orness presented a series of challenges. The first was that Talia had long since lost the star pit. Where had that gone? She had so few things she was usually better about keeping track of them. But she had scoured her pockets and her room after the poisoning and had found nothing. It was possible that she'd lost it in the garden. Likely, even. Perhaps the orness had taken it from her somehow. It seemed a thing the orness would do.

The second challenge was that she could not make the skar door open for her. Neither breath nor hand nor song had changed the stones from barrier to entryway.

She had decided to go alone, over everyone else's objections. "I should come with you," Isera said.

"I think it has to be just me," Talia replied simply.

She didn't say why. Because if, as she believed, the orness was dying, it was because of her. And that meant there were only two ways the conversation could go. Talia could actually convince the orness that the city was in danger and that they could use her help. And the orness would offer to help.

Or the orness could try to kill her.

Either way, she didn't think her case was going to be helped by showing up with a crowd. "Plus, you have other things to do."

But as she stood at the base of the skar, she wondered if what she was doing was some kind of skewed attempt at penance. She hadn't saved those in her life before this one, so she would save those in her life now.

Too late now, and she couldn't seem to get in anyway, no matter how much she scrabbled around the stones. Finally, she threw up her hands. "Orness, if you see everything in this city, then you know I'm standing here and that I would like to be let in."

Pretending that she didn't care, she surreptitiously pressed her fingers to the base of the skar. Nothing. She didn't know why she thought that appealing to the orness would work. The orness had shown herself to care for nothing and no one more than her city. Certainly not her own child or grandchild, and certainly not Talia. Protecting the city was a fair belief to hold, she thought, but perhaps slightly misguided in its execution.

She kicked the stone base. Speaking of misguided. The material was so hard she felt it reverberate in the bones of her foot.

Someday, Talia, you will learn to plan better. I don't mean one step ahead. I mean three. Four even.

One of the mirrored orbs hung at her shoulder. She caught her reflection in its surface. It looked, just for a moment, like a very small version of the Eye. She reached out and grasped it with her hand. The orb shocked her, sending a dull ache up her arm and into her shoulder. She dropped it, pulling her fingers back with a swear.

The orb fell and shattered, reflective pieces going everywhere. "I hate you," she said, and she didn't know if she was talking to the orb, the orness, or the face she saw reflected in the shards.

She dropped her forehead to the stone, letting its rough coolness dimple her skin.

"Mihil," she said. She had stopped talking to the orness now and was talking to the city. Or some entity. Maybe some device. Gods and metal were all crisscrossed in her brain. Who could know where one ended and one began? "Mihil, Enthait. I know I've been a liar and a thief and a coward, but I am those things no longer. And this time, just this one time, I need you to trust me. I need you to let me in."

From above, she heard three clean, clear notes. She

looked up. A tiny fluttering mechanical bird was resting on an outcrop just above her. It opened and closed its wings with an impatient flick, then whistled the same notes again.

She could have sworn she heard Ganeth in her head. *I expect it will come back at some point. Probably when you need it most.*

Talia echoed the notes into the doorway. Or tried to. Nothing happened. She'd always been the storyteller, but not the singer. That had fallen to Kanistl, her sister who sang in a tongue so beautiful and clear that even her joy songs had made Talia cry.

"Again, please," she asked.

The bird sang, and she echoed.

Again. Getting further from where she wanted, needed, to be.

She closed her eyes, and when the bird started, she did too. Matched it.

A moment later, she could put her hand through the material.

"Thank you." She didn't know who or what she was thanking, but the gratitude was enough to make her heart thump to her ribs.

Talia stepped through the door and fell down and down. She thought this time would be easier because she was expecting it, but no. She braced for the fall, and felt the jar in her knees and her spine as she landed.

The garden smelled thick and wet. Not at all the green lushness that she remembered. Fragrant flowers and fruit and honeys. This was the beginning of rot, an undercurrent of things turning toward decay. The air seemed thick, sluggish. Little brown spores seemed to linger in front of her face, falling impossibly slowly. She didn't hear or see another person. What was happening?

The moss was squishy beneath her feet, not soft and spongy but sopping, wetting the soles of her boots with each step. She'd been following the orness last time, listening, and hadn't realized how complicated the paths were. She'd assumed a single curve, following the circle of the Green Road, but that wasn't how it worked. Every path branched and forked, following its own logic.

She remembered a few landmarks from last time – the trees, the beehives, the entryway to the orness' garden. She would walk until she found one of them and then figure out where to go from there.

At the first fork, she took a left. Something about it seemed familiar, and then a right – that too, seemed like a thing she remembered, but it wasn't very long before her memory had failed her completely. This was as bad as being in the tunnels. Worse, because of the sense of urgency she felt. With every step, she could hear the poison dream in her head saying *charncharncharn.*

Soon, she was out of light, and thought that, impossibly, she'd spent the whole day here, lost, sweating, swearing beneath her breath. But after a moment, she realized that she had moved, to be beneath the clave itself. Here, things grew too, bracken and pale green plants that opened into deep wells, half-filled with liquid.

The earth was wetter here, the moss deeper. Water splashed against the bottoms of her boots even when she stayed on the path. Fish creatures with two legs jumped or swam out of her way; their movement was erratic but fast. Around her face, she sensed and heard, but didn't see, winged creatures that seemed to dip and dive. She swatted at them, and their low buzzing moved back, but returned a second later.

A tiny black creature – bird or bug? – no bigger than her thumb, dive-bombed her face with a spray of air that was acrid and bitter in her nose. She sneezed, and the movement carried her off the path just enough to step into water up past her ankle.

Skist.

This was not at all how she'd planned for this to go.

She should go back, retrace, but by the time she realized it, she thought she was already halfway across the clave. She moved straight across, on the one path she'd found that didn't seem to turn and split. The clave was huge, and she had no idea what she'd find on the other side. But she needed to get out of this shadow, which seemed to grow heavier with each step.

Finally, she could see light ahead, slanting in long rays through the trees. She moved toward it, panting a little. The shade was somehow hotter than the rest of the garden, and she was heavily sweating. Even her hexed armband was irritating her skin, sweat and salt, and she popped it off and put it into her pocket. A mirrored orb wafted past her, clinging around her head until she brushed it away. It let out a low squawk, but didn't stick around.

In front of her, a synthsteel building stood there, shaped something like an egg. Archways around the bottom of it. The glass was frosted, but she could see movement inside. Light, blinking blue, then yellow.

"Come, Talia." The orness' voice came through the material. It was still weird to hear her name in the orness' mouth. She wasn't sure she'd ever get used to it.

A door irised open, and Talia stepped inside.

Someone was sitting in a chair. Not a regular chair, but one made of synth and steel, big. Wires and tubes ran from it into the floor. It swiveled around to face her, but Talia couldn't see how it worked.

"Well, that took you longer than I'd hoped."

It was the orness she knew in voice alone. Seated upon the chair, which looked much too large for her, the orness appeared shrunken and hollowed out, as if someone had been scooping at her flesh. Beneath, her cheeks dug into her face like sinking caves. Her eyes too were sunken and bloodshot.

Talia lifted her thumbs to her eyes. Not out of habit so much as for the opportunity to hide even part of her face briefly.

"I am impressed," the orness said, and followed the words with a rasped cough. "And here I didn't think anything could shock you into that expression. You're usually so..." The orness lifted a bent and gnarled hand and ran it through the air in front of her face. "Stonefaced is the expression I've heard. But I appear to have done it. Or, rather, my appearance appears to have done it."

"You really are dying," Talia said. She hadn't meant it to sound so matter-of-fact. It was just that she hadn't entirely believed it until this moment. "I'm sorry. That was–"

"Nothing more than the truth," the orness said. "Besides, I might have had an inkling."

Talia had known in her heart that she was right about the orness, but she could not have guessed it was like this, so soon. Last time she'd seen her, the orness had been standing, as she always did. Tall, straight. Wearing her cloak and her false face and pushing those nailed thumbs against her eyes.

"Each time you live, I die a little more," the orness said. "That's the way it works. The way it's always worked." She lowered her voice a little, as if telling Talia the secret. "Will you talk with a dying woman, Poison Eater?"

Poison Eater indeed. After all the things she'd told her. Everything in her wanted to say *no*. What right had the orness to ask that, even if she was dying?

It wasn't pity that turned her hand, but need. She needed the orness as much, perhaps more, right now than the orness needed her.

There were two chairs across from the orness'. Nothing so elaborate or tall, so she chose the one closest and sat. The heat and wet were far worse than last time, even though there seemed to be a kind of cooling mist coming through the glass. It brushed against the back of her neck, chilling her, before it moved on to some other spot in the room.

At a barely visible movement from the orness, one of the guards appeared, set a pot and a single cup on the table. "Taf?" the orness asked.

"No." It was impolite to refuse – beyond impolite – but she couldn't bear to sit there and sip a drink and smile and make useless prayers as propriety. Not now.

The orness barely allowed a response to show in her face, although she said, "I didn't think so."

"So then, let's talk," Talia said. "About your lies."

The orness coughed at that, and it took Talia a moment to realize she was actually laughing.

"Oh yes," she said, after a moment. "*My* lies. My lies are to serve the city of Enthait. What do yours serve, other than yourself?"

Rather than look at that question and answer – she'd

already done so, thank you very much, and did not care to do so again – Talia felt a pang of something like delight. The orness had practically just admitted that she had lied.

"Were you lying to me? Or did you just not know?" She thought she knew the answer to that. The orness was many things, but she was not naive. Surely she had known everything she'd said and done. Talia wanted to hear her say it. She didn't know why. She guessed it was because it seemed like the time when everyone was finally, finally coming clean. If she had told her truth, she thought it was high time the orness did.

"Of course I knew." She almost sounded offended.

"So you're telling me you threatened your granddaughter just to play with my belief system?"

If the orness reacted to that, Talia couldn't see it. "You believed that I threatened my granddaughter. I quite like the child, even if I never do get to see her anymore."

Anymore. She wondered what that had looked like. Had someone brought Seild down here for a nap and taf? She didn't think so. More lies? Wishful thinking? Or something else?

"Why, then?" Talia said. "Why all of it?"

That sound of disappointment through her teeth. "You are smarter than this. Why do you continue to ask me questions that you already know the answer to?"

"You chose me because I was new."

"And?" As if it was Khee and not the orness. Egging her on. But also helping her understand when she was on the right path.

"Because..." Talia filtered through everything in her brain, tried to put the pieces together. "Because I didn't believe."

"Because you didn't believe," the orness echoed, simply, as if she was surprised that it had taken Talia so long to figure it out on her own. "I could see it in you, each time you came to take the poison. You thought you were false."

"You told me I was. You told me everything I knew was false. I believed it."

"And what…" the orness coughed into her closed fist. It was wet and, if her face was any indication, painful. "…do you believe now?"

That you lied. But more than that. "That I am the true poison eater. That there is such a thing. That I will eat the tenth poison and I will become the orness."

"If the tenth doesn't kill you."

"I was never false, was I?"

"You never were. You just needed to *believe*. Heart and head. Through all doubt, through all the lies, through your own needs. Through me. To serve Enthait, you had to believe in it, so that it could believe in you."

She gave Talia a meaningful gaze. "And so that others could believe in you."

Talia was no longer surprised to understand that the orness had likely seen or heard their entire conversation last night. It was likely that the orness had been watching her from here as she'd yelled and screamed to the sky, trying to get in.

"What if I didn't believe? What if I'd died? Walked away?"

The orness lifted her thin shoulders, barely a movement beneath her shirt. "There are others."

It stung. Not the words so much as the dismissal. Because even now, after everything, in some small part of her heart, she believed in the orness, in the poison, in the eternal promise of all of it. That she was chosen by something – or even someone – greater than herself. *Wanted to believe. It's not the same thing.*

Isn't it?

She didn't know.

"Others," the orness repeated. "But not like you. I think that if that had happened, we would have lost a lot of lives to the Eye after you. But I believed in you. Even when you couldn't. Even when I couldn't say it."

"I think you are a monster."

"As you will be some day, when you are sitting in this chair. As all of us become." She sounded sad and tired, and less like herself than Talia had ever heard her.

She didn't want to pity the orness, and she certainly did not want to like her. Or be like her.

But she needed her. As much as she didn't want to.

"If you know everything, then you know what I am about to ask," Talia said. "I need you to hold a poisoning. Now. Not on the moon. I need to know if they're coming. And when they come, I need you to use the aria."

The woman began to laugh, a taunting, phlegm-racked cackle. And then she stopped and wiped the back of her hand across her mouth. She was an old woman now, Talia thought, and she did old woman things.

"Yes, that's the way it works, isn't it?" the orness said. "It isn't enough that we must die to protect the things we love. It's that we must die in some enormity of destruction. You die before you know whether your sacrifice was for everything. Or nothing."

"Orness, the city needs you to protect it."

At that, the orness lifted one papery hand, put it to her face. "I cannot help you."

Anger, fierce and hot, swept through Talia. She stood, stepped forth. Close enough to touch her. Close enough to strike her. She did neither.

She knelt, looked up into the face of the old woman and made it so she could not look away. "You talk to me of roles? This, this is your only role. To help the city. And you deny it. You are a monster. Far more than I ever thought."

The orness shook her head. Her voice cracked, broke against the hands that covered her face. "You still don't understand," she said. "It isn't that. It's that you still haven't made your choice."

That was unexpected. The orness' admission, the truth that threaded through her words, took all of the fire out of Talia's anger. "What… do you mean?"

"I have been the orness for longer than you can imagine," the orness said. Anger of her own now, flaring up, although Talia didn't think it was at her. "More than a hundred years. I've been kept alive by that damnable device."

She laughed again, and this time it was as bitter as any poison. "I thought I was important, needed, and so I did my role. But the city never needed me. It… made me watch while it killed people. So many people. For what? Nothing."

The city was not responsible for those deaths. Talia let it go, unspoken.

"I kept its secrets. I told myself it was for the greater good. For the promise of an attack that never came. But I did it. At first because it was my role. But then because the Eye demanded it of me. After so many years, I gave up on finding another true poison eater. But I pretended.

Because of Burrin. Seild. I had to keep them safe."

Oh. Oh. "So you put them in the zaffre," Talia said. "Where they could learn to protect themselves."

"Yes. I knew the Eye wouldn't let me die until it found another."

"And here I am," Talia said flatly.

"Yes," the orness whispered. "There you were. You came from the outside, like I did. Those from here, they believe because it's all they've ever known. That's not enough. You didn't believe. But I knew, I hoped, that you would come to do so."

"The lies..." So many lies. Would she have come to believe on her own? Probably. Possibly. But maybe not as strongly. Maybe not strongly enough.

The orness struggled to push herself from the chair. Fell back. Talia did not move to help her, but she did lift herself from her crouch and go to sit across from her again.

"Maybe Ganeth can help you..." Talia started.

The orness shook her head. "Maybe once. I never took him into my confidence," she said. "Although I should have. He always was loyal. So loyal." Her tone suggested there was something else, too. Something deeper than loyalty, once. "It was stupid. But I was still young. And prideful. I wanted it to be a big secret, something just for me. And now it's too late for that."

She lifted one aged hand above her head, pointed to a cluster of mirrored orbs that Talia hadn't even noticed.

"The Eye is watching. Always. I tried to tell you." *CROSA.* Not a threat. A warning.

"What happens now?" Talia asked.

The orness looked for a long time at the orbs, saying nothing. Then she gestured. The two guards stepped forward. "Take her," she said.

A little overkill, Talia thought. She found her own hand resting on the red hilt of her blade. But the orness waved the guards down. "No, no," she said. "Take her to see the cicatrix."

To Talia, she said, "Go and tell me what you learn."

Talia knew the word, but not the place. She'd studied Burrin's map when she could, had found others in Omuf-Rhi's stacks. She knew the names of all the places that were marked on the city, all the buildings and towers and bars. After her first trip to the green she had the names of the skars, although they still slipped through her fingers sometimes, when she tried to recite them.

But she'd never seen anything with that name.

The guards – she assumed they were zaffre due to their blue and bronze, although she'd never seen them before, and had no names to give them – were not rough, but they were firm. They led her along a series of paths, some of which seemed familiar, some of which did not.

"You can probably let go of me now," she said to the one who was still holding her wrist. Some of the paths were not made for two people to walk side by side, and one or the other of them often ended up in the brush. "I don't think I'm in trouble or anything. Am I?"

If the guard heard her, he didn't acknowledge it. She wished she had one of Ganeth's devices now, to send a message and update everyone. She wondered how their tasks were coming along. Hopefully a little less confounding than hers.

The guard stopped before a large door in the garden. Just… a door in a doorframe. No building around it. It was bright red, and bore four keyholes. Plants grew all around it and a little stone pathway led up to it.

"Go," the guard said, as he let go of her wrist.

"Um… where?"

He looked at her, squinting one eye as if he thought she might be a touch slow. "Through the door."

So she did. She opened the door – despite all its keyholes, it was not locked. On the other side, she could see the continuation of the garden and the path she was standing on. If this was another trick of the orness, some kind of ploy or punishment, at least it was original.

"Go," the guard said again.

She stepped through the door – she heard something whir and click above her head – and by the time her foot came down on the other side of the frame, she could tell she was somewhere else. Alone. In a big grey room filled with nothing but windows. Somewhere high up, from the grey tone of the sky and the drop in her stomach. Higher up even than the blackweave.

Out the window, through a glass that warped and bent as she neared it, she could see the entirety of Enthait. All of it. Without turning her head. As if it was condensed into a smaller, tighter version of itself. From here, the clave, the skars. The Eternal Market shone like a silver spiral, like the zaffre's symbol in living, moving form. The thing she couldn't figure out was, if she could see the entire city from here, laid out in front of her, then where was she? At first, she'd thought she was in one of the skars, but that wasn't possible. Not if what she was looking at really was the city.

The city, the city was a cicatrix. Not just in name. It was the shape of a star, one that started at the clave and ran

out through the five biggest skars in the city. You couldn't
tell when you walked along it; the scar was too big, too
ingrained into the elements of it to show itself. She thought
of the rough streets in the moonmarket, how they seemed
gouged from the earth. And the Break itself, how the place
where the wall crumbled perfectly matched the scar that
ran through and past the Moon Skar.

Standing here, you could imagine two things: one, that
a giant creature had come to the city, and attempted to
destroy it, pawing the earth, leaving a scar that would live
on for aeons to come. The other, and the one she thought
more likely: that something had come to destroy the city
and whatever had killed it had started at the clave and
spread outward to the skars.

*And there shall in Enthait be a weapon, so grand, so glorious,
so powerful, it shall destroy all of the enemies and all of the beasts
and all of the living and all of the dead and only the orness, the
keeper of the aria, shall remain.*

The weapon wasn't something inside the city. The aria
was the city.

The guards brought her back to the orness. Who already
looked older, more frail.

"What do you know now?" she asked.

"The aria is the city," Talia said. "The device is too. And
so are you. Threaded together. But the myth says that if
you use the aria, you're the only one left standing."

"Do you believe that?" The orness' words were soft,
mostly breath. It was clear that she was tired. Death was
coming for her on rapid wings. They both knew it, but
neither wanted to say so again.

"Yes," she said. "Because that story isn't about the city,

is it? It's about me. The enemies, the beasts, the living, the dead, they're all the things inside me that make me who I am. That make me human." She felt the push of blackened hands against her lips and suppressed a shudder. She'd always thought that the vordcha had made her less than human, but no. They had only made themselves less so. She understood that now.

"You can choose to save yourself or the city, but not both," the orness said. "The aria has its costs."

Of course it did.

"What did you choose?" Talia asked.

The orness smiled, and in it, a glimpse of her younger self. A glimpse of Burrin and Seild. A glimpse of who she'd once been, once hoped to be. "You thought me a monster once," she said. "Do you think me a monster still?"

Talia chose.

Weirdly, she was not afraid. She leaned in, took the orness' hands in her single hand.

"Will you help me serve the city of Enthait? Will you help me serve its people?"

The orness looked at her, her eyes flickering between the illusion of health and her own white globes, already falling toward blind. "I will try."

SHALL SING

The others spent days preparing the city. Talia helped where she could, but there was so much she didn't know, so often she watched, and gave answers where she could about the charn, the mechbeasts, the vordcha.

Ganeth and the city's mechmakers had gotten the vallum built up even higher than before. It wasn't useful for the charn, which flew, but it would be useful for the things that came on foot. Mechbeasts and vordcha alike.

"Are you sad about this, Khee?" she'd asked. "They're your brethren."

not.

Burrin, Isera, and Omuf-Rhi had taught all of them as much as they could about what was coming, sometimes asking additional questions of Talia. Rakdel had stocked the clave with supplies. The zaffre, too, were ready. Everything was in place, as much as it could be. The only thing they didn't know was when the vordcha would come. And there was only one way to tell that.

Ganeth had made her the belt from his drawing, something heavy and metal, with a series of tabs and buttons and devices across it. "The only one you need to worry about is this big blue one," he said. "I think. I hope... that this will work to keep you here."

"No," Talia said, shaking her head with a laugh. It felt good to laugh. Her body was tense, strumming like a wire in the air. "Tell me what that means. In me speak."

"It should let you go to the... wherever it is you go in the poisoning, to see the danger, but it will also keep you here. So that you can see us, and tell us what's going on. So you can talk to us while you're in the poisoning."

"That sounds... horrible." For you, mostly, she thought. But she understood its purpose, and knew what he was hoping to do.

"So I push the big blue button when I take the poison..."

"Yes, just as."

"And then I will see the poison dream, but I will also see all of you?"

"And talk to us, yes. So that you can tell us when they're coming, or how many there are. Or anything else that you might forget if you were in the dream alone."

"You're sure this will work?"

And Ganeth, who often looked at her like he didn't understand her one bit, gave her a look that went so far beyond that she had to laugh again. "Of course I'm not sure," he said. "But everything–"

"Wants to be something. Yes, I know."

"And that's what this thing wanted to be."

The day before the poisoning was going to take place, all of the group that had gathered around the table with her at the Sisk had gathered at the clave. Seild, too, who gamely took part in whatever was going on, even though no one had told her and she'd somehow got it in her head that they were having the most glorious game of hide and seek ever. Which lasted until she decided to start lifting Khee's sleeping paws, to see what he was hiding beneath them. It was Omuf-Rhi who came to the creature's rescue, pulling Seild away with a gentle word. Khee had opened one eye, watching the two of them walk away, and then said,

like.

And a moment later,

both.

The orness came up from the gardens. She was in her chair, without her mask, and there was a long moment of silence when she first entered. No one, it seemed, knew who she was at first.

So Talia said, as loud as she needed to for her voice to carry, "Moon meld you, Orness," and put both fists over her eyes until she could hear the others begin to follow suit. Seild, ever oblivious, ran right into her. She fell hard enough to the clave floor that her thud almost covered her, "Ow, Tal!" Khee lifted his head, seemed to realize she wasn't hurt, and then dropped it back down.

Talia reached down and helped Seild up. The girl wore the red ribbon in her hair again, as she often did lately. Talia ran her fingers over it. "Did your mom give you this?"

Seild shook her head. "Nope!" Then she leaned in and whispered quietly in Talia's ear. "Burn."

It took her a moment to figure out what the girl was saying, since much of the word became spit and false whisper at that close range.

"Burrin gave you this? Really? It's beautiful."

"I know! And saltpetals!" She twirled it over her fingers. Seild leaned in for another excited spit-whisper, and Talia did her best not to cringe. "He used to scare me, but did you know that he's really very nice?"

"I did know that," she said, wiping the wetness from her ear. "But we shouldn't tell him, right? Because he likes to think he's mean."

With big eyes, Seild nodded solemnly. "Right."

Khee padded over, just in time to get a kiss from Seild on both sides of his head before she ran off.

wet

he said, as he shook his head.

"You're telling me."

Talia watched the others work, sure that they were missing something. Sure she'd forgotten something. Sure that everything was about to go wrong.

From across the clave, she caught sight of Isera, standing in the light of one of the symbols. It lit her up like fire, her blue hair a special kind of flame. Isera caught her gaze, and her face opened up. Lit up. Couldn't close back down.

She felt hope flutter somewhere inside her, soft as moth wings, and she crossed the floor to go to her. Maybe things would go right after all.

This poisoning was different than all of the others. Almost no one in the city knew it was happening. They hadn't waited for the moon. The clave was so silent Talia could hear her own breath.

They went through the rituals of the poisoning, because they didn't know if they had to and it seemed risky not to. Talia had waited in her room in her robe for Seild to come and get her. The three of them had gone through the tunnel, and this time Talia did touch each color of the wall, stroking them calm before they could snap at her, saying someone's name aloud as she did. She didn't think she'd come through here again, although she couldn't say why that was.

For the poisoning, the clave held only Burrin and Isera, Khee, the rest of the greyes, Omuf-Rhi (because he refused to be left behind), and the orness.

The orness could no longer stand, but it was hard to tell. Sometimes you looked at her, and you could see the chair she sat in, the sallow skin. But blink and she stood before them as she always did.

Still, when she pressed her thumbs to Talia's eyes, her hands were firm and barely shook at all.

The orness started to say something, but Talia could tell it wasn't what she should be saying, and she shook her head. She already knew the orness' sorrow, her failure, her shame. But those didn't belong in the ritual. The city needed her focused, or the whole thing was going to go crosswise.

"Do you promise to serve the city of Enthait?" the orness asked. "Do you promise to serve its people?"

"I do," Talia said. "I do."

The orness lifted her thumbs from Talia's eyes. "You may begin," she said.

Talia reached into the Eye, hating the moment of it, that space where her only remaining hand left the world and entered whatever was inside the device.

The poison this time was in the shape of a blue-black blade. Pointed as the one she owned. At first, she thought it *was* the one she owned. But this one was smaller, leather-like and with finely honed edges.

She glanced at the orness, who nodded. *Ready.*

She hoped so.

She looked at Isera, standing upon the light. The mismatched eyes. The tiny scar from the ravage bear. The way she was fiddling with her weapon, anxious, nervous. For Talia. For all of them.

Finwa, she thought. *Forgive me for what I am about to do.*

Then she put the poison to her mouth and swallowed.

She pushed the button on the device on her belt at the same time. Her whole body vibrated, hard enough to shake her teeth, jar the bones in her spine.

For a flicker, she was both here and there, present and memory and future.

She heard Isera whisper across the space, "Stay, Talia. Stay."

And she did her best to obey. But it was so hard. The past pulled and pulled; it ached to have her back, and she nearly went with it. It's like the orness' face, she thought. Look at one thing.

And behind her, through her, the blackweave. Something moving around inside it. She was in both places at once, and yet neither place.

She could still see Isera, but barely, as if she was watching her through Ganeth's device. No, worse than through Ganeth's device. Just her edges moving, as if running toward her.

Once she knew her feet were on the clave ground, Talia focused on the blackweave. And stepped into it.

THE POISONING – ONYSA

The blackweave was waiting for her. Somehow, she had known it would be. Rows upon rows of torn and tangled trees, oily bark dripping, snaked black limbs slithering in on themselves endlessly. And in the middle of them all, towering above the others, its dark branches straight and long and climbing toward the sky, the place she'd once called home, because she didn't understand what home meant. Was supposed to mean.

Darker, bigger, more alive than she remembered. The crisscrossed black tangle breathed and slavered, yellow spittle from its torn-thorn mouths. Flowers grew here and there, so purple they were nearly black, furious fists closed around a dozen deadly insects.

The smell. She'd forgotten the smell. The pungent dirt and festering rot that somehow drew you in and repelled you at the same time. An acrid burnt smell so bitter it made her stomach roil. It was like eating a thousand nyryn petals all at once, being forcefed them by a brazen hand.

The feeling she had in the pit of her stomach was one she'd had before. That wrenching twist that comes from knowing something is about to go wrong, but being unable to figure out exactly what it is.

She moved toward it, although every sense in her body begged her not to, begged her to turn and flee.

"I will not flee," she said. And heard her own voice, and a moment later, the sound of something in the forest moving toward her. She stilled, quiet, listening.

She'd run through this thornforest only once. Snow and fear and her sisters, and she barely remembered it. Other than the tearing. Pushing the pathway through the trunks, they grew so tight together, so coiled and entwined, scorned and thorned, lovers intent on taking the lives of all who stood in their way.

She stood there, on the ground that had once held snow and blades and the bodies of her sisters, and she was ready. She would kill the vordcha. Every one. And this time, she would not run. This time, she *would* go down swinging.

"I am Cathaliaste, the last of the Twelve Martyrs of the Forgotten Compass. I killed your martyrs, your mechbeasts. Come and claim me, if you can."

There was no sound, no response. Everything once alive here was dead.

If this was a waiting game, she did not know if she could win. Make your move, you monsters. Please. One way or another, she needed to finish this. She was a device winding down to its last use. Everything that you run from catches and kills you eventually, and she had been running for too long, dying for too long. Eventually, was here.

The skies overhead went gold. Wing and sting. A million mouths clacked and closed.

Charn, she tried to say, but the words were lost in the press of slick black skin to her mouth, the loss of everything as they cut off her breath.

She found the button on the belt Ganeth had given her. She pushed it. And nothing happened.

"They're coming," she said, and she was back in the clave.

Talia came back to the sound of the world cracking open.

From somewhere behind her, Khee was growling. A silent response that Talia felt like tremors in her stomach.

Everyone else was still watching her, the orness, the Eye, which was spinning wildly, erratically. As if it was going to roll off some invisible pedestal and fall, cracking, to the earth.

Overhead, the strongglass ceiling made a popping noise, like it was being compressed by giant hands. A crack opened up on one side, spread along the curved dome with a series of crackles and pops.

Talia wasn't spurred to action until she felt the first fine shard of strongglass rain down upon her face. She blinked away the sharp dust and then glanced around. It wasn't supposed to happen now, already. They weren't ready.

But they would be. They had to be.

Burrin was already calling the greyes into action. They had been stilled momentarily, in shock, watching the curved dome as it split open.

That ended as the shapes began to come through the holes. They flew down, open mouths and wings like blades. The ceiling came with them, huge pieces of glass falling down in rainbows.

Perhaps it was the darkening of the sky that held their attention. Giant swarms of creatures. Four sets of wings that spun the air so fast they were impossible to follow.

Grotesque fat bodies, wrinkled and sloughing off a stream of off-white wherever they went. Despite their size, they were fast. They were predators to start with, before the vordcha had gotten hold of them. And big – twice as big as Talia. It was amazing that they were able to stay aloft, much less move with such alacrity. They should never have been able to get off the ground.

But they were ravenous and aggressive, and so the vordcha had made them something that they never should have been. Their wings were gold colored, but she thought they might have been built of bones and wire, run across the middle with some kind of skin. It was off-white, thin enough to let through the light, carefully stippled in patterns that seemed designed to catch and maximize the air flow around and over them.

Long spines stood up out of their backs, tipped with a glowing blue substance that somehow looked both dangerous and painful. Two tails whipped around their body, metallic barbs on the ends of both. Their faces were all mouth and teeth, great opening maws that left little or no room for eyes or noses or ears. They smelled their way toward her with their purple, flickering tongues, flicking in and out, scenting the air, looking for her.

"Greyes, in your positions!" Burrin was already running to his. Isera too. The others were running for the posts. Charn circled down around them, reaching and clawing. The other zaffre were doing their best to protect the greyes who stood in the pools of light.

Talia glanced around for Seild, found her and Khee already huddled together off to the side. She knew Khee's every instinct was to fight, and as always, she was grateful for the choices he made.

The orness was moving her chair toward the middle of the clave. Talia ran to help her. As she neared her, the orness lifted an electric prod from her lap and aimed it at a charn that was closing in on her. It met the blue zap of electricity head on and screamed, plummeting to the floor.

The orness had left her chair and was down on her knees, opening a small door in the dais. The door slid back, at first nothing but a black emptiness. And then slowly, slowly, a tall device, a miniature version of a skar began to rise. It shifted as Talia looked at it, almost like the Eye did. Sometimes showing one pattern in its sickle shape, other times showing another.

The orness played across the designs with nimble fingers. Talia couldn't draw her eyes away from what she was watching. A repeating pattern, not complicated, but the timing seemed important. Sometimes the orness would wait a beat, two, before touching the device again.

"Take hold of the Eye," the orness said. "Keep it safe."

"It's going to kill you."

"Everything has its role," the orness said.

Talia didn't want to touch it. She reached for it.

And stepped back into the black.

This time, it was not the blackweave waiting for her. Nor the vordcha.

It was Maeryl. Not Maeryl her sister, not Maeryl her friend or lover, not Maeryl of death in the snow. Not Maeryl of the onysa.

But Maeryl that was all of them and none of them.

Talia lifted her thumb to her eye and bowed her head. The gesture meant nothing to Maeryl, she knew, but in truth, it was not for her.

"You're still dead," Talia said.

"Not dead, sister," Maeryl said, and her voice was venom and metallic spit. "You didn't leave me for dead. You left me for rot and ruin. You left me for them." She spat this time, and a gob of black landed on the ground and began to crawl toward her.

Just a poison dream, Talia. It's not real.

But it felt real. And far off, as if that was the dream, she could hear Isera saying something. *Come back. We've lost her.*

"They've lost you," Maeryl said. "Too bad. You're here now."

"Where are the vordcha? Can you tell me? Will you tell me?"

Maeryl raised and fluttered her bladed hands. "They seek. They search." Talia couldn't think about that, not yet. "And the beasts too. Gnashing teeth. Clashing claws."

"And them?" Behind Maeryl, the blackweave breathed, shuddered.

"I cannot say." Not wouldn't. But couldn't.

Talia nodded. She needed to get back to the others, tell them what was coming, but first, something else.

She stepped toward the blackweave. Maeryl mirrored her. "Do not, sister," Maeryl said. It was half threat, half plea.

"Will you keep me from my task?" Talia asked. She didn't know what her task was, exactly. But she had a wild idea that she would go to the blackweave and burn it to the ground. End it all right now. Even if just in the poison dream.

"If they make me." Her answer told Talia much, as Maeryl no doubt had intended it to. Maeryl was as trapped by them as she'd ever been, perhaps more so.

Maeryl opened her face and–

•••

A searing pain cut across the top of Talia's face. She heard Burrin behind her, the slice of the long blade as he opened the creature's skin, the beating wings as its mouth closed on her skin again and tugged. A moment later, the creature was gone, but the pain remained. She could feel the warm trickle of blood down her face, into her eye. She blinked it away, and again, as it dripped. And still she couldn't pull her eyes from the orness' fingers.

The orness hit one final symbol and stopped. For a long moment, nothing happened. Nothing except what was already happening – the flap of metal wings, the cries of the zaffre as their weapons hit their marks, the triumphant squeal of the charn as theirs did too.

Then: a note. Two. The city began to sing, all around them. Radiating out from the device into the city. A new song. One of woven shadow and the sun's fall across the sky. The dry sound of dust in your hair, the lull of your heartbeat fading to nothing. And then rising into everything.

Talia had never heard the city like this. No one else had either, she guessed, from the way they all stood for one moment, faces trained to the skies, silent.

Outside the clave, a wind rattled the broken roof, sending more shards of glass hurtling toward them. Then it picked up the song. She could hear it the moment the wind wove through the skars, hollowed them out, the haunting moan of metal and blood. The song rose and rose, until the sound became storm, became moving death, whipping everything that moved into a frenzy.

Talia stood her ground, eyes closed tight, felt the sound move around and around her, never touching her. It whipped her hair against her face, the slash of her braids.

Debris caught her on its way by. Blood still dripped, hot and steady, down her eye and she shook her head to see.

She could feel things whipping by her, being pulled out of the clave into the air above. Big things. Metal things. Any moment, she expected to be swept up in the storm.

She felt a hand enter her true hand. It was the orness, paper and parchment, the life slowly going from her.

"Listen," the orness said. "About the tenth…"

"Will it kill me?" Talia asked.

"Do you believe it will?" she said.

"No," Talia said. "No."

But it wasn't the orness' question she was answering. The orness was gone.

NO MORE

Talia thought she crossed back again, but no. Maeryl was here this time. In the clave.

And yet, they were nowhere at the same time. Inbetween. Neither the blackweave nor the clave were in reach. Attor, the space between life and death.

She could hear the oily breathing, far off. And the cries of the greyes, the squall of the charn. Still farther.

She wasn't surprised to see Maeryl here. Again. Mostly alive. Somehow she'd known, even then, that the vordcha would not let her go so easily. She'd known in her heart that this was the path where everything led.

Maeryl had always been a sharp fighter, a hand on each blade. Better than Talia. The vordcha had only made her better in near-death. They'd bifurcated her arms, added hands on the ends, so that four hands and four blades began to whirl. Her chest was open to the air and, inside it, a machine that spun hot and white, giving off smoke.

Talia had her hexed hand. Her red-handled weapon. The blue-black blade. It was so little.

"Where are the vordcha?"

Maeryl stepped forward, blades whirring. The machine in her chest released a stream of smoke that made Talia's eyes water and pull closed. "Gone. I am their hunter now."

"I'm sorry, Maeryl," she said. "I thought you dead. I would not have left you for them."

A small *tsk* from Maeryl. Disbelief. All white smoke and blades.

It was almost deserved, and she let it sink in, a small shard in the meat of her heart.

"If what you said is true, that you did not mean to leave me for them..." Maeryl said, "...then come and save me, if you are true."

"I can't, Maeryl. I won't fight you." She thought of Burrin, putting his fist to his chest. *I won't kill you. But I may hurt you very, very badly.*

"Then you are still the coward you were that day," Maeryl said. "And no sister to me."

Talking to the mech inside Maeryl, Talia said more words, words about how she wouldn't take on Maeryl, how she wouldn't fight her, how she wouldn't kill her. At the same time, she tucked her hand into her pocket and pulled out the sliver of blue-black blade. It was as sharp as it always was, and fit just so into her hexed palm.

I will give you mercy if you ask it of me.

While she talked to the mech with words, she talked to Maeryl with something else. She held her hand open, off to the side until she was sure Maeryl had seen it. When Maeryl nodded yes in the depth of her eyes, Talia said, "Finwa. I am sorry for what I am about to do."

She took a single step toward Maeryl, who met her, blades whirring. "Me too, sister."

Talia ducked, stepped away. Maeryl was slow, clumsy,

the fight between the vordcha's planted mech and her own self causing tremors.

"Ready?" Talia asked. She had been a survivor long enough to know not to wait for an answer. She skirted Maeryl's thrusts and drove the blue-black blade into the back of her sister's neck. Her strike was sure and true and deep, and when she pulled the blade out, Maeryl fell, a slow, languid path toward the ground. Talia watched her hands catch her friend, her lover, her sister, her enemy. Together, they lowered to the ground.

Talia knelt at Maeryl's side. For a moment, she was not Talia. Not Cathaliaste, the last of the Twelve Martyrs. But something else entirely. The secret name she'd been once, before the vordcha, before she'd been given away for so little. She leaned down and whispered the name into Maeryl's ear.

Just for a moment she was that, and then it was over. She was who she'd become, who she'd been made into. They all were.

She cradled Maeryl's head in her lap. Maeryl opened her eyes. One was shot through with black, the vordcha's doing or a sign of her death, Talia didn't know. Her breathing was rough, broken. You could practically hear the air scraping over her raw lungs.

"I'm sorry, sister," Maeryl said. Her voice, out of breath, sounded like the Maeryl she had known, once. The Maeryl who had kept her light in the darkness. The Maeryl of the sea and salt and windswept waves of blue.

"You've nothing to be sorry for," Talia said. She meant it, even though it punctured her heart to say it. "You did everything you could."

"It wasn't enough." She gasped at the end of the

sentence, and Talia realized she must be struggling just to breathe, with the weight of all the mech inside her. It was only the vordcha's imperative that made her go on, forced step by forced step. She was more machine than human now.

"It never is. Not for any of us." She meant that too, more than she realized until she even said it.

Maeryl exhaled, then took a ragged, pain-filled breath in order to speak. "Cathaliaste, sister, will you tell me of the sea?"

Talia, who had never seen the sea other than in Maeryl's words, gave those words back to her now. A woken stream of water and wind, of blue beyond all blues, of the place where water met land and stepping forward buoyed you into weightlessness. She wove a story of blue love around the body that was no longer her sister, and when it was done, and Maeryl closed her eyes one last time, Talia's shard of blue-black blade went back home.

Once again the last of the Twelve Martyrs of the Forgotten Compass, Cathaliaste wept.

AND EVERYTHING TASTED OF SALT.

When she opened her eyes, all around her lay the dead charn and bleeding zaffre. Rakdel was already moving forward to tend to them. The rest of them were standing, harsh breaths and dusty faces. The device had retracted back into the floor. She didn't know if that was something the orness had done, or if it had done so on its own.

She saw Seild and Khee, both all right, Seild looking like she didn't know whether she was supposed to be excited or terrified. Or perhaps both.

Softness

Khee said and there was so much pride, so much love, in that single word that she couldn't have spoken even if she needed to. So she nodded at him, blinking back all the tears that the world had left. Which was surprising how many.

Talia went down on her knees beside the orness. "Thank you," she said. Even though she knew that the orness couldn't hear it. Would never hear it again, not even for all that she had done.

She pushed herself up, found Isera standing there. They

leaned their foreheads together, eyes closed, just breathing.

"Is it over?" Isera asked.

Standing there, with her forehead touching the woman she loved and her hand holding the hand of the woman she would become, Talia wanted to say yes. Yes, it was over. Yes, everything was fine.

But it would be a lie. And she thought that she might be done with those for a while. She thought she would see how it felt to speak true.

"No," she said. "The vordcha are still out there."

"They'll come?"

"Maybe." But maybe not. They were cowards, even more so than she'd once been.

"If they don't come, you'll go after them." It wasn't a question, so Talia didn't answer.

They stood a moment longer, Talia breathing in the scent of cyrria spices and green boughs.

"You're bleeding," Isera said, as they pulled away. "Rakdel will have to stitch you."

Together, they reached down and lifted the body of the orness back into her chair.

Burrin came over to help, and they let him, although they didn't need it, because he so clearly did. Whatever her relationship had been like with the orness, Burrin's had to be a thousand times more complicated.

Burrin turned to Talia, put both thumbs to his eyes. "Moon meld you, Orness," he said. The others, those who were close enough to hear, echoed him.

"I don't think so, Burrin," she said. "I think that's going to be your role for a while."

The moon had only just risen – Talia could see it through

the broken ceiling of the clave. She put her thumbs to her eyes. She'd regretted so many choices in her life, but she did not regret this one.

Moon meld you, poison eater, and you shall shine.

IV. awos

EVERY HEART A DEATH

For the last time, Talia knelt before the Eye. And she saw, as she always did, as she always had, nothing more than the reflection of her own face.

The vordcha were still out there, somewhere. Coming for her. Or going elsewhere to gather new martyrs.

If they were coming, the city would be ready. If they weren't, then she would go after them.

She needed to know. The tenth poison would kill her or it would save her. She was fine with it either way.

Khee lay beside her, the length of his body a comfort in the darkness. Beside him, her pack, filled with what mattered. A device that became a map of the world. A green cup. A hexed armband. A long red ribbon tied into a bow.

"Will you come with me, Khee?" she asked.

yes.

She pushed her hand into the Eye, softly but firmly, as one might push their hand into the chest of someone they loved to save them. She gripped its beating heart in her fist and lifted it toward her mouth.

Finwa, she thought, as she placed the poison upon her tongue. *Protect me in what I am about to do.*

Poison never lied. But that didn't mean it always told the truth.

THE TEN POISONS OF ENTHAIT

tursin – wind damps the lungs

caerrad – shiv upon the breath

oniwer – failure of the skin

itasi – branches bloom in blood

achad – ache in the muscles

aigha – the way the fingers tremble

ebeli – memories cleave the marrow

iisrad – shades ward your eyes

onysa – these tongues shall sing no more

awos – every heart a death

ACKNOWLEDGMENTS

You know that no novel, no story, is a thing unto itself. It is a carefully tended lie, an unspoken promise, buried deep and brought forth from nothing more than pure will and unquenchable thirst. And so, beneath these words, you sense the hands and eyes and minds of those who helped shape this story, breathe life into it, and set it free. Thank you to everyone who touched it, and me, in some way during its creation.

Thank you to Monte Cook for creating Numenera, a place of wonder and weirdness that allows even the wildest stories to take root and bloom. Additional thank yous to editor Susan J Morris, whose wisdom and insight is unparalleled; to Ray Vallese for making sure that every single word was right and true; to the entire Angry Robot team for jumping into this weird water with both feet; to Ben Wootten for the incredible cover and interior art; and to every single Kickstarter backer and first reader who made this book a possibility. And a giant helping of jerky to the world's most amazing rescue dog, Ampersand, who is surely a soul-sibling to Khee.

If you'd like further inspiration, may I recommend a few of the things that kept me going during the writing of this book: the Numenera corebook; *The Book of Symbols*; *The Art of Language Invention*; *The Library at Mount Char*; the Freedom app; the sounds of Brain.fm, *Florence and the Machine, Thao & the Get Down Stay Down, Lost in the Trees*, and *Grizzly Bear; Don't Starve Together*; soy mochas; and you.

Moon meld you, Poison Eaters, and you shall shine,

Shanna

ABOUT THE AUTHOR

Shanna Germain claims the titles of writer, editor, leximaven, girl geek, she-devil, vorpal blonde and Schrödinger's brat. Her short stories, essays, poems, novellas and more have appeared in hundreds of books and publications, including *Women Destroy Fantasy, Best American Erotica, Best Bondage Erotica, Best Erotic Romance, Best Gay Romance, Triangulation, Salon, Storyglossia* and more.

shannagermain.com • *twitter.com/shannagermain*

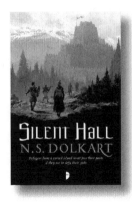
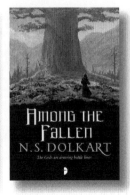
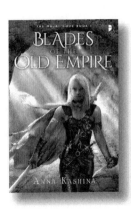

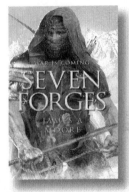
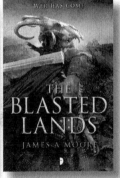
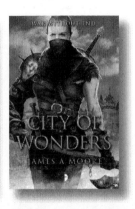

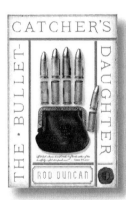

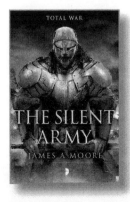

THERE HAVE BEEN EIGHT PREVIOUS WORLDS

Each world stretched across vast millennia of time. Each played host to a race whose civilizations rose to supremacy but eventually died or scattered, disappeared or transcended. During the time each world flourished, those that ruled it spoke to the stars, reengineered their physical bodies, and mastered form and essence, all in their own unique ways.

Each left behind... *remnants*.

The people of the new world—the Ninth World — sometimes call these remnants magic, and who are we to say they're wrong? But most give a unique name to the legacies of the nigh-unimaginable past. They call them...

Explore the Ninth World in the Numenera roleplaying game from Monte Cook Games.

www.numenera.com